THE *Younger* MAN

Zoë Foster Blake enjoys writing her biography because she can write things like, 'The literary world was shocked when Foster Blake was controversially awarded the Man Booker prize for the third time', despite the fact that this is patently untrue.

Things that *are* true include a decade of journalism writing for titles such as *Cosmopolitan*, *Harper's BAZAAR* and *Sunday Style*, as well as being the founder of all-natural Australian skin care line, Go-To.

Zoë has written four novels, *Air Kisses*, *Playing the Field*, *The Younger Man* and *The Wrong Girl*; a dating and relationship book, *Textbook Romance*, written in conjunction with Hamish Blake; and *Amazinger Face*, a collection of her best beauty tips and tricks.

She lives in Springfield with her husband, Homer, and her three children, Maggie, Lisa and Bart.

BOOKS BY ZOË FOSTER BLAKE

Air Kisses

Playing the Field

The Younger Man

Textbook Romance
(with Hamish Blake)

Amazinger Face

The Wrong Girl

Zoë FOSTER BLAKE

THE *Younger* MAN

PENGUIN BOOKS

PENGUIN BOOKS

UK | USA | Canada | Ireland | Australia
India | New Zealand | South Africa | China

Penguin Books is part of the Penguin Random House group of companies
whose addresses can be found at global.penguinrandomhouse.com.

First published by Penguin Random House Australia Pty Ltd, 2012
This edition published by Penguin Random House Australia Pty Ltd, 2017

1 3 5 7 9 10 8 6 4 2

Cover and text design by Allison Colpoys © Penguin Random House Australia Pty Ltd
Author photograph by Michelle Tran
Typeset in Fairfield by Laura Thomas © Penguin Random House Australia Pty Ltd
Colour separation by Splitting Image Colour Studio, Clayton, Victoria
Printed and bound in Australia by Griffin Press, an accredited ISO AS/NZS 14001
Environmental Management Systems printer.

National Library of Australia
Cataloguing-in-Publication data:

Foster Blake, Zoë, author.
The younger man / Zoë Foster Blake.
9780143784906 (paperback)
Subjects: Man-woman relationships--Fiction.

penguin.com.au

Age is a question of mind over matter.
If you don't mind, it doesn't matter.
Leroy 'Satchel' Paige

I

Abby washed her hands and peered at her naked body in the mirror as she dried them on a technicolour Missoni hand towel. It was a gift, but an expensive one, as she had then felt compelled to buy a whole set of Missoni towels to match.

Her face was flushed, her skin damp with a light sweat. Even with the flattering light of a summer morning bouncing softly off the walls she looked like Twitchy the Tramp: her eyeliner had escaped her lashline and was cavorting around what would eventuate into magnificent bags under her eyes, her thick brows, usually groomed perfectly into position, were unruly and dishevelled, her eyes were red and glazed, and her pixie-short honey-blonde hair danced wildly around her head.

She felt roughly as terrific as she looked. Her breath was poisonous with the scent of alcohol; her mouth dry from salt-rimmed glasses and smoking the cigarettes she vocally abhorred in Real Life. Her head pounded quietly; warming up for the rousing drum solo it planned to unleash the moment she thought she had a handle on her hangover.

But Abby did not give a shit about any of this. She had just had heart-pounding, passionate, uninhibited sex with a beautiful man ten years her junior, and she felt fucking fantastic.

Even in her glorious post-coital glow, she was bound by a bathroom habit she'd been doing since she was seventeen. She twisted 180 degrees to check on her (minor, invisible to most) cellulite, wondering if by some stroke of incredible luck and/or magic, it had fallen off during that final, excessively athletic romp, and she now had the pert arse of an eighteen year old. She did not. It was definitely the arse of a thirty-three year old, and while it was fine, almost good, in jeans and passable in a very low-slung bikini bottom and a thick layer of self-tan, it was not an arse that should be paraded around an extremely good-looking young man in the harsh and unforgiving light of morning. Why the fuck she'd chosen to make the master bedroom the one with the skylight, she didn't know. Spectacularly bad for self-image.

It didn't really matter, though, because as usual, her new male friend would be leaving. Abby had a no-sleepover rule. Didn't matter if he had Future Husband potential or was a no-strings rascal like the one currently sprawled on top of her crumpled sheets. Didn't even matter if he was the best lover she'd ever had, and she blushed as she realised this one just may have been. And it wasn't just because she'd had a bit of a drought lately. He was incredible. So intuitive, so generous, so . . . *skilled*.

She fanned her face and grabbed a towel, wrapping it around her body before walking quietly back into her hot, sweaty room. The dark floorboards creaked noisily under her feet and her breath seemed louder than usual, everything seemed exaggerated, partly because of the hangover and partly because there was a handsome stranger in her bed who she had the task of kicking out.

'Marcus,' she half-whispered, half-said.

The toned body remained lifeless; the face, strands of messy brown hair covering it, remained unresponsive. He was young, so young, she thought. Twenty-two years old. He was a baby! Jesus. How did this happen? . . . Tequila, that's how.

'MARCUS.' Nothing. She sighed, contemplating her next move as she perched on the side of the bed near where his head lay, resting next to a bedside table boasting a pile of impressive but unread books. She checked her phone: 6.02 a.m. He needed to leave. *Now*.

'Marcus!'

'Mmmphffh . . .'

'Come on. You gotta get outta here. My fiancé will be home any second and he probably won't be as thrilled to meet you as I was.'

Marcus suddenly sat bolt upright, his face twisted in confusion and panic.

'*Fiancé?* You have a *fiancé?!* Whatthefu—'

'Yes,' Abby spoke slowly and calmly. 'He gets home from his business trip this morning, and presumably will want a shower and a kiss. Obviously I have to clean this place up before he walks through that door. You know, get rid of the condom wrappers and the scent of mating. That kind of thing.'

But Marcus wasn't listening anymore. He was untangling himself from the sheets, and scrambling around on the floor trying to locate clothes that had been removed by two sets of very impatient, urgent hands. He found his undies, simple black Bonds (nothing wanky and designer, thank you) and pulled them quickly up over his tanned legs and white arse before hopping into his dark blue jeans. Without so much as a look at Abby, who was still sitting on the side of the bed, he raced out into the lounge room for his rockabilly checked shirt, tripping over her low mosaic coffee table. She could hear him swearing in hushed tones.

Abby padded to the lounge room and leaned against the doorway as she watched Marcus racing to put his socks and shoes on.

'Got everything then?'

Marcus stood up and patted his pockets for the holy trinity: keys, wallet, phone.

'Yep . . . What's so funny?' Marcus looked at Abby, his eyes bleary but handsome, his hair the kind of cool mess that stylists spent hours creating for arrogant fashion campaigns.

'Nothing. Why? Nothing . . .'

'You're smiling!' he said in disbelief. 'I'm about to be intercepted by a furious man on your front steps and you're smiling. You're a lunatic.'

A giggle tried to escape Abby's mouth. 'I'm *not* smiling!'

'No, because now you're laughing, and that's worse.' He looked at her in disbelief for a few seconds before his outrage softened. God she was sexy, he thought. He had a thing for women with short hair. Even with her eyes smeared in black shit and her hair all crazy. He wanted to kiss her. He wanted to pick her up and take her back to bed and do very bad things to her. He had half a mind to push her onto the lounge right now.

''S just nervous energy. Now, go, go!'

Marcus shook his head. How often did she do this? That poor son of a bitch fiancé. He stopped at the front door, and turned to face her across the room, all coy and shy in her towel, despite having been straddled naked on top of him, panting and theatrically moaning not thirty-four minutes ago.

'Do I get a goodbye kiss?'

She sighed, enjoying his beautiful face and those deep brown eyes for the last time. She wanted to. Very much. Why not? What would one kiss do? Nothing. It would do nothing.

She walked over to him, one hand holding her towel up, the other tucking her hair behind her ear, and stopped before him, looking up into his eyes.

'You do.'

He looked into her blue eyes for one, maybe two seconds before leaning down and kissing her softly on the lips. It was the perfect kiss: gentle, final, lingering. Abby felt her heart do a small pirouette as she pulled away from his lips, and looked into his eyes. Oooh, he was a piece of work, this one. Best he disappeared into the dawn, forever.

'Now scat, young man.'

He turned and opened the door; 'I don't call you, right?'

'You don't have my number, so, uh, no.'

'I could find it if I wanted it.' He smiled mischievously and pulled the door closed.

Abby shook her head and walked back to her bedroom.

The kids of today. Honestly.

2

'You're sick.' Abby half-smiled, her eyes wide with disbelief. It was the kind of demented behaviour generally reserved for psychotic ex-girlfriends in Hollywood films, but somehow, as usual, her friend made it cute.

'Wasn't like I did it on *purpose,* it was more like, well—' Chelsea toyed with her long caramel-chocolate hair and issued one of her trademark smiles, wicked and childlike in equal parts, masterfully created to excuse her of any blame.

'Okay, so maybe just explain how deliberately running up the back of a Porsche was not on purpose, Chels?'

'It was a *tap.* A little bumper kiss. And it was his fault; he was flirting with me in his side mirror. And I just had this moment when we were stuck in this long trail of traffic where I accidentally pushed too hard on the accelerator and it happened . . .'

More laughter from Abby. She tipped her empty cappuccino into her mouth to enjoy some of the chocolaty froth that insisted on clinging to the bottom of the cup.

'Abs, that's so off – what are you, five? *Anyway,* whatever, he said he'd pay for the damage. You're missing the important part – he is hot, funny, *and* generous.'

'Rich. The word you're looking for is rich.'

'Tell me that's not what I've been searching for – hot, funny and successful.'

'It's spelled R-I-C-H.'

Chelsea folded her arms over her perky, expensive breasts and scrunched her mouth over to one side in a paltry attempt to disguise a smile.

'You're an asshole, do you know that? I *like* this guy! And all yo—'

Abby laughed heartily, throwing her head back to allow more room for her jaw to fall and the laughter to barrel out. Chelsea was the most blunt, judgemental person she knew, and yet she could never, ever hack it when it was given back to her. Even when it was sprinkled on jovially, like cute, teasy icing sugar.

'With all due respect for the man, who is of *course* your soulmate, how can you know you really like him when the extent of your interaction with him was a minor car accident?'

'We sparked! It felt very meant-to-be-ish. Anyway, you wait and see. After dinner tonight I'll prove it.'

'Prove what? That he's rich? I guess if you can steal his platinum AmEx, sure . . .'

Chelsea shook her head and checked her BlackBerry for the 689th time.

'What'd you do on the weekend anyway?' she said, changing the topic as she deleted one of the many daily newsletters she received. She opted-in impulsively and was too lazy to work out how to unsubscribe. It was textbook Chelsea. Want, need, race in; lose interest.

'Had that bloody gala thing. Ended up going out with some of the girls afterwards to that new place, Deluxe, and getting absolutely trolleyed on tequila. And then hooked up with a very, very,

very hot and preposterously young boy. Looks a bit like one of those gorgeous boys in the Burberry ads, all olive skin and brown eyes and longish hair and that perfect amount of facial hair. In all it was a very professional, grown-up evening.'

'*How* young? Like, eighteen?'

'No, you sicko . . . twenty-five.' Abby looked down.

'How. Old.'

'Twenty-two.'

'WHO'S the sicko?? Twenty-two! Was he wearing a nappy?'

'Oh, you're an idiot. Twenty-two is an adult! God knows what I was up to at twenty-two, but I wasn't a child. I knew what I was doing.'

'You were being dull as shit with Mr Boring. That's what you were doing.'

Abby's friends *loved* to remind her how different she had been while with her ex-boyfriend, a man she had stayed with for six years, although no one, Abby included, could work out why. He was nice enough. Nice friends, nice family, nice, nice, nice. *Too* nice. Abby had ended it a few years ago when she found a diamond ring in his underpants drawer. She figured it was better to break his heart by saying she had fallen out of love, rather than have him go through the whole proposal business.

'He's actually pretty smart. Funny too. Amazing body, Chels. Fit. Tanned. Delightful. Felt a bit pudgy next to him, but he didn't seem to mind.'

Chelsea didn't dispel Abby's belief she was pudgy. Chelsea always felt Abby could do with a little more time in the gym.

'Did you take him back to your lair?'

'Of course. You know what tequila does to me.'

'Was it worth it?' Chels was in rapid-fire interrogation mode. She needed all the details. Immediately. Then she would conclude whether or not Abby should bother with a guy again. Her decision was final – Chelsea was convinced she knew men. The problem was she dated the same kind of man every time, which fuelled the deluded opinion that she knew all men.

'He might just be the best lover this woman has ever had. Four times in as many hours. With SEVERAL added bonuses for no extra charge.'

All of Chelsea's previous ideas about this man changed instantly. Despite being a huge and loyal fan of the 'No Sex Until Three Months' club, she loved sex. The fact that her ex-husband – Tim, a monstrously successful plastic surgeon who was also a chronic gambler – never gave her any loving might have had something to do with it. She'd had a healthy account at AdultPleasures.com for years. She had been a mess for a few months after divorcing him and his addiction, but had bounced back, or rather overshot, as she was now a serial dater, with a Facebook wall that could pass for Match.com. She wasn't interested in settling down with a man for a while, and with her enormous settlement money, didn't need to.

'*Reaaallly!* Well, you have to see him again, obviously. Twenty-two or fifty-two, if the sex is good, age doesn't mean a thing.'

Abby shook her head and exhaled. 'Can't, unfortunately. Threw him the fiancé line.'

Chelsea closed her eyes and threw back her head. 'WHY do you always DO that? It's so psychotic to begin with, and then, if you realise you do actually want to see them again, you can't, because they think you're a screwy bitch. Which you are.'

'I don't know! I was, I didn't know if, it just fell out of my mou—'

'Did you give him your number?'

'No.'

Chelsea shook her head: Abby was *such a retard* in these situations; she managed to sabotage things before the guy even left her apartment.

'Look. He'll find you if he wants to. He knows about Allure, right?'

'Think I mentioned it, yeah . . . He knew one of the girls, too.'

'Then hopefully he's ballsy enough to contact you.'

'He thinks I'm engaged! Anyway, whatever, it's just sex. I can find more sex.'

Chelsea shrugged, scrolling through her phone's inbox. 'Ohmygod, our new receptionist is so wrongo – she uses Comic Sans for God's sake . . .' Chelsea locked her phone and placed it in her bag. 'Well, my cradle-snatching friend, as delightful as this has been, I must go. Some of us have disgusting, rotting mouths to peer into.'

She stood up, her toned, tiny body resplendent in a body stocking miscast as a dress, and swung her handbag, Gucci of course, complete with gilded keyrings and enormous G's screaming from every square inch of the leather, over her shoulder.

Tim's 'generous' divorce payout meant Chelsea now only needed to work three days a week – which she did as a cosmetic dentist in one of those high-end surgeries in the CBD that had mood lighting and essential oil burners and groovy jazz playing in the foyer – leaving her plenty of time to make her body toned and tiny and tight dress-ready.

'We doing pilates tomorrow morning? Mads is in.'

Abby hated pilates, but seeing what it did for Chelsea's figure ensured she kept up her pricey twice-weekly sessions. Their figures used to be fairly comparable, but then thirty had happened, and *Allure*, and the twelve-hour days and processed, convenience food that came with it. It wasn't *terrible*, but now she had an extra layer of flesh hanging over the waistband of her jeans and cuddling her bra straps. It all just . . . hung. Over. She was a walking hangover.

'Reformer class at eight. Then let's go for breakfast and I can tell you both how Porschey De Rossi fell in love with me over our entrées.' Chelsea winked playfully, threw twenty dollars on the table and bounced out of the café, the eyes of the waiter following her, glazed and pathetic under the spell of her petite arse.

Abby checked the time, it was just after nine, and she was rarely at work later than eight. This – or possibly the second cappuccino – made her jittery with anxiety, and with shaking fingers she picked up her bag and phone, and set off.

3

Abby parked her duck-egg blue, vintage Mercedes in the car park, several layers below the core of the universe, and waited for a lift that operated at the pace of a drugged tortoise. The girls gave her plenty of stick about her car, but she treasured it. It was a complete pain in the arse, always breaking down and needing parts shipped in from Jupiter, but it was such an elegant, timeless beast. She couldn't bear to part with it.

As she waited, Abby felt a little envious of her friend. Chelsea always landed on her feet, or more accurately was caught by a suitor in Hermès and a poorly concealed past as a male model. Admittedly, she'd endured a torturous marriage, but she seemed to fall over a new man on the way to her driveway each morning. Abby hadn't met one relationship-worthy man in over two years. Lately, Chelsea's were *all* dashing and charming and successful! All of them! Not one starving poet or megalomaniacal TV producer among them. Of course, they might very well have been drug lords or clown performers at children's parties underneath the shimmering veneer, but Chels never hung around long enough to find out.

Chelsea's propensity to attract men aside, Abby was also jealous of Chelsea's lifestyle. Not *Chelsea*, she soothed her conscience, her *lifestyle*. Different. Chelsea was terrifyingly intelligent underneath all her Kardashian-style tics. She'd worked her arse off at University and done her hard yards looking into disgusting mouths for years, and now she had it made – time *and* money.

Abby could hardly believe such a thing as 'part-time' existed. She had come from a textbook blue-collar family. Her mum was a primary school teacher; her father had been a town planner and the idea of working less than a fifty-hour work week was inconceivable.

Exactly *why* there was such valour in working yourself to death to earn your money, Abby wasn't sure. It frustrated her that she worked so hard for hers, even though she loved her agency. She'd always done it with the vision of hiring a sterling 2IC she could leave in charge so she could flit about the world selfishly, but there was no way she was ready to leave the business in anyone else's hands. Her clients would have a fit, not to mention the girls. And what if they messed up? They could ruin her reputation in one stupid move. Nope. Not going to happen, at least not in the near future. Abby realised she had created a business that literally could not run without her; at times it felt like a jail sentence.

Her older brother, Sean, was much more enlightened. After inhaling several thousand self-help books and listening to a bunch of 'gurus' spout dribble about taking ownership of *you*, he had created a fully automated, million-dollar business (of 'almost' organic hotel toiletries made in Taiwan and shipped all around the world) which he ran from his laptop wherever in the world he and his business-partner wife, Jamie, were at that time. Presently it was Buzios, Brazil. The photos he sent made Abby gasp with jealousy.

In her more self-aware moments Abby was able to see that her resentment for anyone living a fantastic lifestyle was entirely ridiculous, and was more founded on annoyance at her own path than on genuine bitterness.

When the lift finally arrived, one of her promo girls, Jen, was already in it, tapping away furiously on her iPhone.

Jen looked up, a huge smile etched on her face.

'Ohmygod, did you *hear* about Katie and Tara?'

Jen was a petite Vietnamese girl, who looked like she was finally going to graduate high school this year. This was no accident, for despite being unusually beautiful and having one of the most incredible physiques, Jen loved wearing jeans, hoodies and caps. It added to her charm, Abby thought. As long as she dressed up for jobs, Abby didn't give two burps about what Jen wore during the day.

Abby's face dropped.

'No. Talk.'

'They worked that sailing boat last night? The one tha—'

'Frederic Hamburg, the vitamin billionaire's boat. Yes . . . Go on.'

'And some guy tipped them each $1000 cash at the end of the night, just flat out cash! I effing hate that I get seasick. The boat jobs get the biggest tips.'

'Uh, Jen? Remember how tips aren't actually allowed because I pay you guys exorbitant rates? Remember that part?'

'Yes, but, I mean, it's not like you're going to confiscate it from them or anything . . .'

The lift opened at reception, where a black 'Allure' sign sat elegantly above a minimalist desk manned by the six-foot, feline-eyed Angie.

When Abby had decided to start up her own promotional-girl agency, she'd realised just how few names there were that wouldn't make it sound like a badly disguised escort agency. She still wasn't sure she'd chosen the right one, which made her all the more militant about the chic styling of the office, website, the girls and their reputation. Promotional girls had a bad wrap – they were generally thought to be second-rate girls who couldn't make it as real models, and who existed only for decoration or titillation, but Abby was working to alter that perception.

She had created an agency that embraced promotional work not as the poor man's modelling, or a pathway to being an escort (as so many ruthlessly wrote it off as), but as a legitimate industry where attractive, charming women could learn outstanding socialising and networking skills, and where companies could employ chatty, fun women who looked terrific to endorse their brand or liven up their event. As far as Abby was concerned there was nothing sexist or anti-feminist about it; it was a delightful way to earn good money if you had the perfect cocktail of personality and looks. Her girls were attractive, but they had charisma and smarts too.

She talent-spotted wherever she went, and poached from other agencies with reckless disregard, knowing they'd do the same thing given an eighth of a chance. Only they never would, because Abby paid her girls three times as much, and *never* sent them on shitty jobs. Furthermore, she was vigilant about their safety and intensely protective.

In her time as a promotional girl (she had been at uni and spectacularly penniless), Abby's grubby boss Geoff had hurled her into countless jobs and situations that were dangerous, disgusting and soul destroying. One – the final one – had almost ended in irreversible damage.

It had been a boozy Friday night job in the CBD and Mads and Abby, who'd met at uni in a 'napper' subject, were dressed as Uma Thurman (*Pulp Fiction* era). Some prick in a suit, who mistakenly assumed that his Italian loafers, expensive suit and six litres of beer made him invincible, had followed Abby, all black mini-dress, scarlet lips and ebony bob, to the pokies room, which was deserted, and started grabbing her arse. When she turned around he pushed her up against one of the stools and forced one hand up her skirt while the other groped her breasts. Her screams went unheard because of the music and noise of inebriated morons, but she finally escaped by belting him over the head with her tray of cigarettes and raced upstairs, panicked and crying.

She found Mads and told her what had happened. Mads shot downstairs to find him, but he'd vanished. When they finally found their boss/minder/security, he told Abby to calm down, that it was no big deal and that he'd speak to the manager of the bar. She watched him return five minutes later clutching cartons of cigarettes, the ones Abby had spilled while defending herself. Couldn't find him, he'd said. You shouldn't have left all that stock on the ground, he'd said.

Threats of litigation followed, wigs and slutty dresses were thrown, jobs were quit, letters to the head of the cigarette corporation were written, but nothing came from any of it. It was deflating and fatiguing and, like so many women who chose to make a stand, Abby gave up.

Now, thirteen years later, after a string of well-paid but tedious jobs in marketing and corporate event management, Abby owned her own promotional agency. If she'd been told this on that fateful *Pulp Fiction* night, she would've spat on the idea. But, at twenty-eight, with nothing more than an ABN, a laptop and a mobile phone, she withdrew all her savings and created Allure.

Five years later she had a chic office overlooking the harbour in the city, almost thirty models, and three office staff.

Smiling at Abby and Jen with gleaming white teeth and fuschia-pink lipstick, Angie answered a call as they walked past her. 'Good morning, you've reached the Allure agency, this is Angie. How may I help you?'

'One moment, I'll see if she's in yet.' Angie put the caller on hold and looked at Abby with a wince.

'It's Georgie. She sounds panicked. Said she's on the Visa job and one of the standby girls is, um . . . *wrong?*' Angie whispered the last word.

Fucking fucksticks. Whenever Abby was desperate and asked one of the girls to call in a friend for a last-minute fill-in job, they were undoubtedly atrocious: vulgar in personality, or two hair extensions away from the cover shoot of a men's magazine. It was terrible for the Allure brand, and was the precise reason she had a two-warnings-and-you're-fired for no-shows. To be fair, it *was* an early-start corporate golf day up on the Northern Beaches so the appeal for her regulars wasn't huge, but still . . .

'Give me a minute then put her through. Thanks, Angie.'

Abby walked into her glass encased corner office and placed her bag and coat on the lounge, before taking a seat at her desk and picking up the handset, a fake smile plastered across her face, a deep breath filling her lungs.

'Georgie girl, what's going on?'

4

'Come on, sweettits. Out with it. We know you're dying to tell us all about your date with Porsche guy.'

The three friends were sitting at the health-food shop under the pilates studio, having been served their dull but virtuous breakfasts. Chelsea always had a water-based berry and chia seed smoothie; she was 'allergic' to dairy, if by 'allergic' you meant 'it made her bloat and feel fat so she avoided it'. Mads was hoeing into the bircher muesli, and Abby, who refused to spend twelve dollars for the same muesli she had at home, and whose preferred breakfast came in the shape of pancakes or eggs benedict, had opted for scrambled tofu. She was yet to find a decent substitute for her sugary, dairy-laden staples at this place, and this celery-soy-tofu mess was about as satisfying as nibbling on a chair leg.

Chels tugged her perfectly fine bun out and gathered her long, blow-dried hair up into exactly the same bun, patting it carefully into place. Her tanned skin was free of makeup and glowing unfairly given the time of day. Her brown, almond-shaped eyes were puff free and clear, and her teeth, the recipients of several rounds of high-strength bleach, were dazzling. If Abby and Mads didn't know

Chelsea, it's fair to say they would be surreptitiously bitching her out in a most unbecomingly jealous fashion. But they did know her, and they adored her. Even if she made them feel 75 per cent less attractive, 100 per cent of the time.

'How do I say this,' Chelsea said, knowing exactly how to say it. 'He's perfect. Absolutely perfect. And his name, for the record, is Jeremy.'

Abby snorted. 'Of course he is. They all are to begin with. Am I in any danger of getting a fork, do we think?' She looked around for the waitress who'd forgotten her silverware.

'For the love of lychees, let her talk, woman!' Mads reprimanded.

'*Thank* you, Madeleine,' Chels said. '*Anyway.* I think this could really be something . . . We had so much fun, and I was just . . . myself, you know? Like, I wasn't trying to be this super smart or funny or perfect girl, dropping names or hobbies or labels or trendy music or films or whatever, I was just myself.'

'*Well.* This is *wonderful* news,' Mads said enthusiastically, ever the champion of love and romance. Mads was happily married to Perfect Dylan, a gorgeous, nerdy sweetheart of a man. The two were nauseatingly in love. Mads attributed this passion and romance to the fact that they had lived in different cities for the first two years of the relationship, then lived together, but with separate bedrooms and bathrooms for the next two ('It keeps it sexy!') before finally getting married and Buying A Home Together. Dylan travelled a lot for work and this afforded the couple a lot of time away from each other, which Mad's said was the Golden Key to a happy, romantic relationship.

Abby noticed Mads had switched her crystal; the stone around her neck was now a beautiful golden amber colour, whereas for the last few months she'd worn a deep blue lapis lazuli heart. Mads was big into her crystals, they kept her grounded, she said, kept her protected and gave her strength. Chelsea, who preferred to adorn *her* neck with Cartier, found them to be an endless source of amusement, but Abby loved Mads's attachment to her magic crystals. It kind of kept Abby grounded, too, in a funny way.

Chelsea went on, her eyes sparkling. 'He's funny and he's smart – he owns a digital advertising agency and they have like Vodafone and Coke and American Express and all these big accounts, and he grew up in the country, which explains why he's so genuine and humble—'

As Abby pinched a fork from the next table she couldn't help herself. 'Humbly driving his Porsche . . .'

Mads shot her A Look.

'I'm sorry, I'm sorry. Please, go on.'

'Anyway. He's just a lovely, lovely man. He picked me up on time, and opened doors and all that stuff, we had a beautiful meal and he gave me a kiss on the cheek at the end and walked me to my door.'

'I'm *telling you*,' Mads said in a singsong voice, 'the gentleman is back.'

'And he has these *green* eyes . . . they're insane. You know how you see those images of women in the Middle East with just their eyes on show through slits in their burkas, and they're that icy green colour? They're like that. I just, I kept staring at them all night. Could stare at them forever.'

'When might you sleep with Green Eyes, do you think?' Mads asked mid-slurp on her coffee. Being married, she was incredibly salacious and intrusive when it came to Abby and Chelsea's sex lives. Although, with Chelsea a fastidious student of The Rules, and Abby being mostly dry save for the occasional one-nighter or one-nighter that turned into a month-long hook-up, Mads was definitely having the most sex of any of them, especially since she was desperately trying to have a baby. 'Come now, Mads,' Chels said, tsk-tsking. 'You know I don't sleep with a man for at least three months.' Excluding oral sex, she failed to mention.

'I've always thought your three-month thing is a *trifle* over the top, Chels . . .' Abby prodded gently.

'Just because YOU spent all weekend sexing some kid you just met, and Mads and Dylan shagged on the first night they met . . .' Chelsea was indignant. She loved playing Lady Chastity; it was an exciting contrast to her micro-attire and Latino-esque heat, and she knew it drove men wild. She believed there was power in withholding sex, and any woman who didn't harness it was a fool.

Abby was less convinced. 'You'll be giving him head in that Porsche by next weekend. Mark my words.'

'Wait, hang on, who have you been sexing, Abs?' Mads squinted at Abby.

Abby inhaled. 'Just this boy I met at the hospital gala. He's not *that* young – twenty-two—'

Mads burst into laughter. 'Oh, I'd say that's pretty young, Abs . . .'

'Well he's legal, put it that way. And gorgeous . . . Blemish-free and self-assured and oh *God*, Mads, the skills . . .'

'Abby Vaughn, you are blushing like a fool. Look at her, Chels! Who would've thought the fussy lady would finally find some butter to adorn her toast.'

Even when she was ridiculing her, Abby loved Mads's way with words. She was a terrific writer, as her popular food blog attested. The blog was mostly an escape from the intensity and madness that was her full-time job, teaching a Special Ed class at the local Catholic school. Every day, gorgeous Mads trotted off to work with her wild curls and crystal necklaces and taught kids with Autism, Down's Syndrome and Cerebral Palsy. Sometimes she came home with bites or scratches, or just a new trail of exciting swearwords from poor Luke, who had severe Tourette's and the vocabulary of the criminally insane, but mostly she just came home happy she'd stopped Katie from biting her arm till it bled, or helped Brendan stop counting all the letters in a book so he could actually enjoy the book as a narrative. Abby was constantly in awe of Mads's hard work and selflessness working with these children. Chelsea thought she should quit and get a job on a food magazine.

'I don't care enough to defend myself, because yes, it was amazing, and *he* was amazing, but I'll never see him again, so have your fun.'

'WHY will you never see him ag—'

'Fiancé.'

Mads slapped her hand to her forehead. 'Abby! *What did we say about that?* No more! It's a ghastly thing to do!'

'It's a form of self-sabotage,' Chelsea said significantly, 'so even if she likes a guy, she can't pursue it.'

'Dazzling psychoanalysis aside, why would I want to see a TWENTY-TWO-YEAR-OLD again? He's younger than half the girls on my books! *Not* sabotage. A smart and entirely conscious move.'

Mads and Chelsea looked at each other with a mixture of pity and disbelief. They loved playing Abby's knowing, disapproving parents when it came to relationships and men.

'Darling.' Mads said, her married know-all voice on. 'If the sex is good and the boy is hot, grab it with all you've got.'

'Madeline, I must say I am very disappointed to hear that you, as one who is married, are encouraging me to cheat on my fictional fiancé.'

'I adore you, darling, but you are nuttier than a pecan pie. And that fiancé line is so violently uncouth. See the boy again! Explain that it was a nervous reaction and have a big laugh about it together. And then have fantastic sex. Simple.'

Abby could only shake her head as her two friends winked at each other. There would be no seeing Marcus again. Even if they didn't know it, she did.

5

'Natasha is on line two.'

At eighteen, Angie was the youngest girl Abby had hired for reception, a job Abby took very seriously, since it was the first impression, physically and aurally of the agency. But with her sass and calming presence, her desire to learn and phenomenal efficiency, Angie's age quickly became irrelevant.

Abby was good like that, forming strong opinions and convictions on an area – in this instance the relevance of age – but only adopting them as it suited her. If someone had asked her why it was that she didn't want to see Marcus again, age would very quickly become extremely relevant.

'Oh and also, um, the site is down again . . .'

'*Eff!* Angie can you please find me five good, no *great* web companies I can review. We need a new site immediately, if not yesterday. This is ridiculous.'

'Right away. And Natasha?'

'Put her through.'

'*Hiiii* Abby, I'm *so* sorry I couldn't call you back yesterday . . . things got crazy. Hey, so I'm still okay for Friday night, right? When

I saw your missed call I was all like, "Please don't let Abby be calling to tell me I'm not needed Friday!"'

'No, no, I still need you Friday. You were the first girl booked. Why everyone is so excited to be working at the Channel 8 ball, I have no idea.'

'Because all the TV stars will be there! It's *sooo* exciting!'

Natasha was obsessed with TV stars, radio stars, movie stars, shooting stars . . . any kind of star. It wasn't because she wanted to sleep with them, or even be one of them, she just loved famous people. Was thrilled by them. Thought they were incredible, fascinating creatures and wanted to know every banal minutia of their days. Popular culture ran through her veins, and Hollywood gossip was intravenously inserted daily via trashy magazines, gossip websites, Twitter, *E! News* . . . the medium was irrelevant as long as the content was celebrity.

Incidentally, Natasha, an expensive looking six-foot brunette with a gentle nature that belied her Russian sex-bomb look, could easily have been a star herself, and the way she attracted attention, might become one yet. She was one of Abby's busiest girls, alongside Marie-Claire, a golden-skinned, blonde, girl-next-door, Victoria's Secret type, and Sabrina, a dark-haired, green-eyed pocket rocket who attracted at least four business cards a job from men instantly enchanted with her exotic look and frustratingly aloof nature.

'Okay, well, good, I love enthusiasm. Now, Natasha, that's not actually why I called you. I needed to talk to you . . . make sure you're okay.'

'I'm fine, why?' Abby could hear Natasha's smile vanishing.

'Natasha, you know you don't have to tell me what's going on . . . It's just some of the girls said you've been taking very long phone calls while on shift lately, after which you are terribly . . . visibly upset . . .' Abby took an epic breath in. 'And, well, a couple of them

mentioned some pretty full-on bruising on your arms at the parade
Monday night.'

'Pete doesn't hit me, if that's what you're hinting at.' The bub-
bles in Natasha's voice had burst. 'They were just bumps I did
myself. At the gym.'

An excruciating, awkward silence swept between the two
women. Abby wasn't sure where to go next. Every so often she had
a girl (beautiful women attracted fuckwits like silk shirts soaked up
olive oil) who was clearly in love with an abusive, be it physical or
emotional, boyfriend, and Abby always felt compelled to make sure
her girls were okay, and to offer some help. Help that was invariably
rejected.

'Natasha, I know it's none of my business, but . . .'

'Who has been saying stuff?' The shock and betrayal was thick
in her words. 'And so what if we have fights every now and then?
What couple doesn't?'

Abby took in a deep breath and closed her eyes. She despised
this part of her job.

'Did Pete leave you stranded after that Palm Beach job two
weeks ago?'

'What Palm Beach job?'

'Natasha . . . come on . . .'

'He didn't *strand* me, something came up and he couldn't come
get me after all. I got a cab eventually, it was no big deal.'

'In the rain. At 3 a.m. Natasha, please know I'm not doing this
to make you feel uncomfortable or under attack. I am very protective of my girls, and I just want you to feel you can talk to me if
you're ever unhappy or, you know, in trouble or anything. All that
aside, your safety after a job is paramount.'

'I'm fine. So he didn't pick me up, so what? Why does everyone
think it's such a big deal?! Why is it even anyone's business?'

'You're right. It's *not* our business. And I'm sorry you feel I'm intruding. I won't push it any further, but please know you can always call me . . .'

A sniff. Natasha was crying. Top job, Abby, nice going.

'Natasha? Are you okay?'

Abby could hear Natasha draw in a deep, sharp breath, and clear her throat.

'I'm fine. So, um, I just wear a little black dress Friday night, right? Not the silver one?'

Abby closed her eyes and leaned her elbow on the table, sinking her head onto the phone in defeat. Textbook stuff. She couldn't count the times she'd been through this exact situation.

'Yes. And hair out, please. Be there by 5.30, okay? They get pissed if you're late when it's being filmed live.'

'Got it!' Natasha's overly-super-duper-I'm-fine chirpiness startled Abby.

''Kay, bye Natasha.'

'Bye!' More trilling.

Abby put the phone back in its receiver and put her head in her hand, rubbing her forehead. *It wasn't her issue*, she told herself. She didn't need to worry about it. Natasha would ask for help if she wanted it. And she had her mum, and her sisters and friends to go to if she wanted to talk to someone. Abby would be there on Friday night to ensure the girls were all present, on time and looking sharp, which meant she could subtly check if Natasha was okay, but she wasn't gonna hang around for six hours till the ball ended to see if her boyfriend was there to pick her up, or make her cry on the phone during her break.

Abby *used* to stay the whole shift, back in the early days, but it was complete overkill, and time wasted besides. She learned a long time ago that the best (albeit riskiest) way to earn the girls' respect was to trust them. Of course, if it was an evening job, or a men-only function, she always sent along one of her gentle giants, Uri or Julian, to keep an eye on the girls. There was no way on this earth she would allow what happened to her, happen to one of her girls. Not even a whisper of a hint of a sniff of it. Not a chance.

What she needed was that elusive 2IC, someone she could trust, someone the girls liked and who understood the complexities of the business, who could take some of the pressure off Abby's physical presence at Allure. Escort the girls to the events and do check-ins to see if they were happy and doing a good job. She must get onto that, she told herself. Here it was, February, and she hadn't even written the job description. On some level she was hoping one of her bookers, Charlotte or Siobhan, would demonstrate that they had magically, overnight, become incredibly reliable and impressive, as that would make the whole thing a lot easier. But while they were good at their jobs, Abby wouldn't feel comfortable sending them out as the 'face' of the company in her place. Charlotte didn't have a car, for one thing, and Siobhan was as reliable as a junkie with a fifty-dollar note.

Abby sighed and began attacking the twenty-five new bold names perched in her inbox.

6

Abby stepped quickly but carefully as she and Chelsea power-walked along the footpath in their uniform of three-quarter leggings and singlet. She had developed an irrational dislike of pavement cracks after learning a song about them as a six-year old and, like social smoking and applying toothpaste to pimples, it was a hard habit to kick. She liked to think of it less as pathetic, and more as a sign of a feverish brain, which was always searching for another pattern, another task. She'd heard a guy say that on TV once, and thought it sounded intelligent and admirable. Her last almost-boyfriend, Workout With Wade, an insufferable personal trainer, had immediately picked up on what she was doing and teased her about it mercilessly. He'd push her onto cracks and splits in the concrete, laughing that stupid barking laugh she'd hated at her reluctance to tread anywhere but 'clean' pavement. Chelsea, on the other hand, wouldn't have noticed if Abby had been trailing breadcrumbs behind them as they walked; walks were for Intense Conversation and Buttock Tightening, not judgement of lingering childhood customs.

'So it went well, then,' Abby said, rhetorically. Chelsea had just spent the last twenty-five minutes detailing every moment of her date with Porsche guy, how he'd taken her to Dolce, which *no one* could get a reservation at, how he'd asked her about her job and her life, and actually listened, and how they'd made out – 'I'm talking made out, not kissed, *made out*' – like grubby teenagers for forty-five minutes out the front of her house. When Abby had queried his knowledge of the three-month-no-sex rule, Chelsea had merely smiled knowingly. She wasn't going to be able to hold out with him, Abby could tell. She must text Mads and place a bet on it asap.

'It might just have been the best date in my whole life.'

'And you can promise to me, over my father's dead body, bless his soul, that this is not a swept-up-in-the-cash-and-flash thing?' Abby hated referring to her beloved father like this, but he'd adored Chels, so she had reason to believe he wouldn't mind.

Chelsea looked at Abby with reprimanding eyes. 'Don't take your father's name in vain.'

'Just answer the question,' Abby said, too exhausted to go into battle about how she could utilise her father's memory as she pleased.

'Yes. It's not about his money. Or looks. Both are fantastic bonuses, but I can honestly, *honestly,* say that it's him that I like . . . Guys don't usually care about what I do, or my life. I mean, they do superficially, enough to make them sound like nice, non-selfish guys, but I don't think I've ever had a date ask me why I got into dentistry in the first place, and what satisfies me about the job, and then, you know, if money didn't matter, what—'

'The high price of being super hot . . .' Abby interjected playfully.

'—*what* I would do. As in, what would I wake up in the morning and choose to do? I'd never even thought of that. Would I even have a job? Would I be travelling? Raising a family? Volunteering somewhere?'

Abby snorted.

'I don't know, I just, it was nice to have a bit more of a cerebral dinner companion for once. And also someone who challenged me, you know? Who wasn't pandering to me so that I would like them. I *need to be challenged*. Fuck, I would do *anything* for a boyfriend who forced me to think a bit more, and take some risks, and really dig deep into why I do things I think are arbitrary, but are actually the result of a long and often totally unconscious line of decisions and life turns.'

'Wow. He *has* got the cogs whirring. I almost forgot you were such a nerd for a moment there.'

'But isn't that a good thing? That he has me thinking and speaking in a way that even I had forgotten I was capable of? I mean; I just used the word *arbitrary*. *God* it's a turn on.'

'A lady does need stimulation, after all. And not just via the gentle humming of a small, discrete device.'

Chelsea had quickened her pace in excitement. She was jittery with the idea of Jeremy, of what might become of the two of them, of what was possible.

'I really like him, Abs.'

'He sounds dreamy, Chels. He genuinely does. Oh hey, did Mads get her period, do you know? I forgot to write back to her email yesterday.'

Chelsea made that specific tsk-ing noise that generally preceded not-great news. 'She did.'

'Fuck. They're starting to have an awful time with this, aren't they? It's been well over a year they've been trying now, right?'

'Bet Mads regrets those terminations she had back in the Hugh days now.'

Abby fervently disagreed, on a million levels, but let it slide.

'They're both just so exhausted from it. I feel a bit sorry for Dylan, you know?' Abby said. 'He's struggling a bit with the pressure,

I think. I mean, I get Mads's need to have a baby, but it's not like they've reached the end of the road yet. Dylan has just turned thirty-eight. And she's only thirty-five. It's not as though she's bloody Betty White.'

'You realise we're meant to be on Mads's side, right?'

A small smile crept onto Abby's lips. 'I know . . . didn't she strike out with two best friends in their early thirties who don't want kids?'

'*Oh!* Did I mention he has a place at Claw beach?' And it was back to Jeremy talk.

'So, when do I meet holy Jeremy?

'Leave it with me . . . Shit, that's actually the perfect next date! Group date!' Chelsea fist-pumped the air and twirled around like a delighted schoolgirl after her first kiss. She spanked Abby playfully on the bottom and broke into a run.

'Come on, old man. Let's work it like we love it.'

7

'Alicia?'

A gloss of shiny, brunette hair busy shoving red-pedicured toes into black patent heels peeked up at Abby, all big brown eyes and flushed cheeks.

'You can't wear those shoes. Tell me you have spares.'

A look of utter confusion crossed sweet young Alicia's face. 'But they're closed-toe . . .'

'Actually, that's a *peep-toe,* as evidenced by the way your toes are peeping through the front there.' Abby found it difficult not to sound patronising. This was an ongoing battle when it came to Alicia, a twenty-one year old from an exceptionally wealthy family, who, Abby was quite sure, was doing promotional work just to piss off her parents. It was amazing the number of girls who used the job as a way to get back at their family, boyfriend or ex-boyfriend. Alicia needed the money about as much as Bill Gates did and this was clearly the first job she'd ever had, as shown by her absolute cluelessness regarding things like uniforms, start and finish times and giving notice when you couldn't do your shift because you were now going to be in Paris with your family.

'Ohhhh! Well I guess that makes sense.'

'Spares? Do you have them?' She gave up on Alicia, who was holding one of her shoes in front of her with a newfound respect, and bellowed to the mess of hair, lipgloss and perfume around her. 'DOES ANYONE HAVE SPARE SHOES? What size are you, Alicia?'

'Thirty-eight.'

'IN A THIRTY-EIGHT?'

'I should do,' piped up a long-haired brunette who was doing up her dress. Her face was attractive – black eyes and full lips on an alabaster canvas – and was glimmering with expertly applied eyeliner, bronzer and some might say, too much blush. Her age was hard to place, she had the body of a teenager and creaseless, glowing skin, but there was a hardness to her face, and her eyes lacked the brightness and naiveté of the younger girls. She'd been around, seen some things. Abby knew she was older than the twenty-nine years stated on her employee form, but Yvonne was such a reliable, hard worker, she didn't care. Plus, she looked terrific in a little black dress. Those things counted. Gliding past thirty and perching alongside a Mercedes Benz at car shows as your full-time profession, did not.

'Only thing is my car is parked, like, on the moon. Will I have time to go and get them?'

'No. But Alicia will. Alicia, get the details from Yvonne and get your skates on.'

Alicia obediently put her thongs back on and shuffled over to Yvonne, who was rifling through her bag for her car keys. Alicia had that American Apparel campaign, fresh-faced, bedhead hair with an edge of cool, look that edgier clients liked. It would be annoying to have to fire her.

Abby's ongoing challenge was to find delightful, gorgeous girls who looked like they were twenty-two, but behaved like they were thirty-five. That Alicia was so young – both biologically and mentally – was not ideal, and her Valley Girl slang and silliness was obviously frustrating for the other girls. Natasha was openly dismissive of her, Marie-Claire tried to be nice but gave up after Alicia spilled Red Bull all over her bag, and Yvonne treated her like a painful younger sister.

Abby checked her phone quickly to see if there was anything from Natasha. It was very unlike her to be late, especially when she was so excited about the gig. What if Pete had banned her from working? What if she was in trouble? Abby's mind spiralled into a vortex of worry and imagination.

Natasha are you here? Ax

Texting alleviated a miniscule amount of tension. She'd wait five minutes then call.

Suddenly, there was Natasha. She had poured herself into a Herve Leger–style dress (Abby disapproved, she preferred the girls to wear something a little less . . . obvious), and teamed it with chic, pointy-toe black heels. Her skin was tanned, her hair was salon-swishy, her eye makeup soft and sexy, and her lips shimmered with nude gloss. She looked like she should be hanging off P.Diddy's arm, or advertising Revlon. In short: phenomenal. The event director would be thrilled. They always were when the Allure girls walked in, but there was an added bonus when the Natashas and Sabrinas of the world arrived.

Natasha spotted Abby and smiled and waved, as she kissed some of the other girls hello. Shrieks of, 'Ohmygod where did you get that dress, it is TO DIE!' and 'Have you had your hair coloured? Did Francisco do it?' bustled through the room as the girls put the finishing touches on their faces and welcomed the grand priestess of promotional models into the small back room.

Abby cleared her throat and backed herself against the door.

"Kay girls, stop your air-kissing for ten seconds and listen. You've all been given your jobs – Natasha, you're on the door with Bree, she'll explain what you're doing – and you know how important it is that you do them well. Before any of you ask, yes, you may go to the after-party, but not until you have finished at 11 p.m., and not in your work clothes. So if you brought something to change into, then go for it.' Abby watched as Natasha's face dropped several storeys; she'd come with only a small handbag. 'Any questions?'

'If Jon Harper asks me to marry him, may I?'

Bree was grinning at Abby and elbowing Natasha gently in the ribs. Jon Harper was a devilishly attractive MTV presenter who had mastered looking homeless in a very fashionable way, and was forever seen around town, sucking on cigarettes (and face) with models, singers, actresses, anyone cute and in love with him, really.

'You may. Just have him tested for STIs first. Remember, you're paid to be delightful, beautiful and professional. Not flirty, not ice queen, and not lazy. Okay, go have some fun. Yvonne is your go-to when I leave.'

Last-minute checks were done in MAC compacts, mints were passed around and hair was fluffed. You'd think they were about to take on a runway, but all the girls faced was a huge, dark function room with hundreds of already-drinking, mostly male execs and a few TV stars who attended under contractual obligation. Abby was not complaining. She relied on their vanity, urged it, *demanded* it.

As she'd had zero no-shows, something she never took for granted, and Natasha seemed her usual effervescent self, there was nothing else for Abby to do but head home and collapse in a glamorous heap. Red wine would be poured, some strain of Kardashian show would be watched, a million personal texts she hadn't had time to reply to would be sent. She used to crave a boyfriend on her Big Friday Night In, but hadn't for a long time. She was too tired and too selfish to worry about someone else's needs at the end of a savage week. As long as she got some action every now and then, she was fine. The thought of Marcus, naked in the dawn light, skittered through her brain. Perfect case in point. She could dine on *that* memory for months.

8

'I like the look of these guys . . .' Abby clicked through the slide-show on the site's homepage, a site listed in Webra's portfolio, and which, unlike so many trendy sites she'd seen in other portfolios, didn't exist for the sole purpose of giving you epileptic fits and forc-ing you to upgrade your Flash player.

It was a cinch to navigate but felt and looked extremely advanced. That's what she wanted. The Allure website had to be as beautiful as the girls, very modern and almost embarrassingly easy to use. As around three-quarters of her clients were men over fifty who still asked for comp cards, she had to keep them top of mind.

'Rob? Do you like this one?'

Rob Jackson was Allure's accountant. He came in once a week to go over the books, show off his snappy wardrobe and make all the Allure staff fall a little bit more in love with him. He was a gorgeous-looking man, faintly olive skin, his silver hair almost short enough to be called shaved, and his brown eyes twinkling behind thick black frames. And a big gap between his two front teeth, which was at first arresting, then intriguing and eventually attrac-tive. He looked like he'd fallen from the fashion pages of *Esquire*.

He leaned down to look at Abby's laptop over her shoulder.

'Nice. Very swish. Much better than that ice-cream website.'

'But we're not looking at each individual site, Rob. We're looking at the design and user experience for this whole group of sites. Remember? We're trying to choose a design company, not a water bottle or an ice-cream.'

'Well, these guys seem fine. I don't really know what I'm looking for, to be honest, but I will say that it needs to be useful, because it needs to run your business for you, ultimately. Why don't you just email a few of them and get a quote? That way I can start to feel useful again, because numbers start to be involved.'

Abby sighed. He was right. She'd wasted too much time on this site re-design already; she needed to get onto other work.

'What am I allowed to spend on this?' she asked, already hating the answer. Her current website, whipped up by a friend's brother, Tony, cost her $25k and it was *terrible*. He was the kind of guy who still wore novelty comic book t-shirts, had acne and drank chocolate milk. When he wasn't playing WoW and honing his (admittedly very impressive) version of the stereotypical web dork, he worked from his mother's attic (still honing), where Abby was sure he spent most of his web-building hours 'utilising' the photos of all her girls. She shuddered at the thought.

'As little as possible,' said Rob, packing up his papers and laptop, and sliding them both neatly into a dark brown satchel. 'Think about what I told you this morning – your overheads are too high, you need to downsize your staff. You stand to make a lot more money if you skim off the cream, trim the fat, strip the—'

'I get it, Rob, I understand.'

'It's fortuitous that you want to rebuild your site at this time, because I think your new site is the perfect avenue for exactly what I'm talking about. If you can make bookings via the website only, not phone, then you can cut at least two staff. Taxi companies do it, hotels, airlines . . . It's smart, and it saves a tonne of cash.'

'People are so disposable to you, aren't they?' said Abby. He was right, of course. But it broke her heart a bit to even imagine telling a staff member, let alone several of them, they were being replaced by a website.

'No way. I need them and their incapacity to add numbers.' He smiled and slipped his jacket on, straightening it and smoothing it over his waistcoat as he went.

He walked out of her office, throwing charming remarks to the girls as he strode through, making them giggle and blush, and wonder about what it would be like to kiss him.

Abby turned back to her laptop. Fuck it. She would just send out a few emails, like Rob said. She would ask for a 'business' site, one that could function as a booker, and make it very clear she needed it done soon. These web and design people always seemed to be inconceivably busy, she thought. Perhaps it was their filter, so they could pick and choose the jobs (and clients) they actually wanted to work with. She couldn't blame them. She did the same.

Abby woke up with a start and pressed snooze. It was 6.25 a.m. Why did she set her alarm so early? She always did that, assuming that in the morning she would obviously be inspired to run, or do her yoga video, or if she was feeling particularly ambitious, meditate, but she only ever wanted to sleep more. As usual, her work brain kicked in once she'd been awake for four seconds, and she automatically checked her email inbox, one eye still closed, pirate-style, so as to avoid waking up completely.

The usual emails greeted her, daily newsletters from blogs and websites she never opened, a couple Angie had forwarded on from girls wanting to be part of the agency, and two replies from web companies. The first, from Johan of Intelligent IT, was one sentence long, and as the tail of that sentence featured the number $110,000, was quickly deleted. *Johan, you are off your tree*, Abby thought as she opened the second email, from Marcus at Webra. *Nice name*, she thought, smiling to herself, her mind again springing back to the events of last Saturday night. In this very bed.

> Hi Abby.
>
> Please find attached a rough quote for the renovation of allureagency.com.
>
> Despite the fact we are very busy doing lots of impressive work for brands you recognise and aspire to, we guarantee a 30-day turnaround if 50% deposit is paid up-front. We also guarantee we will produce a site superior – technically and visually – than anyone else will deliver, because we only employ the best. And we don't feed them until they produce magic.
>
> I look forward to hearing back from you.
>
> Cheers,
>
> Marcus.
>
> PS How was your fiancé's business trip?

When Abby's eyes read over the last line of Marcus's email, she bolted upright, her eyes enormous and nanometres from her screen. *Fuck!* It was Marcus! Amazing sex Marcus! Of *all* the fucking Marcuses in all the web design companies in *all* the world, and she chose to email him. Unbelievable.

Her breath quickened and a wash of heat crept from her back up her neck. She felt the same way she did when she and Mads were busted shoplifting back at school. Guilty, stupid and busted.

She quickly re-read her initial email to make sure she sounded friendly, but professional. Yes, all good. The only thing she could be accused of was being a little cold, but she didn't know it would be HIM reading it, did she? She could also maybe, a little bit, be accused of having lied about being engaged, she admitted sheepishly.

Did he know she was lying? she wondered, furiously nibbling on her thumbnail as she ruminated the possibility that he'd caught her out and was deliberately letting her know he had . . . Or, was he genuinely asking about her fictional fiancé and his make-believe business trip? Just as a way to let her know he was *that* Marcus? Well, she supposed, how else was he going to alert her that it was him: 'Hi Abby, It's me, Marcus! That guy you took back to your place last Saturday night for several rounds of energetic and vocal sex? So, anyway, about that quote . . .'

For all he knew there could be two Abbys who worked at Allure. Or it could be the wrong Allure and Abby altogether. He'd played it well, she conceded. Very ballsy. As soon as she concluded that thought bubble, her mind immediately swung back to the thought of him knowing she didn't really have a fiancé. She recognised that this puzzle, and her impatient curiosity, would continue to sauté nicely throughout the day. And it was only 6.32 a.m. Wonderful.

It suddenly occurred to her that she would be required to write back. Was she going to play along with the fiancé thing? But what if he knew she didn't have one? Then she would look even more ridiculous. Maybe she could humbly admit she didn't really have one. Suck it up and move forward.

Oh God, it was too much. It was too far-fetched to even be believed. Serves me right for lying, she grumbled as she swung her legs over the side of the bed, stood up and walked to her 'exercise clothes' drawer.

9

'What's all the fuss, Gus? I got, like, eighty missed calls from you.'
Chelsea had been having a facial, and even though it killed her to
be away from her BlackBerry, she realised having it in her hand
on the massage table was a bit offensive. She walked to her car
wearing her hair under a baseball cap and the kind of colossal sunglasses that used to be reserved for superstars and WAGs, but now
everyone wore. Even though she had exceptional skin, she hated
being seen without makeup, and with greasy, post-facial hair. You
never knew who you might run into. Ryan Gosling, for example.

'I'm pregnant!' Abby shrieked the words in a way she hoped
sounded authentic.

'What are you even *talking* about?'

Abby had momentarily forgotten that Chelsea was too cool to
fall for pranks.

'Forget it, I was calling becau—'

'Well maybe don't use that one on Mads, huh? Might be considered a little tasteless.'

'Oh, *relax*. Since when did you get all earnest? It doesn't suit
you. Now. Can I tell you an amazing story? You will like it. Promise.'

Chelsea opened the door to her convertible and got in. 'Yes. Go.'

'So, Marcus. From the other week?'

'The infant?'

'Yes. I accidentally emailed him, not knowing it was him. Well, actually I emailed the place he works, a web design place, just to the general contact email, and *he* wrote back.'

'Oh come *on*, Abs. I know how to stalk better than anyone. You were stalking. Be honest.'

'*No!* Honestly, no. I emailed a bunch of places asking for a quote because the Allure site is so 1999 and I need a new one. So he has somehow seen my email come in, and maybe that's his job there, maybe he's the receptionist guy, I don't know, but he's replied, all businesslike, and then, at the end under his name, has written, 'How was your fiancé's business trip?'

'Shut UP. He did NOT.' Chelsea's first words of shock and amazement always came in the form of aggressive disagreement.

'He did! He really did. And I can't figure out if he knows I don't have a fiancé, or if that was just his cheeky way of letting me know that it was him . . .'

'Yeah, good call . . . And he said nothing else, just that? I mean, apart from the work stuff?'

'Mm-hmm. I have to write back, obviously, that's why I was being a keeno and calling you non-stop. I need advice.' Chelsea was phenomenal at games with men.

'This is karma, you realise. You've been stitched so that you learn that it's inappropriate to fake having a fiancé. You're just lucky it was a gentle retribution.'

'Says the girl who flirts by car accident. *What do I write back?*'

Chelsea stroked the smooth, cold leather of her steering wheel as she thought.

'Do you want to see him again?'

Abby scrunched up her mouth and thought about the question: *Did* she want to see him again? Sure, the sex was great, but there was plenty of good sex to be had out there; she had the experience to prove it. The idea of dealing with a twenty-two year old, even one as switched-on as Marcus, just seemed like a bad idea. Eventually he would either get bored of her and go back to the world of the youthful, lithe and cellulite-free, or fall in love with her, not because he was actually in love with her, of course, but because like all the others, he was in love with how much she didn't need him. It was the world's most intoxicating aphrodisiac, it really was: if you want a man to go gooey over you, tell him you're not looking for anything serious right now. It baffled her that more women didn't understand this most rudimentary of rules.

'No, probably not, actually. Which means I don't have to admit to no fiancé, right?'

'Unless he knows you're lying. Or you end up working with him on the website.'

'Fuck! This thing is going in circles. It's ridiculous. I've wasted too much time on this little shit and his cryptic email. What if I write back and say, you know, rahrahrah, professional stuff about the quote, and then, um, like, "My fiancé's trip was most productive, thank you for asking." So it cuts it off.'

'Or just go along with it?'

'Chels, this isn't a rom-com movie, I'm not going to put photos of me and my Fake Fiancé on my desk and live a hilarious double life whenever Marcus comes into the office.'

Chelsea sighed. 'Why don't you want to see him again? I know you don't have anything against inappropriate fuck buddies, because that mess of a DJ and that creepy professor guy were both about as inappropriate as they come. So, why? Why not keep him around for some good times?'

'Chels, not once have I ever suggested the men I sleep with are viable relationship material, which, if you think about it, is probably the precise reason I sleep with them, because I don't want a relationsh—'

'Ummm, sounds an awful lot like you're proving MY point?'

'I just couldn't be bothered going down that path. Remember what happened with Victoria? My waxer? That young guy she was totally in love with, he was like twenty-five and she was, well, she's our age, and he SHIT himself two weeks out from the wedding and just fucked off for a week and turned his phone off. Flipped OUT. She called the whole wedding off; couldn't trust him after that. Anyway, whatever, I don't have the energy to be with, as you correctly label him, an infant. No good can come from it. I'm too busy, and also, they are definitely the best web designers around, and I like to keep my biz and my boys separate.'

'Is thaaat why you and Rob have never got it on . . .'

'Pffft. *Please.* That's a nonversation: you know I'd jump him in a second if he didn't have Drab Girlfriend.'

Chels laughed. 'So just keep it business then. And if you have a work meeting, wear something totally hot.'

'Good one. Thanks, Chels.'

'Pilates tomorrow? Come on. Do you good.'

'Do US good, is what you're meant to say, my skinny, arrogant friend.'

'Bye! Kisses.' Chelsea pressed 'end call' on her phone, started the engine and turned up her radio.

Dear Marcus,

Thank you for the time taken with your quote. We're very keen to get this thing turned around fast, and you've offered a very competitive rate and timeframe, so please inform me of the next step and we can get this underway.

We're happy to pay the fifty per cent up-front in order
to complete the job within thirty days.

Abby had so many jokes and witty little asides she wanted to slip into the email, it felt so alien writing in such an official manner. But! She had to. It was strictly *business*.

And yes, my fiancé's trip was very productive.

I look forward to hearing from you re: moving forward.

Abby.

She *hated* the fiancé line. She cut it, then pasted it back in. It felt like she was flirting, playing with him, even though she most definitely wasn't. She'd acknowledged it was That Abby, but hadn't given any hint she wanted to further pursue that train of conversation. It would have to do. If he wrote anything further, she would completely ignore it.

Send.

Not five minutes later, a little envelope icon appeared. Abby braced herself.

Hi Abby,

Great! Webra is thrilled to be able to work with Allure on this project, and not just because it means we'll be working with photos of stunning girls for the next month.

The next step is a meeting with our head designer and our dev genius in order to talk through your vision, and then tell you most of it is impossible.

How are you placed Tuesday at 10am? Webra will come to you, of course.

Thank you for choosing us,

Cheers,

Marcus.

Abby exhaled for what felt like four days. *Excellent*. He was playing professional. What a good stick he was. He was very playful, as she recalled he was in Real Life, but she could handle that. He'd made no mention of fictitious fiancés or wild sex, and this satisfied Abby enough to believe this thing could work after all, and wouldn't just be an awkward mess. She was a little concerned he would find out – if he didn't already know – there was no fiancé, but figured they'd be chummy enough professionally by then that it would be a) cast aside, b) funny and c) utterly inconsequential.

Plus she was spending $40k with his company. That had to account for *something*.

She read his email again to see if he might be one of the two people mentioned, but it didn't sound like it. She doubted he'd be the 'head' of anything at twenty-two.

Hi Marcus,

That time and day sounds fine. Our address is on my signature.

All best,

Abby.

This was good. The Marcus issue was sorted, the new website was underway, things were going to become more streamlined, more money would be coming in, and maybe, just maybe this year was the one she would be able to take some time off and travel. Yes! Good times.

Now she just had the teeny task of firing someone, or Rob's preference, multiple someones.

10

Abby was mid-way through trying to source ten non-slutty bunny outfits for the launch of a new premium whisky, and failing – bunny outfits stopped being adorable and started becoming trampy the moment the wearer had breasts – when Angie's familiar voice came through the speaker.

'Abby, your 10 o'clock is here?'

Webra! Abby closed the three browser windows and swore quietly to herself. She still hadn't completely formed in her mind what she wanted the site to be, and if there was one thing that pissed her off in business meetings, it was when the client didn't know exactly what they wanted. Now she was going to be that asshole.

'Pop them in the boardroom, set them up with water and coffee and I'll be in in one sec.'

She applied some red Chanel lipstick and popped a mint in her mouth for a turbo suck before spitting it into a tissue and into her wastepaper basket. Red lipstick, she'd learned in some dopey, over-analytical and mildly offensive book on being a successful female CEO, was a very effective way of instantly asserting that you were not to be messed with, but not afraid of your femininity.

Abby thought red lipstick generally made men think of sex – but she wore it anyway. It suited her, with her green eyes and dirty blonde hair, and it made her penchant for simple black dresses fall more to the chic and deliberate end of the scale, as opposed to lazy and uninventive. If it earned her some biz points, that was a bonus.

As she walked, laptop, pen and pad in hand, it suddenly occurred to her Marcus might be here. Oh well, she thought. No time like the present to get the awkwardness over with. He couldn't ruffle her feathers with doe-eyed glances across the table, *especially* not when she was in biz mode.

She opened the door to the boardroom, an impressive room with a Florence Broadhurst rug, windows overlooking the city, her favourite fresh David Austin roses on a small art deco-style glass table and a dark brown, antique table with matching chairs. She was very, very proud of this room. That it looked exactly like something out of a design magazine was no accident; she'd modelled it precisely on just that. Warm, chic and beautiful. *So* Allure.

At her table sat one bald, attractive older guy in a black shirt and glasses. And one guy with wild black curls, facial hair and a plain navy t-shirt. And one Marcus. Oh *why* was he here? Dear God, Abby thought, the pity already forming in her mind, please don't let it be because he wanted to see her.

Marcus had shorter hair than she recalled, and a black-and-white checked shirt with a skinny black tie. Jesus. First Rob and now Marcus – when did men start dressing like they were auditioning for a role in *Grease*?

Shit. Maybe Rob should be here! Lend some impressiveness! She didn't even think of it. And now it was too late. Just her, her whorish red lips and three dudes who knew everything.

'Good morning, gentleman, I'm Abby Vaughn. Thanks for coming in to see me today.'

She shook each of their hands as they introduced themselves – Chris, Arthur and of course, Marcus – and they all sat back down. She noticed Marcus was the only one with a laptop; the others had stylish leather-bound notebooks in a grey on white zebra pattern. Ahh. Zebra. Webra. Very good.

The bald man spoke first. 'Abby, I should probably explain why there's three of us, when generally we only send two along to these meetings. I'm Chris, the founder and MD of Webra, and occasionally I pop along to these things to annoy the boys and make them feel incompetent and stutter awkwardly and so on. Keeps things interesting.'

Abby laughed. 'I've been known to do the very same thing.'

'Terribly entertaining.' Chris had a warm smile and sparkly eyes and the kind of skin that spent a little too much time in the sun. Probably less Indonesia and more Riviera, judging by the size and brand of his watch. He was a bit of a silver fox, Abby conceded. Could you be a silver fox if you had no hair? Maybe he was a shiny fox.

'So, Arthur is our head of development, which means he will oversee the actual workings of the site, and Marcus here is our award-winning head designer, so it's his job to make it look incredible and be a joy for the user. It didn't take too much convincing for him to agree to this particular job, strangely.'

Abby smiled, first at John, then Marcus. Marcus was leaning back slightly in his seat, smiling sincerely at Abby. He was outrageously calm for someone who was supposed to be nervous with lust for her.

'Well, shall we get started? If any of you have had a chance to look at our current site, which was created in the time it takes to re-heat a pizza and probably loses me as much business as it attracts, you'll see it needs to be executed, and swiftly.'

'For the sake of politeness, we'll just nod in agreement,' said

Chris, smiling.

'What I'm after, essentially, is a site that can make my agency, well . . . automatic. I'd like to eliminate all phone bookings, and make Allure an agency that, at least for the actual job-booking side of things, can be run entirely through the website.'

'Trying to trim some fat from staff numbers?'

'What? No!' Abby looked at Chris's face. He knew. It was obvious.

'Well, not deliberately.' They all laughed. 'It's more that I want the business to be able to be operated remotely, from anywhere. So that I can have my phone and my laptop and be in, I don't know, *Papua New Guinea* and still run my business.'

'Excellent plan.' Chris said.

'Chris says this because he spends seven months of the year in New York, London, Istanbul, Tunisia . . .' Arthur said wryly.

'That sounds like heaven,' Abby said, dreamily.

'Near enough. Obviously I had to establish great clients and exceptional staff first, but these days I'm fairly free to work from wherever I choose in the world. Liberty is the new luxury. What you're doing is very smart.'

'Automated emails to the models . . .' mumbled Arthur, as he madly wrote on his pad.

'Sorry . . .?' Abby asked, confused.

'Once the client-generated booking is finalised. When a job is booked, and the client enters the date, time and so on of the job, he or she also chooses the models he wants, with two or three backups in case the first choices aren't available. We could make it so all of the details go directly to the girls picked for the job, and they can accept or deny the job, and then that information comes back to you.'

'Well that's just removed about 75 per cent of the agency's work.'

'Easy. And we can set up email, SMS or Facebook reminders to the models the day before the job, for final confirmation.'

'Can we get one hourly on the day, too?'

Chris and Marcus laughed. 'Anything you'd like,' said Arthur dryly, who was writing again.

Marcus spoke up. 'Have you considered penalising the girl's pay if they cancel within twenty-four hours of the job?'

Abby shook her head in bewilderment. 'No . . .'

'Think about hotel cancellation policies. Or salons. Humans value something more if they're going to be punished financially for not showing up. And if you know twenty-four hours out, you can find another girl easier, right? Instead of at the eleventh hour.'

Abby's head was spinning. Who were these people, and why hadn't she met them five years ago?

'That's brilliant. All of this is brilliant. How do you— I thought you guys just made websites . . .'

Chris spoke. 'There's a lot more that goes into an intelligent website than decorative design and a few forms. We love solving big-picture problems as well. You have to be smart about how you use technology. Let it work for you. Literally.'

'The design itself, do you have any ideas?' Marcus asked, as he tapped away at hummingbird-wing pace on his laptop. He was being so professional. It irritated Abby. He was as calm as she had made sure she was. Where were the gooey smiles and nerves?

'Not really, I'm afraid. That said, I feel confident letting you guys drive. Let's keep the black and white theme, though, and lots of white space. The design has to be purposeful; everything needs to work automagically and all of it has to be meaningful for the user. No bells and whistles. Not that it should be barren, of course but—'

'Elegant. Modest. Not like traditional model sites.'

'Exactly, and unfortunately because of the name Allure, a name shared by many of our friends in the brothel, stripping and escort industry, I need it to instantly show we are not that. If that makes sense.'

'Deleting giant red stiletto on the homepage . . .' Marcus smiled cheekily and got back to his laptop.

The meeting bubbled along effervescently for another twenty-five minutes, and with each new notion raised, Abby became skittish with excitement about what her life could become once this site went live. These men, these impressive, clever men, had opened up the possibility of living the life she had aspired to, but had no tangible way of creating. A life that meant, she realised with a whisper of terror, she might not even need this beautiful office anymore. And all in under forty minutes.

Abby bid farewell to the Webra trio at reception, happily, excitedly, and just short of issuing high-fives, and floated back to her office, closing the door behind her. In six weeks she would have Allureagency.com 2.0. She would also have two, maybe three less staff and strong impetus to find a much smaller office, primarily for castings and dispensing outfits. Abby filled with pride knowing that soon she would be part of a brave new world. Her brother would be so proud! And she could actually go and visit him now, so that he could be proud in person.

As she started clicking on emails, her thoughts snuck on to Marcus. He had shown absolutely no hint of interest in her, she realised. Not one lurid smile, not one flirtatious glance. It wasn't even awkward saying goodbye to him. It was all the Right Thing for him to do, of course, but Abby couldn't help feeling deflated. And embarrassed: here she was assuming his initial email was a written declaration of intent, and then in person he was this suave meeting cat. And so clever! His ideas were dazzling; she could see why even though he was barely legal to drink he'd been made department head. She'd been blown away by his rapid-fire genius, each suggestion had been significant, every argument and explanation rational and helpful.

That he was extremely handsome was almost 99 per cent irrelevant. It was his grey matter that had thoughts of him, past and future, swirling through Abby's head.

I I

Mads was in a bad way. This was an entirely alien thing for Happily Married Super-in-love Mads. She'd had a fight with Dylan the night before and had reluctantly agreed to a 'crisis' meet-up at Chelsea's house first thing. It would be a regular fight for most couples, but, as they were as likely to yell at each other as a couple of Tibetan monks, it was epic for them. Knowing there was unhappiness between the Perfect Couple made Abby and Chelsea ill with unease.

The three of them sat morosely around Chelsea's kitchen table, drinking green tea. Abby and Chels looked timidly at Mads and Mads stared with tear-stained cheeks into her tea, fidgeting with the handle of one of Chelsea's prized Versace teacups.

'Jesus, it's like there's been a death,' Chelsea said. 'Not a real death, like, a celebrity death.'

'Mads,' said Abby softly. 'Please don't feel guilty about this. The fact that you want a baby is not something to feel bad about.'

'I don't feel guilty about that,' she said, sniffing. 'I just, I guess I feel bad about how I've made Dyl feel about my wanting a baby. I know he's feeling the strain. We got the quote for IVF last night and I could just see in his eyes he's feeling so fatigued.'

'Oh, honey . . .' Abby said, rubbing Mads's arm.

'He also said, that, that,' the tears started again, heartbreaking, raw tears, tears that Chels and Abby hadn't seen Mads cry since well before Dylan, back in the days of shower-after-sex Shaun and Danny the spray-tan-wearing actor, when Mads was a firecracker of a girlfriend, always ready to explode ' . . . that I'd changed.' Her soft tears made way for harder tears.

'Honey, you probably have changed. Your priorities certainly have. But it's not the end of the world. I mean, this is a man who cried more at your wedding than all of us combined.'

Mads shook her head and tore a couple of tissues from the box next to her. 'That's what's most devastating about all of this to me. I *have* changed. You don't see the half of it, when it's just the two of us I'm a different beast.'

Abby looked at Mads and sighed.

'Sweetie, it's a tough situation. And you mustn't be too hard on yourself. It's a big thing, and at risk of copping a wallop, you both have very valid points. You are allowed to want a baby, and Dyl is allowed to be feeling some fatigue and to be a bit weird about doing IVF. There is no right or wrong here. And you've been trying to conceive for over twelve months, of course it's starting to wear—'

'Of *course* it is!' interrupted Chelsea, clearly bursting after having had to wait so long to talk. 'This is heavy stuff. But it will be okay. You will sort it out. You know that. He knows that. Sometimes you just need to let off some steam to get the pressure back to normal.'

Abby looked at Chelsea in admiration and a teeny bit of shock. This from a woman whose philosophy in relationships was generally along the lines of, 'This is annoying; I'm leaving.' It was testament to how much she – everyone – believed in Mads and Dylan. A great relationship can do that, Abby realised. It can make not only the people within that relationship better people, but there is a flow-on effect to people in the couple's periphery. She knew personally that she had much higher expectations of men, relationships and herself after seeing how beautiful and loving it *could* be. Dammit! *They needed an effing baby! Stat!*

'Where did you leave it, Mads?' Abby asked.

She took a deep breath in and exhaled sadly. 'Nowhere good. After he'd said that I'd changed, I retaliated. It was horrible; I felt the gruesome old Mads rear up, the one who loved a fight. I didn't even know that foul wench still had a heartbeat.'

'What did she say?' asked Abby gently.

'You have to remember this is after trying, cycle after cycle, for almost fifteen months . . .'

'Darling, we're not here to judge you,' Abby said.

'It shits me, you know, that he says I've changed, because it infers I'm the only one this is affecting, which is bosh, because . . . *Anyway*. So, I said that maybe the new Mads didn't like the new Dylan, because he was such an unsupportive twat.'

'That's it?' Chels asked, her brows rose in line with her intonation.

'*Whatdoyoumean?* That's an atrocious thing to say!' Mads said, stoically defending her pathetic cruelty.

'The old Mads would've told him he was a useless fuck and he could shove his wedding ring up his arse!'

Abby clamped her lips together to block the smile forming. 'It's true, Mads. You would've ripped his nipples off, then kicked his motorbike over on the way out.'

A soft smile spread over Mads's face. She nodded, sniffing and wiping her nose. 'It's all relative.'

'Mads,' Abby spoke up. 'You know Dylan's intentions are solid gold, right? He IS being supportive and he wants more than anything for you to fall pregnant.'

Mads turned, rolling her eyes. 'Do you have to keep pointing out the black mark on the X-ray? I know that! But this bullshit could trickle on for another five stinkin' years; he needs to harden up!' She shook her head in frustration.

Abby took a moment to compose her thoughts. She knew Mads had a penchant for the dramatic; it was part of what made her such a fantastic writer and entertaining friend, but Abby couldn't help thinking a little bit of calm might be more helpful at this point.

'What if you were able to relax a bit, Mads? Just leave it to the universe for a bit?' Abby looked at Mads with kindness. And a little bit of trepidation.

'Yes! Em*brace* and enjoy the freedom!' said Chels jubilantly, as though she'd just been asked (for the chance to win $50,000) how one should best regard a year in which they are going to be neither pregnant nor breastfeeding.

'Seriously, you're still so young, babe. Lots of women have babies in their late thirties and even forties these days . . .'

Mads looked at her well-meaning friends and smiled sadly. Their intentions were good, but their arguments were both flawed and exasperating.

Mads stood up. 'All right, my well-meaning turkeys, I'm going home to apologise. I have to believe this will all work out eventually, for sanity's sake.'

Abby and Chelsea were confused as to whether to take this to mean their brilliant suggestion had been adopted as a plan of action. Mads's face suggested that it probably had not.

Mads pulled out her phone, which was illuminated.

'Dyl?' Chels asked.

'Yes, five missed calls.'

'Bless him. Even after you called him such outrageous, hurtful names.'

'He just sent a photo of him kissing the lens.' Mads welled up.

'We're such losers, aren't we?

'The biggest. We're here if you need us, although you definitely won't!' Abs called out to Mads as she walked off down the stairs, hoping it was true.

12

Abby left Chelsea's and headed across the city through dense, lunch-hour traffic. Ever since she'd known Mads, she'd wanted babies. She'd had no siblings; she'd worked as a nanny for years and now as a teacher. *The woman wanted kids!* Mads would get them, Abby confirmed to her self and the universe. And soon.

Her phone rang shrilly. Chels.

'Did I forget something?'

'No, but in all the Mads drama I forgot to ask what you're doing tomorrow night?'

It was Friday, her big night in. She was doing nothing.

'Chels, you know what I do on Friday nights...'

'When you're seventy I'll accept that as a valid excuse. But not when you're young and hot. You're coming to dinner at Cirque with Jeremy and some of his friends. Half because I want you to meet him; half because his friends are probably potential husband material.'

Abby sighed. 'Really?'

'Really. See you there at eight. I would offer you a lift, but Porsches have only two seats . . .'

60

'You're such a wanker. Oh shit, you know what, I actually might not be able to get there, I just remember—'

'Don't start, Abs . . .'

'No, I'm serious, I have a job down at the pier and the girls – there are ten of them – are in full costume, and it's a new client, and I want to make sure no one's arses are being pinched.'

'Don't you have those thugs for that very purpose?'

'Yes, but the client is new, and they have about four billion alcohol clients, so it's worth me sticking my head in for an hour to suck up and check the girls – and the clients – are behaving.'

'Alright,' Chelsea sighed petulantly. 'So what time?'

Abby sighed. Chelsea was factory set to 'bully' and there was no point arguing. 'I'll come for a drink after, at around, I dunno, ten. Will that suit your highness?'

'It will have to do. Dress sexy. Kisses!' And she'd gone. She was such a brat, Abby mused to herself. She knew a lot of her second-tier friends thought Chelsea was a bit of a nightmare, and couldn't quite place how Abby could be such close friends with her. But Chelsea, like Mads, were as good as sisters to Abby. She forgave them their foibles and they offered her the same courtesy. At thirty-three Abby wasn't taking applications for new friends, and she knew no one she could be as brutally frank with, and as relaxed and genuine around, as the girls. She loved them. Full stop. No exceptions.

Abby arrived at work to find only Angie, who told Abby the bookers were at lunch; they'd been gone for over an hour and should be back any moment. Abby walked through to her desk and sat down to get to work, an enormous double skinny 'flatte' in her hand. Forty-five minutes later Charlotte and Siobhan came into the office, laughing and swinging bags plump with new goods, and complaining they felt sick after that Mars Bar.

Abby sent Angie an instant message.

A, how long have the girls been gone?

not sure, abt 2 hours I think but im not positive

One of their birthdays or anything?

nope ☺

Ok, thanks.

Little shits. They were taking two-hour lunches now, were they? And so ostentatious! Walking in with their loot and laughing as though they haven't a care in the world, or a lick of work to do, or a boss who was right in front of them, watching it all.

Not one for confrontations, Abby began creating a savage, but subtle email to let them know she was onto them. Abby was about to hit send when she realised their audacity was actually a gift: If they didn't have much work to do, then *there wasn't enough work*. This was a blessing! It would feel a lot more justified laying them off, if there was evidence of scarce work.

What a shame Angie was so young and inexperienced. She had just the kind of work ethic Abby'd need once she moved so much of the business online: diligent, intuitive, conscientious, self-aware . . . *Was* she that young? Was age really of that much consequence if she had the smarts and the drive? Was it worth training her up a little? Abby felt like it very much might be. Angie would always need time for her castings and band gigs and frog-catching and whatever new talent she was pursuing that week, but that was okay, as long as she was always near her phone and had a laptop – between Abby and the website, surely that would be enough staff to manage thirty models and, say, five to ten jobs a week.

But then, thought Abby, what about when *she* wanted to travel for extended periods? She'd need someone she could send along to check on the girls. Someone authoritative, someone who would whip them into line – and the client too – if there was any funny business. Just a few weeks ago four girls had been booked for a corporate boat cruise with the simple expectation they would serve drinks and provide scintillating conversation from 7 to 10 p.m. When Abby got a call from one of the girls saying that it was less of a corporate shindig, and more of a surprise buck's night – something Abby never allowed the girls to work at – and they were docking at one of the guys' houses to take the party inside, Abby had needed to be around, sober and in driving distance, to get there and rescue her girls. She would never leave them as sitting ducks where drunk, obnoxious men were concerned. They were on her books; they were her responsibility.

She'd toyed with the idea of providing the girls with a driver to take them home, but often the girls went out after a job, or wanted their boyfriends to pick them up, so it appeared to be a superfluous cost. Like that time she'd bought each of the girls a walkie-talkie the size of a twenty cent piece, with the idea they could wear them while on the job, and contact each other if they needed assistance. Half the girls lost them before they'd even had a chance to wear them, a few who did bother to bring and wear them complained they emitted small zaps, and a handful spent the night making fart noises into them to the amusement of the other girls.

Perhaps she was being overprotective, Abby thought. These girls were all in their twenties, some were in their thirties, even if their passport was the only one brave enough to admit it, and they should be able to look out for themselves and each other. But if things got hard or there was a sniff of something that seemed inappropriate, they called Abby. From bringing the wrong shoes, to outfits that were too slutty and girls who no-showed, there was barely a shift that went flawlessly, and didn't result in at least one call or text from a model. It was probably her own fault, she realised with chagrin. She'd trained them to think with Abby's brain, not their own.

Abby placed her elbows on her desk and her head between her hands. Why had she chosen an industry based on pretty girls? They'd spent their whole lives having people wanting to make life easy and enjoyable for them, and now she was doing the same thing. She should've become a cake-decorator instead.

13

'I can't find my gloves!'

'Nat, does your dress fit right? Mine's too big in the tits; think ours got mixed up.'

'My ass looks YUGE in this. I can't go out there wearing this . . . Ohmygod. You can *totally* see cellulite. Ger*oss*.'

'GIRLS.' Abby had to bellow to be heard above the high-pitched statements of fictitious body fat and ill-fitting outfits and the band warming up.

'You all look incredible. That's why you were chosen for this job, and that's why you're here, and that's why you chose this profession, because you know you're gorgeous. So shut it. Now, you need to be ready in three minutes, and you need to look perfect. Remember, this is a new client and potentially a very lucrative and long-lasting one, so I need you all at your sparkling best. Use whatever means you must to be that. Mints, energy drinks, water, lollies, nuts and crystal meth are by the door.'

The girls laughed and then went back to applying gloss, bronzer, concealer, perfume and gently scrunching their perfectly rollered curls to keep the bounce. They looked outstanding, Abby thought, very Julie London. All thigh-high splits and sequined gowns, elbow-grazing gloves, costume jewellery, red lipstick and luscious, smooth curls care of a small team of makeup and hair artists . . . 1940s nightclub singers was a splendid theme. Much better than 'sexy bunnies', which is what the event manager had initially requested.

After peering through the curtains for thirty minutes, watching the usual palaver in which sober men tried not to stare at her girls, the same men who would not one hour later be openly ogling them, and then two hours later, brazenly, pitifully trying to chat them up, Abby felt a gentle tap on her shoulder.

'Abby?'

A pretty, small girl with a full fringe, shoulder-length brown hair and a red shift dress was smiling at Abby. She looked like she might be Audrey Tatou's little sister. With a penchant for earpieces and clipboards.

'Sorry to scare you, I'm Charlie. Charlie Fennessy?'

THIS was Charlie? Abby had assumed it was a male she'd been dealing with all this time. She tried to recall if she'd ever hinted at such in emails . . .

'Hi! Charlie, great to meet you. You must be relieved it's finally here, huh? You've been working on this for months . . .'

'I'll be relieved when the clock strikes eleven and we get to kick all these schmucks out.' Both women laughed.

'Hey, thanks for all your hard work with the girls and their out-fits. They look so cool. At first I wasn't sold on the glittery Jessica Rabbit evening gowns, just so you know, but your girls look amazing.'

Abby smiled and Charlie smiled back; she had an adorable gap between her front teeth, it added to her cute, quirky French girl appeal.

'Now, can I get you some relaxation nectar? Ooh, *I* know: Some Drimms Whisky perhaps?

Abby laughed. 'I don't drink brown spirits – flashbacks of being a weepy, spewy mess at teenage parties – but if you have wine I'd love a glass.'

'Tried whisky, dry and lime? It's good. Trust me.' Charlie looked at Abby with her big brown eyes and a mischievous grin, nodding quickly as the clincher in pulling Abby's decision into the affirmative.

'I'll try one on your recommendation. But if I end up in the corner sobbing because Brendan Winter won't pash me, you've no one to blame but yourself.'

'Ladies and gents, please welcome our newest member to Team Whisky! I'll be back in twelve seconds.'

Abby watched her slip through the curtains and into the opulence of the party, a little girl among giants. *What a dynamo!* Abby liked her immediately. She was so cool. And what an impressive event she had produced. Abby was always very supportive of females at the top of their game. There wasn't nearly enough back-slapping in female business.

As Abby scanned the room again, something in the corner of the bar caught her eye. It was Natasha and Sabrina, looking around furtively as they each quickly slammed a shot of whatever the handsome devil behind the bar had given them. What was their caper? They were supposed to be the eldest, the most responsible, Abby's Best in Show! Abby watched as they laughed and walked away, laughing into each other with linked arms, playing best friends at high school. Abby's breath had started flowing through her nostrils, and her hands were jammed tightly into each other across her chest when Charlie returned with two glasses, her clipboard tucked under her arm.

'Heeeere we go', she said, passing one to Abby. 'I'll bet my bike that you'll like this. It's the girliest way you can drink whisky without being beaten up by cowboys— hey, you okay? You look much more likely to throw something than when I left.'

Abby smiled as she took a sip. To her surprise, it *was* kind of delicious. She took another one, quickly, hoping the alcohol would burn up her fury.

'Bah, it's nothing. I just saw two of my girls; the two I would consider my best, slamming shots of something at the bar. They know they're not allowed to drink on the job. Shits me to tears.'

'Phillipe. If the guy who served them was the best looking man you've ever seen, that's Phillipe. He'll butter them up like a dinner roll in five seconds flat. Could make a virgin take the lead role in a porno. Trust me, they're dealing with means beyond them.'

Abby looked to see if Charlie was kidding, but as she earnestly sipped from her glass and cocked her head to listen to something coming through her headpiece, she looked absolutely normal.

'What do you mean, exactly, by that?'

'Girls are powerless against him. It's well-known in the events industry that Phillipe will brainwash your female staff, woo them, seduce them, make them forget they have a boyfriend and have them in his bed before the dawn. He's like . . . I dunno, a sex wizard or something. It's amazing to watch.'

'He sounds kind of gross, actually.'

'No, no, he's a dish. French accent. Body you'd be stupid to put clothes on. Smart. Plays the guitar. Funny. He doesn't do any of it deliberately—'

Abby sighed. 'Alright. I'll let the girls off. But I might go out and survey how many of them are walking around half shitfaced thanks to ol' Frenchy.'

Charlie smiled. 'I'll see you out there. The client is already pissed and has just told me he wants every guest to leave with a bottle of his best whisky. Which we don't have. But must find.'

She slurped the last of her drink and placed her glass on the table. 'Whisky me luck.'

Abby laughed. She liked Charlie. She was ballsy. She must get her number; maybe they could form a work relationship, throwing each other business where possible.

Before she walked out to make sure Phillipe was not drugging any of her girls, Abby checked her makeup in her compact, gently powdered down some shine on her nose, and applied a new layer of nude lipgloss. She'd opted for a bit of a smoked eye tonight, over her usual bare eyes and red lips. She'd mussed up her hair a bit too, it was getting long and wispy and her highlights needed re-doing desperately, but she kind of liked how it had worked out tonight. Add her fitted olive green dress and new nude heels, and she looked pretty good. Chelsea's Porsche-driving mates would not be disappointed, she nodded smugly to herself.

'Having fun, ladies?' Abby sidled up to her shot-skolling jazz singers, close enough that she could pretend to have smelled their breath. 'Whoa, who's been drinking?' Abby threw the question up hoping it wouldn't get shot and fall back to earth with a blazing gun of denial.

But she'd forgotten who she was dealing with here: Pretty girls. They always had a bloody answer for everything.

'The guy behind the bar told us it was a mock-shot. It has no alcohol in it,' said Sabrina, yelling over the music.

'And you believed him?'

'What?'

'Never mind. I don't care if it's full of rocket fuel or lemonade; you cannot be seen slamming shooters while you're working. Come on, girls, you know this. And I saw you do it with my own eyes, so don't deny it. Just be smarter, please? I rely on you two to be a good example to the others.'

Natasha looked sheepish, Sabrina more like she was trying to construct a physical force field of immunity against being in trouble.

'Okay, you two. Have a good night. No more drinking till you clock off and are out of costume.'

Abby turned around and politely waited while four very drunk men in front of her tormented another drunk man, who apparently had just been brutally rebuffed by one of her girls. Good. She'd taught them well. Finally she was able to sneak past, and scanning the room one last time for all her girls, she made her way to the backstage area. Just as she was about to reach for the black curtain she felt a tap on her left shoulder. Expecting Charlie, she turned around with a wide smile. And was faced with Marcus.

'Oh, God, I was expecting someone else,' she said, her hand flying to her heart in shock.

He was wearing a dark maroon velvet suit, with a white shirt, black buttons and a black bow tie. If she didn't know who he was, she would assume he was in the band, famous or gay.

'Your fiancé?'

She peered at him to see what his eyes were saying. Was he challenging her to lie? Or was he genuinely asking her? She couldn't tell. Just as in the meeting the other day, he was terrific at halting any kind of emotion before it could sneak out via his eyes or smile. He'd make a terrific blackjack player.

'No, a colleague actually.'

'I thought the sexy jazz birds might have been the workings of Allure,' he said, nodding his head back to the heaving, loud chaos behind him.

'Because you've studied them on the website? Or because they're gorgeous?'

He grinned. 'Bit of both . . . Did I stop you from doing something?' He gestured to the curtain. She could smell the warm scent of whisky on his breath, which was probably true of 100 per cent of the people in this ballroom, staff included.

'I was just leaving, actually. But I needed to find Charlie first.'

'Is Charlie your fiancé?'

Abby blinked a few times as she tried to comprehend his bolshiness and the question.

'*Nooo*, Charlie is a woman, and she is the event manager. What's the preoccupation with my fiancé?'

'Well, mostly . . . I'd have to say it's because I don't think you have one. You're not wearing any rings for starters, you have a *very* feminine house and, I don't know, you just don't strike me as a philanderer.'

Abby crossed her arms. 'And why not?'

'You're too elegant. And smart. And careful. And pedantic. The guilt would drive you insane.'

Abby tried to cram the smile spreading over her face back into her mouth. He was too smart for a kid. *Way* too smart. She had an irresistible urge to kiss him. His smiling lips were very attractive all of a sudden.

'What if I knew he was cheating on ME, and you were a retaliation cheat?'

'I'd say you should call off the wedding.'

Abby laughed. 'Alright, Sherlock. You've got me. Tell me, did you already know I was lying in your very first email?'

'Of course. Knew you wouldn't admit it, though. Too careful, like I said. Figured it was something you said to guys you didn't want hanging around.'

'Okay. But riddle me this; how did you know it was me when you got that email?'

'You told me you owned a brothel called Allure when you were trolleyed the other weekend. Just before you ushered me into a taxi

71

so that no one would see you were "kidnapping" me.'

Abby covered her eyes with one hand in shame. 'I didn't. Did I?'

'You did. Luckily Google quickly led me to your not-brothel website when I was stalking you. You know, after you kicked me out into the street at dawn?' He grabbed two potent, Long Island Iced Tea looking things off a tray floating past and held one out to her. Abby checked her phone. It was only just nine. She had time for one drink . . .

Abby took a sip and looked into Marcus's eyes as she did so. He looked straight back at her. *Finally*, he was communicating with them! As he held her stare, Abby felt something race through her that indicated she might have to re-visit the naked Marcus and Abby show again.

'Don't you think it's wild that of all the web companies in the city, you emailed Webra?' Marcus said, once he'd adequately non-verbally communicated his intent. 'At first I hoped you'd stalked *me*, but I never told you what I did, or where I worked, and you never asked because you're kind of arrogant, so I was especially blown away.'

'Arrogant, huh? Is that any way to speak to your elders?'

'Stumbling down that rickety old path, are we?' he said, his eyes glazed with disdain in that way Abby recognised in her young models when she asked them to stop texting while she was briefing.

'Which path? The one where I'm doing grown up things like cooking osso bucco and you're skateboarding?'

He snorted. 'Are you serious? Besides, you're what, thirty? Men fool around with women ten to fifteen years younger than them all the time, and no one bats an eyelid. Age is irrelevant. Brains are what count.'

'While Hugh Hefner has done a great many things in his time, his stance on age-gaps between men and women can't be considered a particularly feasible template.'

He shook his head.

'Alright. Have it your way. Would you like me to call you a cougar from now on? Would that put you at ease?'

Abby sensed that Marcus was becoming genuinely pissed, and she herself felt the hot prickle of indignation climbing up her skin in response to his attitude. Why? She thought they were joking around. He was very defensive. Maybe he always went out with older women. But Abby didn't feel like an 'older woman', she felt sexier and more confident than she'd ever been. She was a mess at twenty-three; so insecure and confused, she'd really only started to figure out who she was at about twenty-eight. Now, five years later, she definitely knew who she was, and it was *not* an 'older woman'.

'I think you have to be at least forty to be an authentic cougar. Perhaps I can be a cheetah? A cute house cat?'

Marcus smiled; the tension was diffused. 'Garfield?'

Abby rolled her eyes. 'Okay. But try not to call me that in meetings if it's all the same? Might send out the wrong message.'

'So if not in meetings, when?'

Abby knew the exact trap he was setting. She just had to decide if she was ready to glide into it. Was the fact they would be working together an issue? Probably. Possibly? Not really . . .

Marcus continued to look at Abby admiringly, his eyes penetrating into hers, challenging her to refuse his play. She was helpless. In that way that meant she wasn't helpless at all, but actually very, very full of energy and focus indeed. In regards to one thing, anyway.

'Oh, I don't know. When you're at my place tonight?'

An excited smile took over Marcus's face, as though he'd just been given the keys to Dad's car for the evening.

'Are you instigating a late-night hook-up, Abby Vaughn?'

'Are you going to bore me with obvious questions?'

He shook his head. 'You're a bully, do you know that? Play me like a fiddle.'

'Or a toy? Isn't that why you're called toyboys?'

'You need to stop it with all the clichés, doll.'

'And *you* need to not call me doll.'

'May I have your address? And a phone number too? That's if it's not too forward and/or your pretend fiancé isn't going to mind.'

Abby grabbed his phone from his hand – it was the new model iPhone, of course – and put her number in. 'Prank me and I'll text you the address. Shall we say . . . elevenish?'

'Whoa, I thought you meant now. Got some other guy you need to meet up with first?'

'For your information, I have drinks with some friends. Not that I need to tell you what I'm doing.'

Abby was very intrigued by her tone. She was used to being confident around men, it was part of her 'I don't need or really want a boyfriend' thing, but with Marcus she sensed an elevated level of bossiness. It had to be his age, she realised. She was asserting her role as the older, wiser one, even though the more time she spent with him, the more obvious it became that he was far from a servant needing a master. Pah, it was all part of the sexual circus. Run with it, she told herself.

'Okay, whatever, I'll be there. Ready to work on those website designs.'

He winked – it was sexy, not cheesy, and walked back into the hub of suits and tanned legs and noise and Latino house music.

Abby walked behind the curtain and saw Charlie talking animatedly to a sweaty, flustered guy in all black, carrying several boxes of what must be expensive whisky. He raced off and Charlie collapsed in a chair and closed her eyes, her head facing up to the ceiling.

'Everything okay?' Abby asked.

Charlie looked over and made the symbol of slicing her wrist with a knife.

Abby laughed as she walked over to Charlie, hoisting her handbag onto her shoulder as she did. Charlie plucked a small red card from her clipboard.

'Take my card, maybe we can go for a coffee one time?'

'Sure!' Abby smiled. 'Hey, you should be proud of yourself – that's a good party out there. Always a good sign when no one's leaving early. Have a fun weekend and please feel free to yell at any Allure girls who take it upon themselves to dance on tables.'

'Can do. Cool to meet you, Abby.' Charlie smiled and Abby walked back through the curtain, into the crowd and into what had recently become quite an exciting evening.

14

As suspected, Jeremy's friends were complete dickheads. It was as though there had been an exhibition of Drunken, Rich Stereotypes in the museum next door, and they'd snuck out after closing time.

The obviously-on-cocaine guy with his shirt open two buttons too many was married, but someone had clearly forgotten to tell him, because he spent the entire session trying to lean lecherously over Abby and flirt with her using incredible Can I Buy You a Drink technology. And the young guy with hair from a 1986 Harvard brochure and a slimy jock-hero glint to match was just as bad, telling swagger stories about his awesome job, and important friends and ordering Dom Pérignon, even though everyone had moved on to spirits, and weren't nearly as impressed as he'd hoped when he had the cute waitress bring it to the table with a bowl of strawberries and $600 worth of insincere fanfare.

Jeremy, though, was a delight. Abby immediately got what Chelsea saw in him. He was funny, charming, quick-witted and spectacularly handsome – Chelsea pretended she was above choosing men for their looks but she absolutely was not – and he was genuine and welcoming to Abby, and not just for show, and not just for the three minutes it took for the platitudes to dissolve. He apologised for his mates' *behaviour*, but not for his mates, which showed he was loyal, albeit a terrible judge of character. He was generous, but not in a showy way for the sake of gratification and adoration. And he was very, very, very sweet to Chelsea. Abby caught him gazing at her more than once as she chatted to other people, or applied lip gloss, just smiling at her in his own little world, thrilled to be in her presence.

But the thing that Abby liked most about Jeremy (surprisingly *not* his friends' chest hair) was the way Chelsea was around him. She really was *herself*. She wasn't playing the coquettish, regal princess she often did around new men, nor was she pretending she was more intellectual/artistic/musical/sexual than she really was. She was just herself. The same Chelsea Abby loved, and the same Chelsea who drove Abby mad. It was special. It made Abby feel warm with joy and jittery with a desire to pull Chelsea aside and tell her NOT TO FUCK THIS ONE UP.

At 10.50, Abby whispered to Chelsea that she had to leave, and why, but not to make a scene, because she wanted to slip out quietly. Unfortunately, after 729 martinis of various flavours and fruits, Chelsea was not interested (nor capable) of being subtle.

'Wooooooo!! Abby's gotta booty call!' she screeched.

'*Chels!*' Abby hissed, irritated.

'Is that why you've been such a sourpuzzzz?' enquired/accused chest hair.

'Bringhimhere! Less meet him, why don't you . . .' slobbered Harvard.

'Is it the toyboy?' Jeremy asked, with a mischievous glint in his eye.

'I will neither admit not deny anything,' said Abby as she smoothed her dress down over her thighs, and tucked her hair behind her ear, unable to contain a smile at what lay waiting for her at home.

'It was so lovely meeting you, Jeremy, and uh, your friends. Night sweetie' – she kissed Chelsea on the cheek – 'Have fun!'

She walked quickly away from the table to jeers, hollers and sloppy wolfwhistles, eager to get home and freshen up before her new friend came over. Once in a cab, she realised she'd forgotten to text him the address, and quickly sent it to the missed call number in her phone.

Hey 'Toyboy', address is 22a River St, Paddington. I'll be there in 20. See you then? Garfield.

Abby sat back in the taxi and took a deep breath. She was excited about seeing Marcus, and it felt delicious to admit it. Well, she was excited about what they were about to do, more accurately.

Once home, Abby tore up the front steps to her stylish semi and barged through the door. She tore her heels off and threw them in the hallway, the sound clattering off the polished floorboards. She raced into the bathroom, taking the corner too wide and slamming her elbow into the door, swearing loudly and rubbing her arm quickly to dull the pain. She was clearly more pissed than she thought she was; she smiled goofily at the memory of Harvard refilling her champagne glass every three minutes, in order to make sure she saw the label on the bottle. Abby looked at herself in the mirror, which served as an instant reminder as to why she rarely did smoky eyes – she looked hellish. Her eye makeup had run and smeared and there was black gunk in the inner corner of both eyes. Hot. She roughly wiped her fingers underneath her eyes and applied some more blush and lipgloss; that would do. Oh, and perfume. And deodorant too, actually – this dress was made from as many natural fabrics as a laptop and Abby was disgusted to find a faintly acidic scent when she sniffed under her arms.

She pulled her handbag open – it was resting precariously on the toilet seat – and checked her phone: 11.25. And no text back. Hmmm. Her gut, ever the optimist, was quick to suggest he wasn't coming. Of course he was, Abby chided herself! He was far keener than she was. He was probably on his way right now. Being as smug and confident as he was, he was probably deliberately not replying, hoping to suavely knock at the door instead, all leany-against the veranda-y and cool, as though he'd happened to be walking past and thought he would pay her a visit. She'd prepare some drinks and put some music on, is what she would do. Would she change . . . ? Naaah. Looks too contrived. Plus, she *loved* this dress. Sucked everything in magnificently, like a sexy, socially acceptable girdle.

At 11.58, Bonobo was playing at just the right volume in the lounge room, and Abby was perched on a stool at her breakfast bar sipping on vodka and ginger ale, wishing desperately that she had a cigarette, preferably housed in a packet with nineteen of its friends. Where. The. Fuck. Was. He?

Maybe he'd gotten into trouble, she thought. Or lost his phone. Or . . . *NO*, her head-voice reprimanded – we do not make excuses for men. Especially when they have done nothing to deserve such a privilege. He was just a little ratbag who was good in bed, why was he making her so angry? Did she even care if he came around tonight? *Really?* If she was honest, it was more the fact that he'd got under her skin and made her angry, that was making her angry.

She jumped off her stool and checked she didn't have an emergency cigarette in the little wooden box of random shit on top of the fridge. No. None in the third draw either. *Fuckit!*

This was such a sad, sad scene, Abby realised. A desperate, pissed fool scrambling through drawers for a cigarette, stood up by a CHILD she didn't even care about. That was it, she decided. She'd give him till 12.15 and then she was cancelling the invitation. She *could* text him, and see what he was playing at, but she didn't want to give him the satisfaction of knowing she was annoyed, or that she was even thinking about him. Not a chance in hell.

She'd go and wait on the lounge, she decided; more comfortable. Maybe reply to some emails on her phone. There'd be no watching TV, that's for sure. It would kill her buzz and send her directly to sleep. Perhaps she could check Facebook, she thought, spying her laptop on the desk. Or perhaps she'd just lay here for a moment and close her eyes, just for one second . . .

At precisely 3.17 a.m. a very confused Abby awoke in an awkward and intensely uncomfortable position on her sofa. Her hangover had arrived early, which was cute, and her mouth tasted like the bottom of a pig's hoof, although she had no evidence it didn't actually taste worse. With one hand rubbing her right eye clumsily, she reached for her phone. There was a text from 'Toyboy'.

Hey Garfield, are you still awake??

It had been sent at 1.46 and it made Abby very, very irritable. *Was she awake* indeed.

He could go fuck himself. 'Cause he sure as hell was not fucking her.

15

Abby pushed the eggs around her plate with her fork, and considered buying another bottle of mineral water. Why she had bothered ordering food baffled everyone seated at this impromptu brunch. But Abby felt stupid not ordering breakfast when everyone else was, so she always did, even though when she was hungover all she could stomach was mineral water. Icy cold. No straw. Until around 4 p.m. when intense cravings for hot chips with barbecue sauce and chicken salt kicked in, and the only thing worth living for was being warm and horizontal and doing something requiring 2 per cent of the brain, like sleep or anything starring tacky housewives or drunken guidos.

'So when do *I* get to meet the wonderful Jeremy then?' Mads asked, after Abby's glowing report. Well, as glowing as she could muster after her brain had hidden 98 per cent of her adjectives and refused to push more than eight words together at a time. And yet she didn't recall drinking that much . . . She hadn't eaten dinner though, that was never much help. Fucking Harvard and his champagne refills hadn't helped either.

'I'm thinking about hosting a barbecue next weekend, so you

should definitely come to that.' Chelsea beamed when she spoke about Jeremy. It was lovely to watch, even if her radiance in light of her drinking irritated Abby. It wasn't fair – Chelsea's skin never dipped below 100 watts, not even after half a vat of vodka.

'Good. Have that barbecue, we'd love to come.'

'So . . . everything cool with Dyl now?' Chelsea was swirling her teaspoon through her coffee at a furious pace, clearly agitated by the two coffees that had preceded it. She often used coffee in place of food; burned heaps of fat, she maintained.

'Of course. Although, poor bastard, I do feel sorry for him. Sex has been so on the clock with trying to get pregnant that when I'm not ovulating, I really, I just couldn't be fucked, so to speak. He was quite keen on some nook-nook last night, but I was so tired, because we'd had an excursion at school yesterday—'

'To the post office?' Abby asked.

'The front gate and back?' Chelsea asked.

'How dare you . . . We went to the shop to learn how to buy a train ticket, thank you. Anyway, so I'm there, rolled over, suffocating under the heavy blanket of fatigue and I feel this big poke in my lower back, and he's kissing my neck and being all foreplay-ish, and do you know what I did?'

'A quick handy and a kiss goodnight,' Chelsea stated, as though it was the obvious answer.

'No, much better: I hooked my ankle up to his groin and I wiggled it around a bit on his balls.'

Abby launched forward and placed her hand over a mouth that was about to furiously spray mineral water. Once she'd swallowed, she burst into laughter.

'You, you—' she was gasping for air, 'you gave him a tickle of the balls, with your heel?!'

Mads threw her head back, curls bouncing around her, and

laughed. 'I *did*. I actually did. As though he was a small, desperate dog and I was giving him the titillation of his life, a stranger walking past with an agile ankle and a perverse desire to see a stray dog happy.'

Abby and Mads dissolved into laughter again, as Chelsea tsk-tsked earnestly.

'Poor Dyl.'

Abby, who was still struggling to breathe, gave Mads's leg a rub with her ankle. 'Oooh, you like that, don't you, mmmm, sexy rubs . . .'

'I know, I *know*. Dyl said, 'Did you just rub my balls with your heel? And we were both quiet and then I admitted my disgraceful behaviour and we lost it. *Just* lost it. I think we needed the laugh, to be perfectly honest.'

'You have to give him sex at other times of the month, Mads, you can't just do it for baby-making purposes, that's hardly fair.'

'Oh fuck off, Chels,' Mads said good-naturedly. 'I'm not in the mood for your dramatic, archaic Stepford wife shit today.'

'I'm just saying . . .' Chelsea said, her inflection rising along with her eyebrows.

'"Just saying" has to be the most passive-aggressive, juvenile non-conclusion a human being can offer,' Mads said, shaking her head. She also hated when people used the word 'absolutely' or 'totally' in place of 'yes', both of which Chelsea was guilty of, daily. 'I was tired, it was funny, Dylan isn't just a sperm bank, he gets plenty of sex, and more blow-jobs than most married men get in their entire lives, so you can just calm the godamn farm.'

Chelsea, finally locating her compassion chip, exhaled and reached over to rest her hand on Mads's shoulder.

'Honey, I'm sorry. I jus—'

'You're a fascist,' Mads said, half-smiling. 'I know. I'm sorry, I hear it's genetic.'

Abby slumped in her seat as she felt the energy of the table soften. 'How wonderful that we all love each other again. Roll credits.' Abby took another sip from her water and a sparrow nibble of her hash brown, more as a token nod to food, her old friend and comforter, rather than for nutrition or taste.

'Well, old sexy heel here has to head. I'm going to the cinema with Dyl.'

'What you seeing?' Abby asked, flirting with the idea of inviting herself along, before realising that involved moving from this table, something she wasn't interested in just yet.

'His choice. Something arthouse I'd say.' She sighed and threw $20 on the table as she stood. 'Have a good day, you seedy tarts. Try not to fall asleep at the wheel yeah, Abs?'

'I'm fine,' she said, straightening up in her chair. 'Don't be so morose.'

As Mads walked out, Chels slapped Abby on the arm. '*Hey!* What happened with the kid last night? Did you let him stay over? You did, didn't you . . . you like-*like* him!'

Abby smiled with closed eyes, shaking her head. 'So wrong. You are so, so wrong. In fact, he no-showed.'

'Shut UP! He *didn't!*'

'I hate when you tell me to shut up, and yes he did.'

Chelsea's hand flew to her mouth, but her eyes were smiling.

'I can't even be bothered to make up excuses to make me sound like less of a loser. He didn't arrive, then I fell asleep on the lounge at midnight, and when I woke at three, I saw a text from him sent at quarter to two, asking if I was still awake.'

'What a d-bag. Well, he's obviously out of the race.'

'I was annoyed, but I'm not now. He was just sex, and it's more my ego that's hurt than my feelings. *No* manners, the yoof of today.'

'He'll text you today, you realise. Or email you tomorrow.'

'Good on him.'

Chelsea's attention had waned and she was applying fresh gloss and gathering her phone and keys. 'I need some cleanser and foundation, wanna come to DJs? Come on. What else are you going to do, wallow in your hangover at home? No. Come with.'

Chelsea's battering ram persuasion was too exhausting to fight against. Abby put her money on the table, picked up her bag and tried to figure out how she could stop her eyes from feeling like they were coated in olive oil.

16

It was there, waiting for her when she got home from an epic shopping trip that had started with a new Giorgio Armani lipstick, some Bobbi Brown foundation and bronzer, then morphed into a new pair of ballet slippers and a skirt, then a full body massage at the Thai massage place, then an enormous bowl of gooey, sweet Hokkien noodles, then a grocery shop. How she had done all of that when just blinking had been a struggle, Abby did not know. She also did not know how much money she had spent. And finally, she did not know what to make of the note that had been slipped under her door by a certain twenty-two year old.

It was written on proper notepaper, which was impressive, because it meant that he'd arrived with the note, instead of writing it on a receipt he'd found in his car.

Garfield,

I'm sorry I didn't come over last night. We went to a horrible new club ("Darcy's – encouraging drink-spiking since 2005!") and there was no phone reception down there, and after drinking my body-weight in whisky I lost track of time.

When I checked, it was after 1 as my pathetic text early this morning confirmed.

I messed up. I know. I'm sorry. Bad form.

Forgive a guy?

M.

It was completed with an illustration of a small Garfield. And it was adorable. That he had left a Real Life, hand-written note, instead of calling or texting, was commendable.

Abby sat down on her bed, dumping her shopping bags on the floor, momentarily getting excited about what lay inside them again, and re-read the note. He had outstanding handwriting, she decided. He was a designer, she supposed, of course he did.

She flopped back onto her soft, mint green sheets and grinned. She had a funny feeling he had just earned himself redemption, but Abby was so stubborn that knowing he'd written that note wanting redemption made her not want to give it. She'd let it simmer for a bit.

It was amazing how a little note revived a girl's spirits, though. Abby even toyed with the idea of a glass of red wine as she ran herself a bath, despite the fact her hangover was still lingering by the door, sipping on tea, unwilling to leave. A crazy thought entered her mind: *what if he came around tonight?* They'd both be hungover, but maybe that was better. Less expectation. Less drunken fumbling. No, wait; the drunken fumbling was the best part. It was the sweet nectar that heralded the arrival of fantastic, non-emotional, non-vanilla sex. And *hang on*, since when did random men get a Saturday Night In invite? You had to earn that. That was boyfriend-girlfriend gear. All cosy, shunning the world, the natural night of the sofa snuggle and the DVD . . . No. No, no, no. *What was she thinking?* They hadn't even had a proper hook-up yet. She would have to hold tight. And besides, he wasn't just going to weasel his way back in that fast; now he could experience some of his own delayed gratification.

Still, she thought, as she undressed, it *was* nice to feel wanted. And to regain the power. She'd text him, perhaps, that would be enough. As she sat in the bath, gripping her phone and praying she didn't drop it in the jasmine-scented water, she sent her response. She secretly hoped for a flirty text rally as she hit send. That would be the perfect end to the day.

Nice note. Not as impressive as sky writing, but better than a text, I suppose.

Satisfied she'd been playful without being too forgiving, she relaxed into the bath and waited for her phone to vibrate on the windowsill. She loved her bath so much; it had been a gamechanger when she'd looked at the apartment, perched under a large windowsill, with views over the hills and down to the city. It had a dazzling vista, and with the dim lighting of a few candles, and the window thrown open, she had an incredible view of a million glittering stars. It was truly her oasis, she often lay there wondering if she would ever find a man to lie in here with her, and gaze up at the evening sky with her. She knew that at the rate she was going – one-night stands and fuck buddies – it wasn't that likely in the near future, but she'd get there. Once she'd sorted Allure out, and had some more time, she'd be able to focus more on attracting a man who wasn't inappropriate, dull or twelve.

Bbbrmmmt. Abby snatched up the phone and read the text from Marcus which was lit up on her screen.

I deserve that, I suppose.

What was that? There's nothing to respond to there! That was a horrible response from him! Oh please don't let him be a shitty texter. It was such a crucial element of hooking up. How could he be, when he was so wordy and clever? Bad texting was akin to being bad in bed; such was the power of a good SMS.

Abby placed the phone back on the sill in disgust, just as it started vibrating with a call. She checked the screen; Marcus. Oh God no. He was a *talker*. Abby wasn't, it reminded her of being at work. Abby much preferred the control and highly edited parameters of texting. Calls were too on-the-fly, too personal, too intimate. And she hated unknown numbers with a passion usually reserved for perpetrators of public flatulence.

She let it ring out, knowing exactly what was coming next. Bang. And there it was; the text that accused her of screening. So predictable.

Cat got your tongue? Or in your case, have you got your tongue?

Fine. She'd play along. And win.

I can't chat. In the bath. Don't want to drop my phone in.

She smiled self-righteously. Ah yes, the ol' bath line. The finest and most powerful texting ammunition a lady could use. It immediately threw men off-guard, because now all they'd be thinking about was your body naked and wet. She'd possibly used it a little early in the piece, but this was a booty call, not a boyfriend. The filthier the better.

Silence. Silence. Silence. Abby waited twenty minutes, and got out of the bath. Was he still playing? Or was he on Facebook chatting to girls his own age? Whatever. She didn't have the energy to care, she decided. He could chase her from now on; she was weary already and they hadn't even managed an authentic hook-up.

Bbbrmmmt.

Before the phone could even finish vibrating, Abby clutched it in her hand.

> I'm at your front door. You cannot send a text like that and not expect immediate action.

Abby's heart began thumping, the sound of blood rushing through her head suddenly akin to the roar of a jet. He could not be serious. She cocked her head to try and hear anything at the front door. She didn't want him at her door! *No!* Too much! This wasn't the plan! He was meant to write back something disgusting and they'd rally from there! Jesus, the *hide!* Now she was scared to walk through her own house, lest he really be there, and she had to open it and awkwardly tell him she wasn't interested in guests, not even handsome ones with perfect-sized man bits.

Bbbrmmmt.

> Gotcha. Did cross my mind, though. When can we try for Your Place, V2.0? Monday night? Come on. I'll make it up to you.

Abby sighed an epic sigh of relief, and rolled her eyes. Little jerk. She didn't have the power longer than twenty minutes before he thieved it back, and she didn't like it. He should be a breeze! He was supposed to idolise and respect her, she was the older woman; he was meant to be chuffed to score her!

Abby sloppily slip-slopped through her skin care regime and

pulled her skimpy nightie over her head; it was polyester and made her sweat midway through the night, but she kept forgetting to buy a new one. Plus it had fake tan stains on it. Gorgeous. After putting all of her delicious new purchases away, Abby looked at her bedroom and wondered if it was time for a rearrange. Mads was mental about feng shui, and was always banging on that if you wanted to attract love, you needed to not have your bed facing the door, and to put lots of red around. Abby's bed directly faced the door, and as her colour scheme was soft duck-shell blues and grey and mint and white, she was as likely to put tacky red ornaments around the room as she was a Miley Cyrus poster.

> What about if I bring a bottle of the best pinot you've never tried and some olives and some cheese? Is that a more tempting offer? Say, 8? I'd suggest a proper dinner date, but I know you'll hit 'deny'.

Abby read Marcus's next effort a few times and smiled. He was pretty cute, she decided. He possibly didn't deserve the ice out just yet. What the heck, live a little, Vaughn.

> Make it 8.30.

She still had to make sure he knew who was boss.

Monday in the office was the equivalent of a minor car accident. No one was seriously injured, but there was definitely some damage.

It started with Pete, Natasha's caveman boyfriend, sending Abby a threatening email along the lines of: you bad lady, you make Natasha dress in slutty clothes, make men look at her, Natasha not work for you anymore.

Abby chose to not respond to his uneducated, vitriolic tirade, a decision that was roughly as hard as choosing between a cyanide smoothie or patting a docile calf. Natasha would come to her if she really was leaving.

The next treat came in the shape of Angie telling Abby that she had been offered the job of singer with a (legitimately impressive, successful and moderately famous) DJ called Matchstix. Of course she had. She was irresistible to look at, would look terrific in glittery bikini tops, and could actually sing. Duh. He wanted her to sing several tracks on his new album, star in the film clip of his new song, 'Stop Dancing', and then tour the UK festival scene starting late April, Angie told Abby excitedly.

Despite Angie's age and level of hierarchy in the company, it was highly entertaining to watch as she *told*, not *asked*, Abby that she'd now be taking Fridays off. Oh well, thought Abby, she knew her worth. Good on her. It had taken Abby another ten years to figure hers out.

The third slice of awesome pie came via Rob, who said that in order to be able to warrant the ('immense and hopefully justified') amount going towards the new website, one staff member had to be made redundant by the next payroll, and new premises, cheaper, smaller, new premises, were strongly advised. As soon as possible.

Abby sipped on her third latte of the day, a horrific idea given the circumstances and level of stress already hissing and bubbling away in her gut, and a sure way to send her off the edge of coping and into the sea of minor breakdown, and tapped her pen frenetically on the desk.

Well, Angie, the one staff member she *didn't* want to leave had kind of solved the first issue by getting all famous and sneaking off. Which actually, she realised, left her with an even more irritating problem, which was that she still needed a PA-type role, not two bookers, so not only would she have to let go either Charlotte or Siobhan, she'd have to hire another junior . . . Or *would* she? Did she really need an office administrator type in the brave new web world? Could she handle it herself, like when Allure first started, and it was just her and her laptop at her kitchen bench? Abby wouldn't know what she'd need until the site was functioning and she could comprehend the actual workload. What a mess. Chicken or the fucking egg.

Maybe, Abby thought delicately, as though the idea were a spoon of piping hot soup, maybe she should get rid of *all* of the office staff and could hire an equal a few days a week, someone who could replicate her role in the company, that is, look after clients, find new girls, book girls for jobs, then book new girls when those girls cancelled, and go along to events that needed client sycophancy, or a watchful eye. That actually sounded like the most intelligent idea – a business partner. Who this person was and which horrible job they were in that they needed saving from was anyone's guess. Abby would have to pay them well because the role was so senior, and she'd need to trust them, obviously. But it could make life a lot easier, a shared responsibility. And with only two staff, and small premises, the profits would be greater. Yes! It was good. Really good. Rob-would-be-pleased good.

Abby wobbled her head side-to-side, mouth pursed, as she did some rudimentary numbers in her notebook. It made sense. She'd ask Rob his thoughts immediately. She knew his first question would pertain to how exactly she was going to locate this magical gypsy, but he could calm down. She would find them. And anyway, he should be happy that she had not only already sent Angie on her way/allowed her to go, but was thinking of Rob's favourite picture in the whole world, the Bigger one.

As for the office space . . . Could she move it into her spare room? She'd always resisted, on the grounds she didn't want to take her work home with her, but that was complete horseshit because as long as her phone was on, she was working. And if it was just her and one other person, well, why not? Her home was neat and stylish enough to entertain the occasional casting, so that was no issue, and she would just meet clients in restaurants and cafes, like normal people did. The more she thought about it, the more Abby felt like a wanker for even having a big, showy city office. It was such a dick-swinging move, such a false symbol of wealth. It was appropriate for a company who needed to host a lot of meetings and have a powerful, impressive base, but Allure was not that company. Allure was a company that did almost everything remotely – all the girls were booked via phone or email, castings were rare these days, and clients were either regulars, or word-of-mouth recommendations, or they called after a quick perve on the website. Few meetings were booked for her boardroom, as beautiful as it was.

Allure, Abby decided, was about to grant her the four-hour work week, which was the premise behind a book her brother had given her last Christmas and which she'd thought was a preposterous idea. Now it seemed not only feasible, but possible. In truth it was probably going to be more like a fifteen-hour week, but even that was an astonishing concept to Abby, who'd been working twelve-hour days for the last three years at least.

Rob,

I've got an idea. And if it doesn't light your fire, your wood must be wet because it's absolutely, brain-bendingly perfect . . .

17

Marcus was polite enough to wait until they'd had a glass of wine and a small cow-full of extravagant cheese from regions that were impossible to pronounce before he kissed Abby.

He'd brought a very impressive selection, especially given his age. Abby was mostly eating Doritos on white bread when she was twenty-two, a result of either marijuana or poverty or both. Abby presumed he came from wealth, and that if he wasn't still living at home with his well-liked chiropractor father (handsome, late fifties) and glamorous private-school-teacher mother (just on fifty, stunning, probably European), he would be there every weekend for a brunch featuring not only quince paste, but fig and tamarind also.

They had been sitting on stools at her breakfast bar, politely scoffing the delicious spread he'd brought, Abby awkwardly filling in the space a very quiet Marcus was leaving by babbling about her desire to buy the semi they sat in, all the while utterly preoccupied by the fear of leaving crumbs around her mouth, and Marcus constantly drawn to Abby's mouth, which in his mind was the perfect shape, and begging to be kissed. So he did. He simply stood up, walked around to Abby's side of the bench, and kissed her, just as she was explaining how she'd never liked blue cheese, but actually this one wasn't so bad and where was it from, because she'd never had one tha—

The kiss was equivalent of finally being given permission to enter the best, most incredible party you'd ever witnessed after standing in a queue for forty-five minutes making small talk with someone you didn't know very well.

Abby was intensely grateful Marcus made the first move. For some reason, possibly because of a lack of tequila in very small glasses, she was all twitchy and nervous around him tonight, and couldn't for the life of her figure out how they were going to make the transition from Chit Chatty People in the Kitchen, to Primal Beasts in the Bedroom.

She had been repulsed hearing the drivel fall from her overactive mouth and, for a moment, when she'd finished her fascinating dia-tribe about property prices in Paddington and he'd said nothing, she thought that she'd not only made an error in inviting some kid over for a sober (it was all relative), school-night hook-up, but also an error in thinking he was worth any kind of contact, ever again. He was just there, watching her, smiling serenely. Clearly they had nothing in common. That's why he was so quiet. But then he kissed her. And it all made sense again; he wasn't here for conversation, he was here for *pene*tration.

As they kissed, Marcus gently bustled himself in between Abby's legs and kissed her harder. She hooked her thighs around his legs, and kissed him hungrily, her hands behind his neck, pulling his face down onto her so he could kiss her deeper. Then he took her hands in his, and led her, looking back at her with twinkling eyes as often as he could without tripping over the furniture in her lounge room, to her bedroom, a room Abby had prepared with two soft lamps for maximum sexy-silhouettes. He turned and fell back onto the bed, pulling Abby down onto his chest as he went, the pursuit they had both been looking forward to all day – all weekend – finally before them to feast upon.

Abby woke up and was surprised to find herself nestled in Marcus's arms in a terribly romantic and loving fashion. She gently extracted herself, secretly enjoying the scent of his skin as she did, and crept to the bathroom. What did she do now? she asked herself as she grabbed a towel to cover up. He couldn't stay, no way. *Especially* not on a school night. She needed her sleep and besides, Chelsea was coming by to pick her up for stupid hot yoga at 6.30 – what, was she just going to leave him here in her house alone? No. No, no, no. And he couldn't walk out with her, Chelsea would have a heart attack, and Abby would've signed a contract for weeks, possibly months, of teasing. He had to leave now; there was no other option. Boys were not allowed to sleep over; only boyfriends were, and he was a couple of solar systems off that.

As she washed her hands, her mind raced back to what they had done just hours earlier, and as usual, because she was just a dork despite her flashy shoes and grown-up makeup, she blushed. Even Marcus's kisses were exceptional. As for everything else . . . He was so *experienced!* So intuitive, so . . . *generous* a lover. How did someone that young become so good? Practice, she supposed. He'd probably slept with hundreds of women. Good-looking men usually did. Abby couldn't understand how they did it, until she became single in her thirties, and had her own apartment and a good income, and figured out you didn't need to feel guilty after sex, you were allowed to just enjoy it, and that to feel bad about it was just a social construct placed on women to stop them from feeling confident and powerful and awesome and taking over the world.

Maybe he had always gone for 'older' women, she thought. Maybe instead of girls his own age – girls who interpreted having good sex as being theatrical and doing filthy things they read about in magazines or saw celebrities do on home sex tapes – he preferred women who were confident in what they wanted, and what they could offer, and who'd taught him how to be a good lover. Abby decided this was a Definite Positive, and would benefit her greatly. It should be compulsory for all men.

She walked into her room and saw him there, naked from the torso up, his bottom half concealed by her crumpled sheets, sleeping soundly. He looked like he could be advertising the sheets; a hunky linen angel. Everything about him, from his full lips to his perfect olive skin and hairless chest was beautiful. She sighed, sitting carefully on the end of the bed. How was she going to do this? Part of her was mature enough to admit that she would love to fall back into bed with him, into his arms, but that part was, as always, quashed by the bigger, stronger part, which demanded he leave, because it was The Rule, and if you break the rule, all kinds of events may unfold, none of them much good in the long run.

She tapped him on the leg. 'Marcus?' As had happened last time, nothing. This time, she was too exhausted to play.

'*MARCUS.*'

'Wha?' He woke with a start, his eyes adjusting to the situation. 'Your fiancé on his way home again?' He smiled sleepily, flattening his short hair with his hand, obviously a hangover from when he had longer hair to flatten down.

'No, he's not, but you gotta go, Cinderella. I have an earl—'

'Hot balloon ride? Half-marathon? It's okay; I get it: you don't like sleepovers.'

'No, hang on, it's not that I don't like them, I just . . .'

But he'd got the message. He sat up and swung his legs over the side, grabbed his undies and pulled them up.

'Garfield, it's fine. When you send me on my way with a $100 bill, then I'll feel like a cheap hooker. For now, I just feel used. They're two totally different things.'

Abby couldn't see his face and so couldn't tell if he was joking. She had the feeling Mr Sensitive was not, despite his tone.

'Are you serious?'

'No, but I think I *do* want to know why you won't let me stay,' he said, pulling on his jeans, cool, skinny black ones that stopped just above the ankle, black t-shirt and brown leather loafers. No socks, of course. 'Did you come out of a long relationship recently?'

'No! I genuinely have a 6.30 a.m. pick up.'

She couldn't believe he'd said that about a long relationship; it was in fact, one of her most cherished lines, her Get Out of Jail Free card when guys started getting too close, or asking too much of her. Dammit. He was a tricky cat. No such thing as string-free sex. It was a fallacy.

'Alright, well, maybe one day I'll be lucky enough to break the 2 a.m. barrier. Till then, I'll be on my way. Hope I've got some Richard Marx in the car to accompany my tear-stained face.'

He stood up, a smile on his face, and walked past Abby to the kitchen to get his phone and keys. She followed, feeling much worse than she thought was appropriate. Why did she feel bad about sending him home? Probably because he was doing such a terrific job of making her feel bad, she guessed, which immediately made her want to stay firm in her decision.

She followed him, trying to think of a smartass quip to lighten things, but falling just short each time something bubbled up.

Ready to go, Marcus turned and pulled Abby in close to him,

kissing her lightly on the lips. His taking control of the situation and establishing something a little bit romantic was a shock, and Abby was surprised to find herself allowing him to hold her.

'I'll call you,' he said, pulling back to look her in the eyes. 'And you will answer.'

Abby smiled. 'So confident . . . and bossy . . . and cocky.'

'Jealous I've stolen all your best attributes?'

He kissed her on the nose and walked to the door. 'I hope you don't have nightmares; cheese always gives me nightmares. Pity you don't have someone to cuddle you if you do, huh?'

The signature wink, and he was gone.

Abby sat on one of her black stools, clutching her towel around her, and tried to figure out exactly what breed of beast she was dealing with here. She was positive she held all the cards just a few nights ago, that she was the catch, now he had her rattled and thinking that *he* was the catch, and she needed to behave. *This was not right.* He was just another kid who'd been raised with far too much self-assurance and the mantra that he could have whatever he wanted, just so long as he put his mind to it. It was impressive, admirable and entirely revolting. He was fantastic in bed and clever and funny and was better at wine and cheese than her, but so what?

Well he was about to get a shock, she thought as she cleaned up the cheese and wine. She was about to remind him exactly what this was, which was nothing more than the occasional drunken hook-up. Even having him over on a school night was a bad idea. Far too 'date'. She shouldn't have allowed it.

Abby wouldn't see him for a whole week, and when she did, it would be on her terms, and late at night, and not all pre-determined and ridiculous like tonight.

Yes. Good. He could put that in his pants and stroke it.

18

'And THEN guess what he did? He left little notes all over my bed, little post-it notes with little things he likes about me, like my smile, and my eyes—'

'Or the fact you know pi to ten decimals and can shear a sheep.' Abby couldn't resist having a dig.

'Shut it, it was very romantic. See that's the kind of thing a *man* does, doubt the kid would do something like that.'

'You're kidding, right? First of all, the *kid* is the one who should be doing dopey romantic stuff like that, not a man in his forties, and second of all, the kid would never do stuff like that, because I would set those pieces of paper on fire before he even finished writing on them.'

Chelsea laughed in spite of herself. 'What would be so bad about falling in love with the kid?'

'Don't even finish that sentence. Marcus is a bit of fun, just like all the others. And anyway, why are you suddenly championing *him*?'

'Because I think you like him, is why.'

'What on earth makes you think that?'

'*Because he's annoying you.* If he didn't come over last Friday and you didn't like him, you wouldn't have been pissed. Same with the sleepover thing. You have never, ever even entertained the idea of a guy staying over, and you just spent ten minutes asking me who he thinks he is, wanting to stay over, and that you almost considered it, and rahrahrah.'

'Chels, did it occur to you that maybe the reason I talk about him differently is because he is amazing in bed? And that maybe that's worth enjoying a little longer?'

'What's worth enjoying a little longer?' Mads dumped her enormous handbag on the spare seat and sat down at the Spartan café table outside the pilates studio.

'Getting it off with the kid. Abby just admitted she's into him.'

'Mads, ignore her. How are you? How did it go at the clinic? I tried calling you yesterday, but no joy.'

Mads exhaled and ran her hands through her hair, gently finger-combing it back as she did so, then tied an elastic around it carefully. Mads's curls needed special treatment, or she swiftly morphed into Elaine Bennis. Early episodes.

'Yeah, as good as could be expected, I s'pose.' She smiled sincerely.

'Hey, on your blog yesterday; what was that thing you put in that walnut and baby spinach salad? It was something weird . . .' Chelsea was either incredibly good at conversation gear-changing, or bored of talking about something that appeared to have sorted itself out, and wanted to get back to her.

'Oh, the meringue?' Mads's eyes lit up; it always delighted her when she had proof people actually read her blog. Real proof, anecdotal proof, conversational proof, not just numbers on a Google traffic chart and email subscriber lists.

'Meringue with baby spinach and walnuts, Mads! How *controversial*.' Abby took a sip from her water, smiling. Mads was a cook

102

with a talent and creativity that bordered on savant. She'd never work in a professional environment with it, though; her love of it was too fierce. Instead she generously shared her finest recipes and insights with greedy, anonymous internet prowlers, most of whom found her by googling insipid things like 'how to cook prawns' and were treated with not only a simple way to cook them, but also how to construct dazzlingly mouth-watering garlic chilli prawns with linguine with parmesan and rocket, of the calibre that makes people return to the same restaurant for decades in order to enjoy such gastronomic delights.

As Mads explained the relevance and flavour that smashed up meringue offered in surprising scenarios, Abby quickly checked her phone. It was now Friday, and she hadn't heard from Marcus. Not one stinkin text, not even a work email, although Arthur had very much taken over the Allure dealings for now.

She wasn't foolish enough to lie to herself and pretend it wasn't killing her a little bit, but it also killed her a little bit that it killed her a little bit. He'd definitely said he'd call, she knew he had, he'd made a grand point of it, so she needed to stop thinking about it. Anyway, if she recalled correctly, her plan was to initiate the next contact, and on her terms; drunk, late, weekend. A small smile snuck onto her lips as she realised it was Friday, which meant that technically, she could beckon him this evening. Terrific. She wanted to see him, she realised. A lot. If he was playing hard to get, it was working.

'Now now now! Miss Vaughn, how IS it going with the toyboy?' Mads's eyes lit up excitedly.

'They're banging, and she likes him.' Chelsea answered bluntly and stood up to walk into the studio, following the instructor, who'd just arrived and was doing her best to make even the slimmest girls in the class look enormous.

'REALLY? You like-like him?' Mads's eyes bulged with excitement, standing up to go through the doors.

'*No,* Mads!' Abby said, swinging her bag over her shoulder and walking behind her friends.

'Remember the rule we have about ignoring everything Chelsea says? I don't like-like him; we're just hooking up is all.'

As the three girls placed their bags against a wall and walked to get their mats from the cupboard, Mads turned to Abby. 'I think I'm with Chels on this one, actually. When you don't care about a guy, you don't bother to get defensive. You just agree with us and we all laugh gaily about his bad shoes.'

Abby dropped her head back to her shoulder blades and sighed loudly with exasperation.

'Although I'm too much of a gentleman to place a monetary bet,' Mads said elegantly, 'I might be forced to place a verbal one, in which I insist that you and the kid will eventually fall into some kind of groovy love rhythm.'

'That didn't even make *sense.*'

'*Shoosh,* you two.' Chelsea was already on her back, taking deep breaths, eyes closed, hands resting on her diaphragm.

'It's on, Vaughn.' Mads did a pathetic excuse for a seedy wink, and lay down.

Abby tried to relax and focus on the class, but she was frustrated. Frustrated that the girls had it in their heads she liked Marcus, and frustrated that Marcus wasn't chasing her like a hopeless, besotted fool. It was a paradoxical frustration, but Abby was too wound up to see the irony. All the others chased her! She couldn't ignore their texts and calls, or turn them down enough! And they STILL came back for more. Why was it always the ones she didn't want to chase, did, and those she would've quite liked to be chasey, weren't? Or did chase, but in a pathetic, lacklustre fashion that felt more like they were doing it out of boredom, booze and horniness than genuine attraction. Jesus. And this had been her life for the past two and a half years. What a tedious and predictable chain of events. *There had to be more than this*. Abby was positive the man she wanted was not from this country – he was sexy, confident, take-chargey, well-read and well-travelled, and completely obsessed with her, in a healthy, loving way: the stuff of love poetry, not restraining orders.

Waiting for a twelve year old to send her a text message to ease her mind and make her feel happy? That was what it had come down to? No. This was not on. Marcus would have to go. She was prepared to suffer a headfuck from a genuine and potential suitor, but not from a smarmy little rockabilly with far too much confidence for his age and experience. She was over him. Out. Gone.

19

Despite her tough guy talk at pilates, Abby's big Friday night in was fraught with temptation, oscillation and indignation. She wanted, *willed* Marcus to call or text, but her phone remained silent, its screen mocking her with its black face. She *was not contacting him*. As far as he knew she was in high demand, probably on a date with a dashing, yacht-owning media tycoon right now, sipping on Bollinger and laughing at his terrifically witty jokes about the size of the lobster in Monte Carlo. It disturbed her that he might be out, being cute and funny and adorable at cool bars with gorgeous young women fawning over him and his silly neckties. She had to not think about that, and more importantly not care about it. Who cared? Not her. Caring was for morons.

She drank half a bottle of Otago pinot, one that she was disgusted to realise she'd bought with impressing Marcus in mind, and ran a bath, the dialogue of an unintentionally hilarious chat show in the background:

'My first question is for Jasmyne, a not-for-profit yoghurt farmer.'
'Yes?'
'Where did you get those sandals?'

After soaking until she was withered, Abby sent her mother a long email, even though she checked her email account as often as Santa Claus dropped down chimneys. She really should call her this weekend, she thought, the familiar taste of guilt and obligation seeping into her mouth.

To say she had a bad relationship with her mother was neither fair nor accurate, because actually, she had no relationship with her at all. There was no way they could be accused of getting along well, or having a loving mother-daughter bond. It was perfunctory, undertaken with a strong sense of duty. They went through the motions; occasional phone calls, bi-monthly visits (always Abby to her mother, never the other way around), but Abby struggled to feel anything other than resentment and irritation when she was in her mother's company. At least it had softened from her teenage years, when she flat out despised her mother, and made it known in as many channels as possible as often as possible. She remembered the day she left home to move to the city, her mother didn't even come with her and help her settle in, even though Abby was eighteen and comically green. She didn't even walk outside to say goodbye, just stayed inside washing up, like some kind of deranged martyr.

Thankfully Sean was there to blur Abby's rage, and make her feel like someone in the world of the same bloodline loved her. Ever since her dad had gone, Abby had wrestled a deep and simmering bitterness for her mother. If she was brutally, sinfully honest, she was angry that her mother had lived, and her father hadn't. He was a generous, loving man who saw beauty in burnt toast and salvaged humour from horrible situations. Abby figured her mother must've been a different person before she and her brother came along, judging by the way her father's love lingered for his wife, despite the fact she was such a miserable woman. Her father saturated Abby and Sean in love, pride and affection, but he was no pushover. He was a role model and a renegade and a rascal. Her mother had resented her children for consuming her husband's love and attention, to the point where she kept his swiftly deteriorating condition in his final weeks a secret from them, so she could inhale all his last moments herself.

Abby had tried to forgive her, to be at peace and accept who her mother was, and turn the boat around so they might be able to rescue at least a glimmer of a relationship before her mother went completely senile, but their current situation was far from a promising movie trailer for a glittering conclusion.

As Abby settled into bed, utterly disenchanted with her evening and with her personal life in general, she heard her phone chime from the lounge room where she'd left it. Adrenaline surged through her – could it be? No, he wouldn't. It was after midnight, even for a booty call that was disgusting behaviour. It was probably Sean, his texts always came in at odd hours, being that he was on Brazilian time.

Unable to resist, Abby plodded out to retrieve her phone.

Garfield, darling, your website is killing us. Would a gorgeous housecat be awake and interested in a nightcap with a very tired-but-wired web designer? He's going to be driving past your house in 10 minutes . . .

She clasped the phone to her chest and grinned like another famous tabby cat. *He was working late!* He'd been working like a dog all week and that was why he hadn't been in touch. He wasn't out sliming all over nineteen year olds, he was working on her website! Abby's ego beamed with satisfaction and relief.

A housecat would. (Purr.)

Abby hit send on her very non-ice-queen text then tore into the bathroom for some invisible makeup – curled lashes, cheek stain and concealer on a pimple that was thankfully on its way out – plus some tuberose and gardenia scented body oil on her décolletage and arms. A boof-up of the hair, a touch of gloss and it was into the bedroom where her sexy City to Surf t-shirt and boy leg undies were replaced with a silky Calvin Klein nightie and lacy black French panties. She felt her heart racing, her lips stretch into an excited smile. It was ludicrous the way one text message from this boy could change her entire physiological and mental state. Moments ago she'd been cursing his name and placing juvenile hexes on his weekend; now she was pulling her cleavage up so that his eyes would be greeted with two jubilant, sexy bulbs when he arrived.

As that confusing clarification came through, so too did the ding of the doorbell. *Fuck!* He was here. She opened the door in that cute sexy way she always did when a guy came over – half-concealed behind the doorframe, head on an angle, cheeky smile.

'Jesus. You'd give a jellyfish a hard-on in that outfit.'

Something flashed in Marcus's eyes and he pushed the door open, pulling her out from behind it, taking her in his arms and kissing her passionately. She kissed him back, instantly feeling herself tingle with excitement of what was coming next. She felt his hands slide down to the hem of her nightie, and slide back up, with the nightie clasped in his hand so that he could feel the skin of her thighs. He created a soft gap in the kiss and pulled back to look at Abby.

'Is it wrong to say I've been looking forward to that since Monday?'

Abby smiled wide, forgetting all of her ice-queen instructions.

'No. It's exactly the right thing to say.'

'Do you feel like that nightcap . . . ?' Marcus kissed her neck as he spoke, making Abby's spine quiver with pleasure.

'Maybe in a little while,' she said, pulling away from him, kicking the door closed and leading him to the bedroom.

'So, the website is looking pretty amazing, I gave the mouse a glittery trail wherever it goes.' Marcus said, as he held Abby in his arms in the darkness, pondering whether he could be bothered to shower.

'Hang on, you left all the hot website talk till *after* sex?' Abby said, in faux shock. She pulled back from her position against Marcus's neck, where she had luxuriated in smelling his aftershave and sweat mixing together in a heady cocktail of sexual male scent. She was beginning to understand the appeal of young, modern men – they were just the perfect blend of metrosexual and masculine. It was dizzying.

'Well, you seemed pretty primed; I didn't think I needed to use such powerful foreplay.'

'Don't underestimate the effect a bit of HTML coding can have on a broad.'

He laughed. 'You're funny, aren't you. I think that's what initially attracted me to you. Your smartassy sass.'

'Lies. You liked me because I was dragging you into a taxi for a good time within an hour of meeting you.'

'That too. But we have more than just outstanding sexy times. I like your company.'

'And I yours. Which is why I'm paying said company so much to make my website.'

'Ooh, very good. But I mean it, Abby. I like you.'

Abby's ears clicked into the 'high sensitivity' range.

'Are you trying to score an invite to stay the night, sir?'

'*Pfft.* I know your policy. Plus, I'm sober and have my car so I don't have to do my usual 3 a.m. taxi hunt. And double plus, I'm too exhausted to challenge you on your screwy rules tonight.'

Abby should've felt relief, but she didn't. She suddenly didn't want him to go. She wanted to sleep in his arms, and go get coffees for them in the morning and then fool around some more.

'What . . . what if I granted the prince permission to stay in the queen's chambers this evening?'

'Well that would be creepy, because the prince would be the queen's son, so that's a bit off, and also because you think you're the queen and I am just a lowly prince, when for all you know I could be a wizard or at the very least a powerful duke from a neighbouring province.'

Abby laughed. 'All right, you've got me there. It came out wrong.'

'Maybe if you ask me properly and don't disguise it with a bad joke sitting under a thinly veiled power play, you'd get a better response. I know you like to call the shots, and feel in control, Garfield, and that's fine. Just be honest about it.'

For the 629th time since meeting Marcus, he had thrown her. She did like to call the shots, she did love to be in control, and he'd picked it. She hadn't even really been able to articulate it, and he had. Impressive. But a bit annoying. He was too big for his fancy vintage brogues, he really was. 'You really want me to grovel? That's the best way to make me not ask you, you know.'

'Are you really doing this?' he said, kissing her softly on the hand. 'Just admit you want your handsome young stud to stay over, already.'

She exhaled dramatically. 'Marcus. Would you do me the pleasure of staying over tonight?'

'Oooh,' he said, making that smacking noise in his mouth people make when they're faking sincerity. 'I'd love to, but I have to get up early to go fishing with Chris.'

'Classic stuff. Do you want a glass of water?' Abby stood up to walk to the kitchen, wrapping her cream throw around her as a cape.

'You think I'm kidding?' he said.

'Are you ever not kidding?' Abby said, as she walked down the hall.

When she returned to the bedroom, Marcus was fully dressed, and putting his shoes on.

'What's all this?' Abby asked, stopping dead in the doorway.

'Told you, I'm going fishing; Chris is picking me up at five . . .'

Abby's face was twisted in confusion. 'But it's, like, 2 a.m. now . . . can't you cancel or something?'

He walked over to Abby and took the glasses from her, placing them on her dressing table, and coming back and taking both her hands in his.

'I'm not playing games, Abby. I am going fishing, and I need to go home. I don't *want* to go, only a moron would, but I can't let Chris down. It's our thing, you know? Some dudes surf, some gamble and chase sliz, some whittle small animals on sunlit porches; we *fish.*'

'I see,' said Abby, seeing nothing but annoyance.

Marcus kissed her tenderly on the forehead and then tilted her head up to his so he could kiss her on the lips.

'I'm secretly thrilled that you're pissed, you know. Means you want me. And! You even asked me to sleep over! I'm breaking you down, aren't I? Admit it.'

'Well, you only get so many chances, you know.' Abby hated what was coming out of her mouth, her defensive, arrogant clichés, but they were uttered before she could reel them back in. She *hated* that this implied that her feelings were hurt.

'Ooh, is that a threat? I love them. Turn me on.'

'You're a goose. Get out of here then, and let a girl get some sleep, why don't you.' She tried to re-ignite some funny before his last impression of her was of a whiny, always-gets-her-own-way woman.

'Fine. But I'm seeing you tonight. Maybe I'll take you for a delicious cocktail at my favourite bar.'

'Oh, but you're fishing, remember? Or have you already forgotten your own exit lie?'

'*After* fishing. We don't sleep out there. I'll call you.' And he began walking down the hall, checking his pockets as he went.

'I'm busy tonight, you know,' called Abby down the hall, even though she absolutely was not busy.

'You're lying,' Marcus called back, mimicking Abby's intonation perfectly.

'Oh, and Garfield?' he called as Abby heard the front door open and his footsteps on her tiled porch. 'Thank you. You're REALLY TERRIFIC AT SEX.' He finished bellowing and closed the door, leaving Abby giggling like a schoolgirl.

As she lay in bed minutes later, thinking about the night they'd had, and how worked up she'd been before he came over, then how much she felt she was 'giving of herself' to eat her pride and ask him to stay, then how shitty she'd been when he rebuffed her request, then how disappointed she'd been when she realised he wasn't going to stay with her after all, and then how disgusted she'd been with her taking-my-ball-and-going-home attitude, and then relieved his reaction was to be *even cuter and funnier,* she realised the girls were right. *She liked Marcus.* That said; she knew nothing of him except for his name, job and what he looked like naked. After all, *fishing?* And where did he live? And who with? And what were his friends like? Why was he out fishing with Chris, his fifty-something boss? Abby was going to find out all of this tomorrow. When he called. And they hung out. And he was the first man to spend the whole night in Abby's bed since she was with her ex.

20

Abby awoke – sans alarm – and luxuriated in her cotton cocoon for a good forty-five minutes, thinking about her delicious late-night caller, and her plan-free day ahead and her total lack of yoga and pilates. It was a gloriously sunny day; the kind that might enthuse one to head to the beach, if one didn't hate sand so much. Abby wished there was a magical beach where the grass went right to the edge and there was no stuffing about with sand in your shoes, bag, swimmers, ears, hair, bum crack. One existed, of course, it was called 'a pool', but Abby simply chose not to swim instead.

As if reading her thoughts, a text from Chelsea flew in.

> Beach day. We'll go to Mackenzie park so u can't whinge abt sand. Breakfast on deck. Mads is in x

She could feign sleep, but Chels was the type who would just show up at Abby's door with her big fancy Ralph Lauren towels and bang on the door until Abby emerged.

Don't you have a boyfriend who should be taking you to
the beach? (In St Tropez?) Where is he today?

Brmmmt.

He works weekends. I've subtracted points for that dont
worry. See u in an hour x

Abby reluctantly left her cosy nook and walked into the bathroom
to study her hair, skin and body and see if any maintenance was
required. Hair, yes: roots were now critical stage. Skin seemed okay,
though a facial wouldn't be the worst thing that could happen to it.
She could see a constellation of blocked pores having the time of
their lives on her nose; to take them away and prevent them from
causing pimples seemed somehow mean. Body . . . Body was *okay.*
Probably her smallest bikini would be required, going by the old
adage of, 'the smaller the bikini, the smaller the body looks'. Abby
had possibly made up this adage, and it might even be completely
untrue, but it seemed to work, in the Pamela Anderson sense of
making everything look as though it's meant to be busting out sexily, not because it's spilling over due to too many days with cheese
toasties with a side of pinot acting as a 'nutritional' full stop.

Pah, she had a hot, twenty-two-year-old lover, she remembered.
She couldn't be doing too badly. If someone that young, that gorgeous and with that many choices for sex had chosen *her,* then
maybe, just maybe, she wasn't as chopped liver-y as she sometimes
felt. Maybe she was actually – gasp – hotter than she thought!
Maybe he saw something she couldn't, like that thing men in chick
flick movies always saw in their average-looking best girlfriend. And
maybe having Marcus around would inspire her to lose weight and
tone up, she thought, gleefully. Maybe she should be going for a

run right now, she thought, with less glee. Nahhh, not enough time. She had sunscreen to apply, hats to locate, and a dozen bikinis to be angry at.

As they lay on their towels in the sun, Chelsea's tight, taut, gorgeous little body made Abby feel like a sloppy sea lion. Abby went through the usual mind lecture of how Chelsea was a sparrow who ate three nuts a day, and how she exercised twice as much as the amount of nuts she consumed each day, and how it was Abby's own fault she had slipped up a dress size. Or two.

Mads, with her tall, elegant frame and perfect, pale skin looked no different than when they were promo models, and just as she did back then, she covered up completely from the sun with a hat, shirt and a fresh layer of SPF 1000+ sunscreen every three minutes or so.

Once she'd finished reading her highbrow arts supplement in the newspaper, Mads turned her attention to her friends' love and sex lives with a voracious need to know everything, or make up her own version and aggressively implement that instead. Thankfully, because Abby's post-coital glow was being nicely camouflaged by the sunshine, Mads's first target was Chelsea.

'So, how come we haven't met him yet?'

'You *have*! Well, Abby has. I had to cancel my barbecue because he had something come up. But you'll meet him.'

'And has he invited you to his place yet?' Mads's tone was that of suspicion. A little bit of curiosity, but mostly suspicion. It was her preferred tone. After doubt and delight.

Chelsea squirmed and reached for more tanning oil from her bag. 'No, but who cares? My place is the perfect love nest.'

'And now for your *real* answer . . .?'

'It's fucking me off. Big time. It's been over a month; what's he hiding?'

Mads seized the chance for fantasy with both paws. 'You don't think he has a girlfriend hiding back there, do you? Oooh, or a *WIFE!*' Her eyes were wide with delight at the thought of a big, fun pool of drama for her to muck about in.

'Mads? Not helping. Pipe down. Chels, I'm sure he's not hiding anything'.

'What if he's GAY and his handsome vet-nurse boyfriend, Dennis, lives there?'

'MADS,' Abby said firmly. 'Put your imagination back on its leash.'

'Sorry. I'm sure he's lovely, hetero and the reason you've not been invited over is simply because you haven't put out.'

Chelsea sighed dramatically and rolled her eyes. 'Gee, thanks Oprah. What's your giveaway today?'

'*Have* you put out, Chels? That would be highly premature from Miss Padlocked Panties, no?'

Chels sighed and looked at Abby and Mads, both gawking at her like excited monkeys being handed a banana-shaped present.

'Of course I haven't. You have to be *militant* about this when the guy is a legitimately good catch, stupid. Otherwise you blend into every other ho he sleeps with on the first night.'

'I sleep with guys on the first night,' Abby piped up. 'Does that make me a ho?'

'Yes. It does.'

'Awww, that's sweet,' Abby said, tousling Chelsea's hair patronisingly. Chelsea was beyond being able to offend her on this topic anymore. 'You're the best friend a girl could ask for.'

'When will you do it?' Mads asked. 'Are you waiting for rose petals up the hallway and patchouli massage oil?' Mads and Abby snorted with laughter.

'Fuck you both. You're dull and childish, and I've heard better jokes from a three year old.'

'Oooh, pretty kitty can *scraaaaatch!*' said Mads, teasingly.

'I know what I'm doing.' There was an edge to Chelsea's tone, but the girls didn't care. She ran her mouth so often that she earned her teasing good and proper.

'So what are we talking, another month?'

'Two. It's already been a month and he hasn't complained, so that's earned him some points. Anyway, what about you, Abby, how's your infant? Ready to admit you like him yet?' Classic Chelsea. If you can't take the heat, aim the torch blower at someone else.

'I knew this was coming,' sighed Abby. She had resigned herself to the fact she had to run the gauntlet at some stage.

'Okay, you know what? I'm just coming out with it: Yes, you were right, you're the best, you're awesome, you are all-knowing super-humans with incredible powers of prescience, because I think I DO like him, even though it's preposterous, and I could very well just be in the post-sex glow and he's entirely wrong for me.'

'*Why* is he wrong for you?' Mads asked loudly in order to compete with all of Chelsea's laughter and knee-slapping and 'I *knew* its'.

'Because he is, Mads! He's a kid! And also, I don't know anything about him. He could be living with his mum and dad for all I know.'

'Better than a secret wife in the basement,' Mads said, without missing a beat. 'Abs, why can't you just roll with it for a while? Stop predicting the future and just be frivolous and fun and foxy for a bit?'

'Well, I am, for your information. I even invited him to stay over last night, in fact.'

'You RASCAL!' Mads exclaimed in excitement. 'Was it amazing and romantic and sexy and did you wake up in each other's arms and have despicable morning sex?'

'No, because he left. He was getting picked up to go fishing – who *fishes*? – at 5 a.m. by his rather handsome boss who, Chelsea, would be just your type, actually now I think of it.'

'I have a boyfriend, but thank you. So wait, you actually got over your "thing", and asked him to sleep over and he brushed you? Oh, this is too funny.'

'Glad my vulnerability provides you with adequate amusement.'

'He would've stayed though, if he wasn't off killing fish?' Mads asked, her eyes gleaming with excitement at this new development in her friend's irrational need to sleep alone.

'I'd like to believe so. He got snarky the last few times when he was sent home . . . Anyway, he wants to take me for a drink tonight . . . do you think it will look a bit wrongo? Like I'm taking my nephew for a cocktail?'

Both girls groaned theatrically.

'HE ISN'T TWELVE, HE'S TWENTY-TWO. You carry on like he'll be wearing a Harry Potter t-shirt and riding a BMX,' Chelsea said, exasperated.

As she so often did, Switzerland stepped in. 'Abs? No one will think anything of it. You look about twenty-five anyway. Let the man take you out for a drink. He probably saved up all his pocket money just for this very occasion.'

Abby sighed and pulled her legs up to her chest as she contemplated what her friends were saying.

'Before you both fall in love with him, he didn't text all week – did I mention that? Did my fucking head in. Why can't people just text or call when they say they will?'

'You mean people like you, who never text men back?' Mads asked in a singsong voice.

Abby smiled in defeat and recognition.

'So you'll go into public with Marcus then, do we have confirmation of that?' Mads asked, pushing romance and coupledom as subtly as a bulldozer.

'Fine, fine. But only if Chels breaks into Jeremy's place and checks in his basement for dead bodies.'

'I might just fucking do that, you know,' Chelsea said, frustration ringing in her voice.

'Don't worry, darling. I'm sure he's done everything to make sure the scent of rotting flesh is gone,' Mads said, reaching over and tapping Chelsea's leg comfortingly.

21

In a move that delighted both parties, Marcus called Abby – *who answered the phone* – at precisely 6.04 p.m. and arranged a place where they could meet and have an Old-Fashioned at 8 p.m., a drink which Marcus assured Abby would become her new favourite way to drink bourbon, and which Abby flatly rebuked, due to the fact she would never find a way, let alone a favourite way, to drink such a filthy spirit.

As Abby finished the brief phone call, she realised she had completely failed to stick to her original lie, which was that she had plans tonight. The pace at which she was thawing out since having met Marcus was both electrifying and terrifying. Despite the heckling, the chat with the girls by the ocean today had helped. Abby knew her hang up with Marcus's age wasn't about to just switch off, but she could at least stop carrying on as though she had whisked him away from the day care centre in her Zimmer frame.

But pretending it was completely normal was so *hard!* She was kissing her first boy when Marcus was on the delivery table. Travelling through Europe when he was hitting puberty. Things like that wouldn't stop swirling through her mind. But after spending

121

an hour and twenty minutes on choosing her outfit – it had to be sexy, cool but not look like she'd tried; an *impossible* equation – she had convinced herself Marcus's age was an issue only for as long as she made it one.

After all, she'd dated thirty-eight year olds who were less exciting, less talented, less intellectual, and far more childish. At least Marcus knew better than to text her at 2.30 a.m. when he was off his head and tell her he was out the front and they were going to the McDonald's drive-thru in their pyjamas, like that fuckwit Ryan had done. God she'd dated some dipshits. Ryan was one of the worst; his Big Guy on Campus Finance Job was the prefect breeding ground for one of the most enthusiastic and badly disguised cocaine addictions she'd ever witnessed. This was a man who had a line before going to yoga; who excitedly took Abby back to his *American Psycho* apartment to show her a gun he'd bought. He was a real catch, ol' Ryan.

It was a bit depressing in hindsight. But Abby was convinced that when she put her light on, when she actually *wanted* a boyfriend, they'd all come crawling out of the woodwork, ready to be the Best Boyfriend Ever. She didn't have her light on yet, but she was definitely starting to think about *maybe* reaching for the switch. It would be nice to travel with someone when all of this newfound freedom came bouncing in with the new website, she'd decided. She could go alone, of course she could, it would be amazing, but a life in which she was deeply in love *and* had the freedom and money to travel? Inconceivable.

Abby arrived at the bar first; (Marcus had offered to pick her up; she had declined) or at least she hoped she did. It looked more like the wine cellar of a restaurant, dark wood, underground, capacity for no more than ten people catered for with three small rickety tables. Abby understood this brand of speakeasy was 'hip' but it was also a bit of a wank. We aren't in the middle of the prohibition anymore, guys – we are allowed to drink, we don't need to hide in underground lairs in case the cops bust in and confiscate our moonshine. Abby much preferred to drink in a place with a view, or at least some daylight, or at the very least, a cocktail list she could read without shining the face of her phone over it.

Turns out she didn't need to.

'What do you think you're doing?' A familiar voice from behind her asked.

'Trying to see what Batman's serving down here in his cave,' she replied, taking him in as he sat down in the chair opposite her, having kissed her lightly on the lips before he did so.

'Well, don't you look gorgeous,' he said, taking her in appreciatively. 'I'm the luckiest bat in the world being able to sit with you here and buy you a drink, do you know that?'

It *sounded* like hyperbole, but somehow when Marcus said it, dark eyes focused intently on Abby's face, voice soft, lips curled into a small smile of delighted disbelief, it sounded entirely sincere.

'And what might that drink be, do we think?'

'Told you,' he said, standing up to move the 23 centimetres to the bar, 'an Old-Fashioned. It's timeless, it's artisan and it's about to be in front of you, winking deliciously for you to sip it up. It's a bit of a love letter to bourbon – or rum or whisky – but there are some notable appearances by sugar and citrus, too. You'll *love* it.'

She loved the way he spoke, Abby realised. He and Mads would have a field day bantering back and forth with their witty turn of phrase and thesaurus-esque vocabulary.

He sat back down and faced Abby directly.

'So, you gonna ask me about the one?'

'What?' Abby froze.

'The *one*. The one that got away today! It was magnificent, obviously. Probably as long as that bar. And made of pure gold. With diamond scales. Pearls in its mouth. And I had it, totally had it, but then the bastard slipped away just as I was pulling him up.'

Fishing. Of course, Abby thought. Duh.

'Well done. Catch any non-fiction fish?'

'Course we did. I generously donated all of mine to Chris so he could cook them up.'

'Or his wife could, anyway.'

'No wife. And he's a brilliant cook, actually. We should go over there for a meal one day. He thinks you're great; would love to have us over.'

'Well, you're awfully matey with the boss, aren't you,' Abby accused playfully.

'He was my friend before he was my boss, actually. Known Chris for about seven years; met him through my older brother Troy, he was his boss back then. He's such a good man, Chris . . . I guess you could call him my mentor. One of a kind. So full of life, and hungry for new adventures and experiences. Webra is only one of his companies; he has three. Stupidly successful, a real entrepreneur, you know? He has an idea, he implements it, it succeeds and he moves onto the next thing. Can't sit still.'

'Impressive. Is he single then? Gay?'

'Straight. Single. Always single. Has plenty of dalliances, of course, the occasional girl he'll see for a few months, but he just . . . he just operates better single.'

'I think a lot of people do. I think maybe even I do.'

'Two Old-Fashioneds?' A tall, thin man with several thousand tattoos and a thin moustache presented two tumblers brimming with ice and orangey liquid. A cherry completed the picture.

'Thanks, man, they look incredible. Thanks so much.' Marcus was so well mannered, Abby decided. He was a child, and yet he was a gentleman. A chentleman.

'Try it. Fall in love with it. Go.' Marcus took a sip of his drink, watching Abby intently as she sipped hers.

To her surprise, although it hollered of strong brown spirits, her least favourite kind, it had a sweetness and warmth to it that was rather pleasing indeed.

'Actually, it's not bad . . .'

'He makes them strong, but that's how they're intended. Delicious!' Marcus's happiness levels upon knowing Abby was enjoying her drink rocketed; he was literally bouncing in his old wooden chair with glee.

'Now that we're becoming a little more lubricated' – he winked in a deliberately over-the-top fashion – 'I think you were saying how you prefer being single, and my heart was breaking a little bit.'

Abby grinned, the heat of the bourbon worming up into her head instantly. 'Some people . . . they're better when they're part of a couple; they feel secure, like a team . . . they can't handle being alone. But I don't equate being alone with being lonely. I like being by myself. I get more shit done when I'm single.'

'Hmm. It sounds suspiciously like you haven't fallen in love with me yet, because if you had, you would be telling me you love being in a couple, especially with people called Marcus.'

'You're in a good mood tonight, aren't you?'

'I may have had a few cleansers on the boat, and then maybe one at home. But I'm not drunk, just fun.'

'Yes, you *are* fun. So, where is home, anyway?'

'I live in the city, down by the wharf. It's this converted ware-house studio loft type thing, one living area. It's got huge windows built into the roof for light, so you feel like you live outdoors, you know? I love it. It's exactly the kind of place I lived in in New York and I never thought I'd find anything like it here.'

Abby's mind was calculating all of this information at roughly the pace of a five year old trying to work a Sat Nav system, set to Danish. Loft? Lived alone? New York? Abby had done none of those things at his age.

'When did you live in New York?'

'I did a year of uni there, at NYU. I'm hustling to get back; told Chris we needed a New York arm of Webra. He hasn't bought the idea yet, but I'll add some sugar to my recipe and I'm pretty sure within a year he'll take the muffin.'

His lexicon was confusing sometimes, Abby realised. Like she was out of the loop and a new language had been created specifically to ostracise non-loop dwellers. 'Thankfully' this happened often enough with her models that she didn't experience a sting of feeling old or obsolete, more just a light pinch. She nodded and went along with it, praying his journey into the argot of hip dudes in their early twenties would be short-lived and was largely fuelled by alcohol.

'Well that sounds like a *lot* of fun. I love that city. It instantly buoys me up . . . the energy is amazing.'

'It's incredible. It was a bit hard coming back here after that place, everything feels so insular, like, I love this city, of course I do, but it can't compare.'

Abby was trying not to be too excited at the revelation that not only was he travelled, but that he had a hunger to travel again. She realised all her reasons for not being with him had started to dissolve; that this was occurring in direct proportion with the amount of bourbon she'd consumed on an empty stomach didn't.

'Shall we – have you eaten?' Marcus asked, hopping off his chair to grab a bar menu, perusing it quickly before looking up at Abby. 'How would we feel if I did the ordering? I'll get us some tasting plates.'

Abby *was* hungry, and was thrilled to have him make all of the decisions. So often she was the one left in charge, organising and choosing where to go, what to do, which wine to drink . . . It was so refreshing to have someone come in and take charge. It was incredibly attractive, too. He was on fire, tonight, Abby realised, watching him chat convivially to thin moustache, ordering their food. His friendliness was so attractive.

Marcus sat back down with a happy plop, clearly delighted with the way the evening was transpiring. 'So, didn't you say you were busy tonight? Was that from the Fake Fiancé book of lies?'

'I *was* busy, thank you,' said Abby, who most definitely was not. 'But it was a stiff dinner party, and I am pleased to have snaked out of it, to be honest.'

'As in, you're happier here with me?' He placed his hand on her bare leg under the table, gently stroking it. She tingled at his touch.

'I'm having fun, yes.'

'So you admit you have fun with me? Even though you think I'm young enough to be your daughter?'

Abby laughed. 'Yes! Yes, stop pumping yourself up, you maniac.'

'I will admit I was surprised you came out in public with me. I thought you were going to pull some "Abby" move and cancel, to be honest.'

'An "Abby" move?'

'You know, asserting yourself. Reminding everyone who's running this show.'

'Am I really like that?' Abby was taken aback. Partly at his comment, partly at the fact she was almost certain he was right.

'Of course you are! It's part of what makes you so sexy. Well, no, actually, the fact that you're *aware* that you do it, that's what's sexy. If you were genuinely a control freak, that would be unsexy. This girl I was seeing for a bit, Naomi, she was a real pleaser, you know? She always wanted to make sure I was happy, and that everything was fine, and she never wanted to cause a fuss, or push her own needs, and at first I thought it was unreal, because we gents love to feel like kings, but after a bit, it became . . . kind of repellent, actually. I was so worried about disappointing her, because she relied on my happiness for her own happiness – is this too deep? Too much? You're not meant to talk about ex-girlfriends, are you? Shit.'

Abby smiled warmly. 'Not usually, no, but it doesn't bother me. It bothers girls who like to believe they're the only girl who was ever in your life, or who prefer to think you were a virgin monk before they came along. We're adults. We can talk about whatever we like. Go on. It was interesting.' And it was. Abby loved how emotionally aware Marcus was. And he was smart and a brilliant conversationalist. And he was sexy.

'There's not much else to say; it was basically a long-winded way of saying I think your self-assurance is very attractive.'

'Thank you. That's very sweet of you to say. Your self-assurance is equally appealing.' The bourbon was making Abby extremely congenial, which was a surprise since she'd always figured the harder the spirit, the more revolting the drinker became. 'What *I* want to know is how you know to use a word like "self-assurance". Your parents brought you up well.'

'Mum did. She's an incredible woman. Dad's not, he's not even an incredible man; in fact, he's not even a man at all. He's a dog.' He took a long sip of the new Old-Fashioned positioned in front of him. 'He walked when Troy, Katie and I were kids; I was five. He's still alive, as far as we know, but he hasn't bothered to contact any of us.'

'What a pig,' Abby said in disgust. It made sense now that Marcus was a gentler breed of man; he'd been raised by a good woman. 'Did your mum re-marry?'

'No, but she's had a boyfriend for about seven years. That his name is Dwayne is forgivable only because he adores Mum and treats her well. I'd be forced to resort to Disney teen-movie style tactics if any guy came in and started making Mum unhappy. Dad did enough damage to last a lifetime. I wish him many sexually transmitted diseases and an acute gambling addiction.' Another long sip of his drink, as if to soothe the fire in his body that arrived when talk of his father arose. 'What about your parents?'

'Well . . . Mum's still around, she's up in the valley in one of those revolting aged "lifestyle resorts", where they get their own little apartment and garden and stuff and they all live together and pretend to not hate their children for never visiting.'

'Jesus, that sounds pretty rough.'

Abby laughed. 'No, she likes it, strangely. Chose to live there, in fact. They all do once they get used to the fact that this is their life now. She had me when she was nearly forty, by the way, she's not some vivacious fifty-something fox living in an aged-care facility, secretly harbouring her escape.'

'. . . And Papa Vaughn?' Marcus's face was prepared for something bad.

'He died when I was twenty-five. Pancreatic cancer. It was horrific, and I still miss him deeply. He was my favourite person in the whole world.' Abby smiled in memory of her father, and as a signal that Marcus wasn't about to witness some kind of teary breakdown.

'Oh, shit, Abs . . . that's awful to hear.' He reached over and placed his hand on hers, his thumb moving back and forward, stroking the side of her hand. It was such a simple, loving gesture;

and coupled with the familiar abbreviating of her name . . . it didn't take Abby's breath away, but it certainly borrowed it for a moment.

'It's okay. He was the best dad I could've hoped for while he was around, so I'm grateful for that. You didn't even have that much . . . Gosh. It's all a bit shit and unfair really, isn't it?'

Marcus smiled, and was about to answer, but four small plates of delicious food arrived, and the attention shifted to them. Marcus passed Abby her cutlery and napkin, and re-filled her water glass. Then he served her all four dishes before serving himself. Abby watched him as he went, quietly mesmerised by his chivalry and shimmering manners.

She thought about his childhood, his life, tried to imagine what his mother looked like, and what she would think of Abby: would she be angry with her for stealing her son away, not only from her, but from the constellation of young women who were closer to him in age? Or would she pour her a glass of wine and warmly tell her to sit down, instantly accepting her because Marcus had? Abby had no idea. But as she watched Marcus delicately shift tantalising meatballs from one plate to another, she realised this evening had gently pushed her down one prong of the fork in the road she faced.

22

The website was due to go live this week, which kept Abby awake late at night with anticipation and excitement and intensely irrational and stressful thoughts about it all failing. Plus, she'd had to 'let go' both Charlotte and Siobhan. She'd done it on Friday, they'd been pissed off and shocked and petulant as expected, but she hoped the weekend and their bonus payout sweetener had helped them thaw out. Their contract stated under these circumstances they had two weeks' notice, so either they would be a real help as the website started to take over, or they'd be resentful, sullen brats who moped around the office and chewed up bandwidth on YouTube.

Rob was impressed with the way Abby had managed to 'callously and cleanly' ditch not only all three of her staff, but also her office (and only pay out two of the remaining seven months of the lease) within the space of a fortnight, as if she'd done it all in a movie-style montage, and swivelled on her office chair smoking a cigar at the end of it all. In truth, it had been incredibly stressful, and she felt terrible, especially for the girls. Plus, she now had no staff. Well, Angie was going to come over and help out on

Wednesdays and Thursdays until she started touring, but Abby knew it wouldn't be enough.

Abby felt her phone vibrate in her bag as she waited for the lift, consciously ignoring the slimy looks her probably too-short dress was attracting from the bored businessmen hovering around her.

She pulled it out, it was a number she didn't recognise, but she answered it anyway. She needed a distraction from the world's slowest lift.

'Abby speaking.'

'Abby! Hi, it's Charlie. From the whisky event? How are you, have I caught you at a bad time?'

'*Charlie!* Hi! No, not a bad time at all, how are you?' Abby was delighted to hear from Charlie. She couldn't recall giving her her phone number, but nonetheless, it was good to hear from her.

'Oh, cool. Hey, sorry for the random call. Shit has been real heavy here at work . . . In fact, they actually let me go, which wasn't at *all* a kick in the baby maker after having bought in their three biggest accounts and worked my bony little ass off to keep them, but anyway, that's boring, so I'll get back to why I'm actually calling . . .'

'Shit, Charlie, that *sucks*. I'm so sorry to hear that.'

'Did me a favour, I'm sure of it. You don't want to spend your life working to make someone else money, it doesn't make sense, I'd rather be doing what you're doing, my own thing, answer to nobody, free as a bird.'

'Well, yeah, I mean, kind of,' Abby laughed. 'It's not quite at that stage yet, but I'm literally in the process of making it more in that vein, yes.'

'Would that mean you're too busy to catch up for a drink this week? I'd love to pick your brain 'bout something, if that's not annoying and you have time? Also, you know, we'll chat and have fun, but I wanted to be up-front because the worst thing to do to another person is invite them out under the guise of fun then make it a leeching session.'

Abby laughed. 'Of course I have time. Can you do . . . actually, tonight is probably the only one I can do?'

'Perfection. How about Jack and Jills? At, say, seven? Let me buy you some chicken schnitzel.'

'Can we make it 7.30?'

'Of course. See you tonight, Abs.'

So familiar! Abby thought. But somehow Charlie could get away with it.

'Have a good day, do something fun for us suckers stuck at work; play with a frisbee or hire a kayak or something.'

Charlie laughed and said goodbye, just as the lift finally arrived. Abby stepped in, excited that someone as talented and cool as Charlie would be soliciting help from her.

Things were demonstrably less cool in the office, where neither Charlotte nor Siobhan had showed up, despite it being 9.27 a.m., and the Angie-less answering machine was blinking irritably at Abby. Fuckin' office phone. That was the first thing that was going. People could use the website for their enquiries from now; an email was so much easier to deal with. God, she could not wait to have that great electronic screening device in action. Everything would be siphoned through it, even her girls would be forced into using it to check their jobs, or contact Abby. Abby was done with calls. It was SMS or email from now on, thank you very much.

Abby continued through to her office and dumped her bag on her desk, waking her computer up with her mouse as she did so. She looked around the office and wondered where all of this shit would go. What did people do with second-hand office furniture?

She needed Angie to be on top of this, she had other things to think about, like why Williamson Pearls had cut their request for ten girls down to two for an event this Friday. She'd be sending them a stern email; they couldn't just do that on a whim, things were quiet at the moment, which while a blessing for the website/staff-firing side of things, was a bit shit finance-wise. Maybe she needed to implement a cancellation fee for clients as well as the girls . . . Another thing to ask Arthur about. Poor guy, he was about as enchanted with Abby's questions and requests as an agoraphobic was with a trip to the desert. But it was his own fault for telling her there were no stupid questions, just stupid people who didn't ask questions when they should. She didn't want to be one of those morons, especially not when her whole business was riding on it, so she asked around 729 questions a day, pretty much all of them stupid.

The girls finally walked in laughing loudly, holding giant coffees and brown paper bags with their Turkish toast and peanut butter, like two BFFs in a commercial for A Really Awesome Café. Charlotte caught sight of Abby looking at them as they walked in and offered a modest head dip as a hello. She was less juvenile than Siobhan, Abby decided. She understood that it was just a business decision; she wasn't letting them go because she wanted different girls, or their work wasn't up to scratch. Whatever. Abby wasn't interested in talking to them, either, and instead chose to sail down the river of passive-aggressive with an email detailing what she'd need them to have done by the end of the week and their final day. She felt less shitty about being an email witch when she remembered the Miu Miu clutches she'd bought them both as their farewell present.

An email from Marcus popped up. There was a chance it was about the site, but there was vast evidence to support that it might be a YouTube clip featuring a micro-pig stumbling through puddles awkwardly in gumboots, or a song he'd found that he thought Abby would love, or a link to Yahoo! Answers with a question on how to get the courage up to tell your new boyfriend you love him.

As it turned out, it was a photo of him holding a takeaway coffee cup inscribed with the words, 'Marcus, I love you, call me!!!' written on it in thick blue texta.

> Found a new coffee joint, it's delicious. I can't be sure, but I think the barista is flirting with me. He gave me extra chocolate. Hope you're having a great day, and try not to miss me too much. It's a bit desperate. X M

Abby laughed out loud and shook her head. He was a funny boy, and flirted in the best possible way: with humour. As usual, she had neither the time nor the cleverness to reply with anything on a competitive level, so stuck to what she knew.

> Why are you emailing me? Finish my website already! Faster! FASTER!

'Your office is filthy,' said Rob from the door of her office, looking resplendent in a navy suit with waistcoat, with the kind of stubble that looked accidental, but knowing Rob, was highly calculated and at the Perfect Length.

'And *you're* overdressed, but who's accusing anyone of anything?'

Rob grinned and walked in, taking his usual place opposite Abby's desk, moving several folders and a stack of headshots to one side in order to set down his tablet.

'She's cute,' he said, looking through some of the comp cards as he settled in.

'Good, put her to one side, they're all potentials and I haven't had a chance to look through them yet.'

'Tough gig.'

'Half of them look nothing like their photos, so actually it *is* a tough job. I usually get Angie to add them as a friend on Facebook so she can go through their photos and see what they *really* look like.'

'Possibly illegal; but impressive. Why do they even bother with these things anymore?' He continued to peruse the photos as he spoke. 'It's all email these days anyway, surely?'

'Will be for Allure. Now the girls just upload their own photos in the "Submit an application" section for us.'

'Who's "us", again, exactly?' Rob had a glint in his eye as he spoke. If Abby hadn't banned herself from ever thinking about Rob in a sexual way, *ever*, she could've sworn he was being rather flirtatious today. Perhaps it was just the confidence that came with his new facial hair. Who could say with Rob? Part of his appeal was the fact he was almost impossible to place – some thought he was gay, some thought he was a rampant flirt; some – Laura – thought he was their boyfriend and that he was neither gay nor a flirt.

'Shut up, you. You know I'm working on it.'

'Work is the operative word, because that's what you'll be doing a lot of until then, madam.'

'But that's what the website is for – to do everything while I read magazines and drink coffee. You're not suggesting that . . . you can't be . . . it's not – you don't think I'm going to have to actually *do* anything from here on, do you?'

'I know you think you're joking right now, but actually, I think you mean that a little bit.'

'Well of course I do! That's why I did all of this staff-firing and office-lease-breaking, isn't it? You know, all that stuff you told me to do? So I could be more flexible and free, and less desk-bound and rat-racey.'

'I love your optimism, Abs. If only it could be bottled and drunk in shots with lemon and salt.'

'Rob? It's cool. I know what I'm doing. You said yourself that it's going to make the business more profitable.'

'Yes, dear Abby, but not by itself. You can't just switch this website to "run business" and hit the shops.'

'I know you think I'm in a fairy princess land where I've just outsourced my business to Flash and forms, but I understand the implications.' Abby watched Rob shake his head as she spoke.

'Well, I guess if you can pull it all off you *will* have more time with your toyboy . . .'

Rob looked at his nails effeminately as he said this, assuming a terrible impression of insouciance.

'Pardon me?'

'Oh, come on, don't play coy, we all know about your little web concubine.'

Abby crossed her arms across her chest, and sat back in her chair. 'And who is "we" exactly?' Had Marcus been running his mouth?

'Just people.'

'Rob. Come on. Who? Not that I care, obviously, because it's nothing.'

'Oh, yes, you definitely sound like someone who doesn't care and is trying to dismiss nothing.' His playful, teasing smile was excruciating.

Abby sighed. 'It's just a hook-up. You know, something temporary and inappropriate? Now, please, in all honesty, who told you?'

'Chris is a friend of a friend and we were at a fortieth on Friday night, and it transpired we both worked with someone that was you or Marcus.'

'Jesus.'

'So, is it as good as Madonna makes it look? You know, the youthful buck thing?'

'For your information, of which you seem to have plenty already, he's very mature for his age.'

Rob laughed raucously, his head rolling back with pleasure at Abby's sensitive and defensive outburst.

'Well I'm happy for you. You could do with some fun, you're so bloody uptight when it comes to your personal life.'

'What does *that* mean?'

'Don't be defensive. In all honesty, you're living the dream; fooling round with some dreamy young stud, and who cares if he can't enter licensed premises? I think it's good for you.'

Rob was going hard on the teasing, Abby thought. A little *too* hard. How utterly inappropriate and unprofessional and magnificent, she thought. The idea of Rob being jealous was breathtaking.

'And, you know,' Rob said, finally finishing up his stand-up routine, 'you have 24-hour assistance should anything ever go wrong with the website, too, so that's a win.'

'Terrific stuff, Rob, great work.' Even though she secretly loved his teasing, she had to maintain her position of outrage. 'Now, can we get back to work, please?'

'Finally! I thought you'd never stop talking about your new boyfriend,' he said as he fired up his tablet, a playful smile etched onto his lips.

23

Charlie looked terrific at dinner. Her hair was jammed up messily in a high bun, her wispy full fringe grazing her lashes and very Chanel-esque, she wore winged eyeliner and a white blouse with a bow-tie tucked into high-waisted, dark denim jeans. Straight from a streetstyle blog. Or a Topshop campaign. Abby felt conservative, dated and overdressed in her corporate dress by comparison.

Charlie smiled as she greeted Abby, but didn't go for the hello kiss, which was strange and foreign, and very obviously awkward for Abby, who did, pulling back and laughing self-consciously. It immediately made Abby question if she was one of Those People, who air kissed anyone, everyone, even if they're not at the cheek kiss level of familiarity. She didn't want to be one of Those People. She wanted to be cool and aloof like Charlie. Charlie definitely impressed and even intimidated her a little, Abby realised. Not a bad thing; she was used to being around young girls who looked to *her* for intimidation.

Both women sat down, and Abby immediately grabbed the wine list, jealous of Charlie's fish-bowl glass filled with a deep burgundy liquid.

'What a day. Excuse the sailor speak; but *fuck me*. Intense.'

'Oooh, don't miss that one bit,' said Charlie as she sipped from her wine and moved her chic, python-skinned notepad and pen to one side. 'I'm living the life of unemployed luxury.'

''Sbeen mental. I've fired all my staff and am moving out of my office this week . . .'

'Whoa, how come? Not enough business?' Charlie's eyes were squinty with interest.

'No, no, no, I just— I wanted to work a bit smarter, get the work coming in and going out purely through the website. It's stupidly obvious now that I'm doing it, makes so much sense.'

A clearly overworked waitress almost ran into the table and asked if Abby 'wanted' a drink, simultaneously snatching the wine menu from her hands. Abby quickly ordered a glass of pinot.

'So hang on, you're going to manage that whole business, all those beautiful, excruciating girls and those diabolical clients, all by yourself? Won't that be too much for you?'

'I'll have to for the next little bit, but I'm actually trying to find someone who can help out. Probably part-time, but more of a senior position than the girls I had working with me. I need someone to be able to manage the girls and keep the clients happy, and show at events and keep an eye on things and so on. It's a pretty simple role, but finding someone who doesn't mind working Friday and Saturday nights and being on call? Not so easy.'

'But they don't work the shift, they just get there and make sure everything's in order, yeah?'

'Yep. It's a bit of a mother-hen role, I guess. And a client suck-up role. And there'll also be office time, of course. I'm thinking I might hire a contractor for three or six months and see how that goes. Thinking maybe a mum with young kids who wants a little bit of work would be good.'

'So it's a pretty lucrative business then? This promo agency stuff?'

'Ummm . . .' Abby laughed awkwardly. What an odd question. 'Sometimes. Ebbs and flows.'

Charlie tapped her index finger against her cheek, her lips pursed and to one side. Abby's wine arrived, was sipped urgently and placed back on the table clumsily.

'Would this be, and this is merely a brain vomit, so just indulge me, would this be a role *I* might be able to do, do you think?'

Abby's hand flew to her chest, and her eyes went dead with seriousness. 'Are you kidding? But you're so *accomplished!* You couldn't be, don't you think that . . . would you really be up for that?'

Charlie took a sip of her wine and tucked an imaginary hair behind her left ear.

'Well, as you know, I don't got no job right now. Which isn't the best sell to your potential boss, but you already knew that, and that's why we're here anyway, so no skeletons rattling 'round there. And second of all, I don't mind working weekends and nights, because I've done it for years, except my call times were a bit longer than the ones you'd be requesting, by about ten hours, so to me, this role sounds pretty tops, actually. Plus it would allow me to work on my own business and get that all started through the day.'

'Your own business?'

'Yeah, the event management stuff.'

'Of course. I can't see any conflict of interest there . . . can you?' Abby smiled broadly.

'Nope. So, do we reckon this might work?' Charlie looked at Abby with a half-smile.

Abby asked herself if this was the most mental idea ever conceived, right up there with the Segway. Or was it one of those glorious moments where everything falls charmingly into place, and the universe smiles softly from above, happy that it created another Perfect Moment in small-business staff hiring. Maybe *this* was why she met Charlie all those weeks ago, for this exact situation to be able to blossom! Abby started to fidget with excitement, her right leg tapping furiously on the ground as it did when adrenaline was given an opportunity to scream through her veins.

'So, just to confirm, there'd be office time as well,' said Abby, 'which actually is based at my place now'. . . Actually, there's no reason you can't work from home, and we'd just meet a couple of times a week, maybe. The whole idea is that it's flexible and malleable, and we help each other out. I guess I basically wanted to clone myself, if I'm being honest. The big plan is to travel for a while . . . I wanted to be able to leave the company in capable hands while I did that.'

'How long we talking?' Charlie peered into Abby's eyes in that arresting manner of hers.

Abby got nervous for a moment, as though she had to justify herself.

'I don't know, say, four/five weeks? I've never done it before, I always had to work, y'see. I don't need to disappear on my life and backpack or any of that shit, I love my life and this city, but I do want to explore a little. I'm nearly thirty-four and I've only ever been overseas for two weeks at a time.' She was babbling. Why did Charlie make her feel like she was a kid?

'I did London for three years, Paris for two, and a stint in Berlin for six months. It was awesome, but I was ready to come home. The weather drove me fucking nuts, for starters. But you gotta travel, course you do.' Charlie sipped from her wine, her eyes still locked onto Abby. Despite her cute wardrobe and adorable fringe, there was something a bit scary and Angelina Jolie-ish about Charlie, Abby realised. Probably has a flock of Satanic tattoos on her ribcage and a penchant for death metal. Meh, who cares; she would keep the girls in line, that's for sure. Plus, the clients would be very impressed by her take-no-shit attitude. They'd be impressed by *all* of the new elements of the business, Abby thought excitedly. How slick and professional and successful she would look if she could launch the site, move offices and have an extraordinary new contractor all at once.

'So, how would a regular week go, for example?' Charlie asked, perusing the menu as she spoke.

'The primary vessel of communication for Allure is the new website. So all bookings, all enquiries, all applications for work from new girls, it all goes through the site.'

'So what do *we* do? Sounds like the web robot has it all under control.'

Abby laughed. 'Kind of.'

'Hey, you hungry? I am – shall we order from our charming waitress so we can get food on the way?'

'Great idea. And also, let's talk about *your* business! That's why we're here – not for me to seduce you into the glamorous and exciting world of promotional models.'

'Oh, it's such basic shit. Like, how do you register the business, who's your accountant, what can you claim, who is your web design company, which brand of instant coffee is cheapest and most effective . . .'

Abby smiled. 'More than happy to help. Wish I had someone to impart all of that stuff when I was starting out. I was like a drunk stumbling down a dark hallway, feeling around for things and hoping they were what I was looking for.'

'You're smashing it now, though. What a fun boss I have.' Charlie had a grin on her face as she sipped her wine.

'Are you serious? You definitely want to come on board? You don't even know how much I'm paying or anything, an—'

'I think you're forgetting it's actually me who benefits most from this. And as I'm currently earning nothing, and have a mortgage and a highfalutin' lifestyle I have no intention of giving up, any job that affords me flexibility and pays me more than $5 a week is a win.'

Abby could not quite believe her luck. How glorious it would be: they would both be teaching each other things, and Charlie wouldn't get under her feet or be hopeless, she would be a rock she could depend upon.

Well, she hoped as much, she'd only met her once but she seemed professional. A small voice in Abby's head said she should get a reference from her old job, but she didn't want to offend Charlie by asking for one. Maybe she would just call them anyway. Nahh, no need. Charlie was legit.

'Let's do it. And if it makes you feel more at ease, yes, you can wear an earpiece around the office.'

Charlie laughed and lifted her now empty wine glass up to cheers Abby.

'To promo girls!'

As Abby sipped her wine, she saw her phone vibrate and light up on the table: it was a text from Marcus. Her heart immediately quickened. She wanted to read it, but didn't want to be one of Those Tools who read every text or email as they came through.

'Be right back.' Charlie stood and strutted off to the bathroom, leaving Abby free to check the text.

I've been thinking of those little yellow knickers you wear to bed. Also, let's go for a nightcap. I'll come pick you up in an hour. X M

So *bossy*. Abby loved it. She checked her watch; it was not yet even half-past eight. She could do a nightcap, why not? It was a celebratory night, after all.

> If you're lucky I'll wear them tonight. If you're even luckier,
> I won't.

Thirty seconds later, her phone vibrated.

> Abby! That's so unhygienic. Yuck.

Abby blinked a few times. Again, her phone vibrated.

> I JEST. Skip the bra and shoes too, if you like. See you at
> 9.30. XM

'Why so smiley?' Charlie said as she sat back down, wiping her hands on her lap.

'Just a silly text from a silly boy,' Abby said, still shaking her head.

'There's no better kind.' Charlie said, smiling devilishly.

'I tend to agree.'

True to his word, Marcus arrived at Abby's house at precisely 9.30 p.m., leaving the car running as he bounded up her stairs to knock on the door, with a small bouquet of neighbourhood-picked roses and a gleeful, pleased-with-himself smile.

Abby, who'd changed into jeans and a lightweight, short grey singlet over a very-visible black lace bralette, opened the door. 'Uh, you know I prefer David Austins, right?'

'Ah yes, but these are better, these are . . . Derek Boston roses.'

'You're a nonce.'

'Bah, roses are roses.'

'Some would argue that, but thank you all the same.' She took them from him and immediately a small thorn pricked her finger.

'Ow, fuck!'

'Oh shit, baby baby; I'm sorry.' He grabbed her finger and kissed it several times, then began creeping up her arm, Gomez Adams style.

Abby laughed. 'It's fine, stop, *stop!*' They kissed tenderly on the lips before Marcus pulled back suddenly, his eyes flashing with excitement.

'You look gorgeous, but you'd look better in my car.' Marcus said, before breaking away and clapping his hands in excitement.

'Come on, let's go! Bring a jacket! Dump the Derek Bostons! Let's go!'

'Okay, okay, I'm coming . . .' Abby grabbed a lightweight anorak off her coat hook and her bag and closed the door behind her, wondering what he had in store.

As they drove along, Marcus insisted Abby listen 'properly' to Washed Out, which was playing via his iPhone, because she'd never heard them, and they were 'fucking gorgeous'. Abby asked where they were going, but Marcus continued to sing along, as though he'd not heard. She opened her window and listened to the pop-synth music Marcus was singing along to enthusiastically, enjoying the excitement and exuberance of her passenger, and the delight of being taken on a surprise mission.

After ten minutes, Marcus pulled up and parked the car on the shoulder of a major highway, and what looked like the perfect scene for a swift, anonymous execution.

'Uh, Marcus? What are we doing h—'

'Sshh, sshh, fortune favours the bold. Come on; get out. Lock the door, bring that jacket.'

He went to the boot and pulled out a large blanket and a brown paper bag. It was a picnic. Abby smiled, despite herself. It was all so hilariously clichéd, but she was feeling convivial and open-minded and promised herself not to judge.

Marcus slammed the boot closed and grabbed Abby's hand. 'Follow me.'

They hopped over a crumbling barrier fence and walked down a path that ran perpendicular to the highway, walking over a small cusp to be greeted by a spectacular view of the city and half a football field worth of grass. Lights from the highway lit up the area just enough to keep it from being terrifying.

'What IS this place?'

'No idea. I helped a mate shoot a film clip here last week and thought it would be a beautiful place to bring you for a glass of wine and a pash. It's just like that hill Bart and Lisa are always on in *The Simpsons*, looking over Springfield.'

Abby followed Marcus, her eyes locked onto the twinkling lights below her, until he found A Good Spot and arranged the blanket for them to sit on.

'Bit of a cliché, I know, but you gotta admit it's good, right?'

'It *is* good. It's creepy, a bit serial-killer, but it's very beautiful too.'

He was busy arranging some fancy nuts, dip and crackers on the blanket, which Abby thought was incredibly endearing.

'Chilled rosé, madame?'

He rustled around in the bottomless bag and produced two plastic wine tumblers, and a bottle of rosé from a zip-up bottle cooler. Abby laughed when she saw he'd written 'Babe' and 'Hunk' on them. He filled them to hangover-inducing levels and handed Abby hers carefully.

147

'To a total babe.'

'To a complete hunk.'

They tapped glasses and looked into each other's eyes. Abby saw a boy who was potentially in love with her. Marcus saw a woman whose resistance was finally breaking down. They kissed, each calmly confident that they were in control. Both were wrong.

24

Abby woke up overtired, cranky and unexcited about the office clean-up ahead of her. Thankfully Marcus had left early and wasn't privy to her foul mood. She'd started letting him sleep over, which delighted Marcus, and secretly Abby as well. He kept her in a vice-like cuddle grip all night, chasing her if she rolled the other way, immediately fastening his arms around her torso and kissing her shoulder before settling back into his slumber. Abby loved it, and the illusion of long-term intimacy it created. She hadn't had a proper boyfriend for so long, and the softness of his skin against her as she slept reminded her of the secret world of two people in love, in their own little cotton cocoon each night, safe in each other's arms. It was becoming addictive.

They had returned from their picnic, then carried on drinking till midnight on her kitchen stools, talking about life, work, Charlie ('She's *definitely* not a spy, is she?') the website, the possibility of the two of them maybe sneaking off for a dirty weekend sometime soon. And also three rounds of Uno. Just enough to determine that Abby was *unquestionably* better at it than Marcus, even if she did occasionally cheat by slipping Wild cards under her arse and pulling them out when he was refilling their glasses.

It occurred to Abby as she sat there in knickers and singlet, laughing and sipping and kissing and talking that Marcus was a very good friend, as well as a terrifically sexy lover. She knew this was dangerous territory, because while it was hard to break up with a lover, it was even harder to shed a friend *and* a lover, and Abby couldn't stop thinking that no matter how delicious and fun and gorgeous a time she was having with Marcus, the chimes of doom had to eventually sound.

They had to! Sure, she was enjoying herself now, but she knew that there was a huge, stinking mess waiting around the corner. Either she would implement a break-up, and that would be heartbreaking because there was a good chance it would be because she couldn't take him or the relationship seriously, or they would 'give it a chance', and their inevitable differences would eventually scream so loudly that they would end up breaking each other and hating each other, too. She tried to push those thoughts out of her head and stop forecasting, but it was in her DNA. She did it with every man.

Before Abby could even get into her car, Chelsea was calling. She considered screening, but figured she owed Chels a chat, as she'd been a little absent from her friends for the past couple of weeks. Pah, she'd let it ring out then text her back. Chels, like Abby, was allergic to leaving voicemail.

Sorry honey, about to go into meeting, what's up?

He has a WIFE AND CHILD.

Jeremy?!

Abby knew she should just call. But now she'd lied, she couldn't. *Shit*.

Knew he was 2 good 2 be true. He's such a fucking skidmrk ☹

How did you find out??

Abby was risking several traffic violations and possible death with her texting and reading, but Chelsea was taking ages to write back so she kept driving.

Last night I put foot down, said I wanted to 2 go 2 his place. It's been 2 months! He had usual excuse but I wdn't take no for answer. We drove there n I asked whwwat he was hiding. Thought he was going 2 show me a S&M dungeon or retarded pedo broth

The text cut off, she had obviously written a novel and it was all still filtering through.

. . . er, n then he says I haven't told u full story – DUHHH! He has wife who lives up northrn beaches, they split last yr n have a 2 yo son. He was 2 scared 2 show me house, because his son has bedroom n toys n shit there n he knew that would freak me out

Abby pulled over. Death or serious injury for Jeremy's secret life wasn't worth it.

Whoa. So, so heavy . . . I'm so sorry honey. Let me call you
as soon as meeting over??

Abby's guilt over her call screening was suffocating.

What sicko dates a girl for 2 months n keeps that stuff a
secret?

Abby couldn't take it anymore. She dialled Chelsea, who picked up immediately, and started talking as though they were mid-conversation. Technically, they were.

'I mean, I can see how telling me he has a wife and kid was never going to be easy, but when the fuck was he going to come clean? How long did he think he could keep the charade up? I hate how men think playing little boy scared permits them to perform bigger atrocities, and then when they get found out, they get to play the "But I didn't want to upset you" card, as if it wipes the slate clean.'

'I'm surprised one of his frien—'

'How do you just put a sheet over your whole life like that? I fucking knew something had to be wrong, it was all going too well . . .'

'Hang on, so where did you leave it with him? What's the exact situation he has with his wife?'

Another deep sigh. 'They've been separated for eleven months, and she's moved in with her parents till she finds a place. He sees Oliver once a week, for twenty-four hours.'

'Sheesh . . . that seems a bit unfair.'

'It's just till he gets a bit older and she feels he can "take care of him adequately".'

'Oh. So does that explain all those times he was working on weekends?'

'Yes! Urgh, I can't believe he lied all those times, Abs. Lied to my *face*.'

Abby was silent, thinking about how she could best sneak in some perspective without copping a verbal serve.

'Would it be fair to say, though, and just hear me out, would it be fair to say it would've been hard for him to find a way to tell you this? You're not the most placid of girls . . .'

'Don't you devils-advocate me, Abs, not today. He could've told me on the first date and I would've digested it and dealt with it, and then decided if I wanted to pursue something with him. Now that I've fallen in love with him, and I've found this out . . . I'm fucked, you know? I don't want children, or did you forget that? And now, if I am to stay with him, I immediately inherit one.'

Abby hadn't heard Chelsea this emotional for a very, very long time. She felt like she'd missed some crucial ingredients in the Jeremy/Chelsea love story, she had no idea Chelsea was so into him. Guilt crept in as she realised it was because she'd been so caught up in a tapestry of work and Marcus.

'Chels, I'm not siding with Jeremy. But it seems like despite his terrible decision to keep this from you so far, he *was* doing it with good intentions . . . in as far as the idea of you leaving because of it was too awful an idea to entertain.'

'Can't you just be angry *with me* for once? Instead of trying to sprinkle fucking pixie dust all over everything?'

'Chels, I'm just trying to talk it through with you, like adults do.'

'Well maybe I don't feel like being an adult right now.'

And she'd gone. Hung up. Left Abby with a dismissive symphony of beeps and a sick feeling in her stomach. Abby called Chelsea back, but it rang out. And then she got cross, a combination of too little sleep, too much wine and being reprimanded for trying to help merged into one simmering hotpot of rage: what was

153

Chelsea playing at? Were they in high school? She'd send a text and let it go. Who got to their mid-thirties and still hung up on people? Who did that? Abby tried to calm herself by remembering how supportive and solid Chels had been for her over the years. That despite being testing at times, her veins and arteries were paved with gold.

> Honey, I'm sorry. I didn't mean to upset you. You know I
> back you without exception. Please call me Xxx

Of course, even after Abby arrived at the office, she'd received no response. She dialled Chelsea again once she reached her desk. No answer. She left a long-winded, apologetic voicemail and again pleaded for her to call back.

> I'll come around tonight and we'll talk, okay? And Mads
> too. We're your friends, let us help you and love you and
> shower you in wine. Xxx

She tried calling Mads. Voicemail! It was all too much, especially since Abby's headaches were breeding, paying no heed to the paracetamol she'd guzzled with her double coffee.

> Mads, have you spoken to Chels? Think we should go to
> hers tonight with bottle of red and a kilo of Valium. Let me
> know what time suits X

There. She'd done all she could for now; the girls could get back to her when they were ready. Or else she'd just show up at Chelsea's tonight. Right now she had emails to write, an enormous desk to clean out and petulant staff to dictate.

Just as Abby inhaled her first ulcer-inducing mouthful of teri-yaki salmon, Mads called.

'Hello, handsome.'

'I've just spent my whole lunchbreak being yelled at by Chels because her boyfriend is a twat, but how's *your* day?'

'Yeah, she hung up on me when we spoke this morning—'

'Because you were pro-Jeremy, you muppet. Don't worry, I heard. A lot. In Dolby Surround. For many hours.'

'Hey, just before we go down that path, can I ask how things are with you and Dylan and . . .? I had so many good intentions to call you last Tuesday night, but I didn't. And I'm sorry. What a shitty friend I am these days.'

'Hold the theatrics; I've had enough of those for today. Every-thing's fine, we're going to try IVF, and it will send us broke and make me into a hormonal dragon, but we'll be united and optimis-tic as we eat our two-minute noodles and try not to kill each other.'

Abby laughed gently. 'Well, I'm glad. And I wish you all the very best. You sound happy.'

'Thanks. I feel pretty good about it, you know? Feels nice to have some help with all this finally.'

'So how *is* Chels? Will she ever return my call, do we think?'

'She's still furious at him. She even had a couple of menthol Vogues. During the *DAY*.'

'*Whoa*.'

'As far as I can tell, she told that naughty Jeremy he'd done irreversible damage and never wanted to see his obnoxious face again.'

'That poor guy, he's obviously been anxious about this secret all this time, and then when it comes out he gets punished anyway.'

'He should've been honest with her, Abs. Only the very evil or very stupid would deny that.'

'Would YOU have told her if you were him? No chance! She'd be gone in a whiff of Chanel before you could even explain.'

'Still. Terribly deceitful.'

'Of course it was. But you have to see his rationale; he just wanted to wait till the right time . . . Hey, do you think her anger is amplified because she slept with him?'

'Almost definitely.'

'But from the sounds of things he and his wife are legitimately separated, and Oli—'

'But the scoundrel is not yet *divorced*. And that's what Chels is annoyed abo—'

'Does he plan to?'

'Who knows, she didn't let him explain.'

'Well, I'm going to go 'round tonight – I feel like a bad friend for making her hang up on me today, and I need her to get some perspective.'

Mads laughed. 'Most friends would be, "I want to be there for her", and we're both bulldozers, ramming our opinions down her gullet until she's gasping for air.'

'As if she wouldn't – doesn't – do the same. That's why I love you two and why you love me. Now, will you come over, do you think? Or have you reached your limit on this for today?'

Mads sighed. 'Regrettably I have work to do. Give her a wallop for me, take wine and be prepared to smoke thin cigarettes that taste like Colgate.'

'Can do. Love.'

'Love.'

As Abby finished her lunch, mindlessly scoffing it down, she decided she wanted Marcus's opinion on the situation. As she called his number, she realised how much she respected him and his take on life. He had a far more gentle approach than she and the girls did, he took time to weigh things up, assess all angles and deeply consider each party's feelings . . . whereas *their* preferred speed when leaping to conclusions was more suited to an autobahn. How he could be so wise at such an age, she didn't know. She was certain when she was twenty-two she was screaming at other drunk, aggressive girls in tacky nightclubs when they dared speak to whatever lucky guy was on her arm that month. Should she ever meet his mother, she was going to thank her for producing such a lovely young man.

25

Chelsea wasn't home when Abby arrived and knocked and called and texted and emailed and then called again.

She waited for thirty-five minutes in her car, desperate to crack open the bottle of pinot gris and neck some – it was a revoltingly humid evening and she'd been looking forward to a glass of wine all day – but finally gave up and drove home. Her instinct was to call Marcus, and see if he was free and wanted to come over, but she knew he'd be in the office, working hard on her website. But maybe he could come over after? She'd text him and see . . .

Then stopped. As Abby realised what she'd been about to do, she shook her head in an attempt to dislodge the thought from her brain. She *had* to stop automatically choosing him as her free-time activity! What had she used to do with her time? Lots of things, surely! Surely there were some hobbies . . . showing dogs or crochet or bingo, *something* must have eaten up her spare time. Now all she really wanted to do was hang out with Marcus and eat tapas and drink wine.

Abby walked in the door, kicking her shoes off and immediately removing her painful, diggy-inny bra, and tried Chelsea again. The phone rang out.

Fine. Text it was.

Can my friend stop hating me so much and know that I
want to know if she's ok? xx

Forty-five minutes later:

Hi honey thank u. spent the evening with a friend, took my
mind off things a bit xx

A friend. Abby knew immediately that she'd gone and seen Graham, which made her want to cripple one of Chelsea's permanently
erect nipples. Graham Blackman was Chelsea's kryptonite. He was
a greasy, thieving, drug-dependent compulsive liar who cast a spell
on Chels a few years ago, and had never bothered to take it off. He
ran a very popular restaurant and bar in the city, which according
to the law of Small Cities made him some kind of deity. He and
Chels had shared a tumultuous six months together, in which he
was definitely seeing and sleeping with other women. Chelsea had
loved the heady faux-gangsta life he led, and leapt into it with the
same gusto she leapt into the partying, champagne and cocaine. To
say Mads and Abby disliked Graham was like saying water irritated
the Wicked Witch of the West. He was Satan, right here on Earth,
practising sin and disruption daily. He'd made Chelsea insecure,
aggressive, combative and eventually, weak. She'd kept sleeping
with Graham long after they 'broke up' but wouldn't admit it to the
girls. They found out through ancillary friends, or from his entou-
rage of baboons, who roamed the city and its bars as though they
owned them. Most of which they did. All of Chelsea's wits and
smarts melted when Graham was around. She became a strange,
dependent groupie; another of his dazed wenches, constantly drunk

because Graham didn't like anyone being too alert around him for fear of them being able to see what he was really like.

Abby started to call Chelsea's number, then thought better of it. If she'd been out drinking with Graham she would be the furthest thing from receptive.

> Jeremy been in touch?

> Calling, texting all day, flowers, as if that's going to make me forget he has wife n kid.

> Is it not worth hearing him out maybe? Then you can boot him for good if you need to. I understand you're upset toots, but I also know you really like him . . .

> Ur a godamn dog with a bone sometimes, u know that?

Yyyess! Abby could sense a micro-breakthrough. Time to ram it home. She typed so fast that she kept messing up the words, furiously deleting and re-writing in her panic to sustain the goodwill.

> I get the sense Jeremy is worth it. You're every guy's dream girl so why would he do something to risk losing you without having some kind of strategy??

> Alrite, dalai, that'll do.

> Dinner tomorrow? Lunch? Come on, I'll let you boss me into eating something disgusting made with quinoa and bark . . .

> K, I'll text u x

> xxx

Abby felt much lighter seeing a kiss on the end of Chelsea's text, and knowing she was softening her stance on Jeremy. Abby wasn't sure why she was standing so firmly in Jeremy's corner; she put it down to how happy, patient and calm Chels was around him. That deserved support.

She looked at her phone: 9.44. If she was smart, she would put the wine in the fridge, run a bath, and go to bed. If she was embracing the 'I'm in my thirties and I've supposedly hit my sexual peak and I have a toyboy to play with,' side of her, she would send a suggestive text to Marcus and get him into her bed later this evening.

> How is it going, handsome? Looking like another 1am finish? Looking like an Abby's place finish?

She placed the phone on her kitchen bench and opened the wine. She'd earned it. She even had some leftover noodles – everything was coming up Abby.

> Beautiful woman, it's going to be a ridiculously late one. I'll crash at home so as not to bother a lady xxx

Always with a school of kisses.

> It won't bother me at all, I'll leave a key in pot plant x

He was sweet, she thought as she poured herself a litre of wine and sat down to enjoy her scalding hot dinner. Very thoughtful.

I'm a bit wrecked, Garfield. Probably better I just head
home. You know I wish I was there doing naughty things to
you, right? Xxx

Abby's face arranged itself into a scowl. Don't feed me your filthy
wish list and then knock me back, she hissed internally. She picked
up her phone to say as much. What difference did it make whose
bed he slept in? It wasn't like he'd get any less sleep. He kept spare
t-shirts in his car, so he wouldn't even have to go home before work
in the morning!

She thought about why she was feeling so incensed. Was it
because she wasn't getting her own way? Because he was bold
enough to stand up to her? Because she actually, genuinely wanted
to see him? Because he put himself first for once? If it was the
latter she was very disappointed in herself. Especially since she'd
been the one to rebuff men in the exact manner he'd just rebuffed
her – sweet, sexy but final – a million times.

Abby put the phone down and sat with her head in hands. She
was being a moron. She was overtired, exhausted and reacting in
a stupid and juvenile fashion. Who cared if he stayed over? Thank
GOD she hadn't texted him again. She was embarrassed just thinking about it. He was working late because of HER, and even if it
wasn't her website, big deal. He had a job; he couldn't just drop
everything and be with her whenever she whistled. The problem
was that he *did*. That very first booty call aside, Marcus had always
been front and centre whenever Abby had requested it. Obviously
the moment he pulled back, it was going to feel strange and uncomfortable. She had to grow up. This wasn't a one-way relationship.
Was it a relationship? She supposed it was . . . They spent three to
four nights a week together – that was far more relationshipy than
Abby had been in the last few years. Oh well, she concluded, it was

fine for now. She was having fun, it wasn't serious and when she had some time she would figure out how to gently extract herself from it before it became anything more than what it was now.

Some research for her trip would take her mind off Marcus she thought happily, pulling her laptop onto the bench and tapping in her password to bring it to life, failing to see that she was subconsciously plotting her escape plan from Marcus in doing so, in the shape of a plane ticket. She had to start getting serious about where she was going and when, so that the universe, and Allure and Marcus and everyone would know that this was serious, and it was happening, and nothing would hold her back from rambling through France or Italy or Greece and putting on ten impossible-to-shift-but-intensely-enjoyable-to-accrue kilos.

26

Even though Marcus had showed her exactly how to do it last night, and even drawn a cute diagram, complete with love hearts and stick-figure Abby and Marcus kissing, the laptop refused to come through Abby's TV. Meanwhile, sixteen models, all putting small dents in her floorboards with their five-inch heels and talking at a level usually reserved for people calling their children in for dinner, sat and stood around her small lounge room and waited. She had forgotten to even offer them a drink or buy some snacks, she realised as she felt the sweat beading on her forehead and pooling under her armpits.

Finally, her desktop screen came up on the TV. Some of the girls clapped.

'Sorry, girls. As we all know, under state law no presentation is allowed to proceed until at least one technical difficulty arises.'

The girls giggled and those standing shifted noisily from hip to hip; they'd already been waiting a good fifteen minutes.

'Okay, I'll be brief; I know you're all busy and thank you for stopping by. So, as you know, Allure has, for the most part, become a fully online operation. From here, it's just myself and my new assistant, Charlie, who you'll love, and who starts next week. Think Zooey Deschanel, but cuter. Charlie and I will be your point of contact, but we will be your last point of contact: the website should be able to do most things for you.'

'It's really simple . . .' Abby got the home page up and navigated around as she spoke, mousing over and clicking on different tabs as she went.

'Abby,' Sophie, a picture-perfect, all-American looking girl with the most glorious head of naturally long and thick hair Abby had ever had the pleasure of hiring/being jealous of, spoke.

'Yes, Sophie?'

'Um, Belinda said we get fined if we can't do our shift now?'

'Well, kind of. There's a penalty if you cancel after the reminder text. It's only $10, but you have to appreciate the amount of work that goes into finding your replacement. Of course, if you're sick or you can find your own replacement, there's obviously no fine.'

Murmurs rumbled through the room. Which Abby had expected.

'Guys, do you know how many phone calls and how much bribery has to occur when one of you doesn't show or pulls out with an hour to go? The penalty doesn't exist to take money from you, but to compel you to let me know with plenty of advance if you can't do your shift.'

'What if we get sick just a few hours before the shift?' Amelia piped up.

'Or our apartment floods? Mine did the other day, you know, and I had an appointment with my eyebrow threader and—' Jacqui's face was frowning and indignant.

'Caroline? In Hayes street?' Lucinda piped up.

'Yes!!' Jacqui confirmed, as though she'd been asked if she'd like a million dollars.

'OMG, she's the best. She isn't to die for, she's to die *five.*'
Lucinda closed her eyes and placed her hand on her chest in
respect for the eyebrow threader.

'Yes, isn't she AMAZE?! I was so annoyed I had to lose my
appointment, but I couldn't just leave my house because, like, my
whole floor was totally flooded, but you're saying I would be fined
for that? When it's not even my faul—'

Jacqui spoke in a tone and manner that demanded an uproari-
ous *'Yeah!'* from surrounding troops. Which predictably, it was.

'Okay, everyone calm down, life happens, and I get that – we'll
deal with those incidences as they come up. It's more about times
when you have a clash, or circumstances change, and you can't
do your shift. It's not that big a deal, it's just a pre-emptive strike
against me calling twenty-nine of you in a row, leaving voicemails
and emails and sending texts, trying to fill a shift within an hour.
Okay? Are we clear on that?'

Some of the girls whispered to each other, but most stared at her
blankly, on some level knowing they were guilty of that exact behaviour. Sian and Kylie had their arms folded and supercilious gazes on
their faces, mostly, Abby assumed, because they NEVER cancelled
or let her down and were resentful they were being treated like
criminals without having committed a crime. Abby didn't have the
energy to appease them and tell them how wonderful and reliant
they were right now, she'd email them later.

'Okay, where was I? So, alright, you each have your own login
and password, and then – we created them for you, it's just your full
name as login, and your mobile number as your password, you can
change it if you like – you'll have your own area that tells you what
jobs you've been requested for, when you're working next, who else
is working that shift, their phone numbers and emails so you can
co-ordinate lifts or whatever, which outfit is required, and of course

where each job is, and the Google map of it so you don't get lost. Not that any of you ever would, of course. Especially not you, Tara.'

Everyone laughed. Tara was renowned for her horrendous sense of direction and terrible driving. She'd once been forty-five minutes late for a job because she thought she knew the bar. The bar was called 'The Local', and there's one in every suburb. Not surprisingly, she went to The Local on the other side of the city, and sat there innocently sipping lemonade at the bar, dressed as a retro air hostess, waiting for the other girls to arrive.

'Also, we've got a Facebook page now, and as well as on the site in the gallery section, we're going to start posting a few photos of you girls at work.'

Instant panic.

'Can we approve them first?'

'Yeah, and can you not, like, tag us or anything please?'

'I don't want ANY photos of me in that disgusting silver dress on there.'

'Yeah, or the white suits. Gerooss.'

Why was it the most beautiful were the most vain? They were the ones who looked great! They shouldn't have a care in the world! Should be flaunting their ability to look sexy in silver body con! Abby was always reminding them of how blessed they were, how flawless they were, how grateful they should feel, but with great attractiveness came amplified insecurity. There'd come a time (maybe) when their arse *did* have cellulite, but for now, they should be wearing tight, tiny, taut outfits as often as possible. If 98 per cent of the population couldn't, it was the least they could do.

'Girls, not that it is possible for any of you to look anything less than gorgeous, I assure you the photos will be few and they will be flattering. It doesn't serve the agency to have you looking anything less than ravishing, believe me. And no, they won't be tagged with your names. It's just for clients to get an idea of the kind of looks we can put together, and to see what a force you girls are en masse.'

'My agent will need to approve them, actually.' A haughty voice piped up. Without even seeing who it was, Abby knew it would be Holly Brennen. Because Holly, being a Real Life Model, found any way she could to remind everyone that she was a Real Life Model, usually at the expense of people being able to take her seriously.

Abby sighed. 'Holly, your agent won't have to approve them. When you signed your Allure contract you agreed that your image could be used – within reason – to promote Allure as a business. So I'm exercising that right.'

'Well, what if it's bad for my image to be seen on Facebook in tasteless outfits? How embarrassing.'

Abby stifled a laugh – half of these girls' default on Facebook was them busting out of a bikini, yet they were worried about a few snaps of them in promo gear. It was a bit offensive actually, once Abby thought about it. She worked hard to ensure they only ever looked gorgeous.

'Holly, if you're that concerned about being seen in your promo garb, why doesn't it bother you when you pose for so many photos with guys at the Grand Prix in it? You *know* those photos are going on Facebook.'

A few girls sniggered; Holly was endured, but not overly liked. Abby wouldn't have usually arced up at her, but she was suggesting she was embarrassed to be seen working for Allure, and that pissed Abby off.

'Fine, whatever. But if I really don't like a shot, I'll be asking for it to be removed.'

'Let's chat about that in private, yeah? Okay girls, so as you can see it's all pretty simple. Basically instead of Charlotte or Siobhan contacting you about jobs, it will be done via automated email and text, and ditto your confirmations. Just like a booking for a hotel or spa treatment.'

'Will you still be at jobs?' The tone was that of being abandoned.

'Either Charlie or I will still be on location when it's required, or Uri will if security is needed. Of course. And you can always call us if you need us.'

'So is this the office now? For uniform pick up and stuff?'

'All uniforms are now to be picked up and dropped off at TLC dry cleaners on Marsh Street.'

Abby was particularly thrilled with this element of the New Allure: dealing with uniforms had always been her least favourite part of the job. Half the girls took them home, or left them at their boyfriend's, or in the boot of 'someone's' car, and when they were needed for the next shift they were a nightmare to track down. Many a job had commenced with a size eight swamped in a safety-pinned size-twelve dress because it was all Abby could find in the ten minutes leading up to the shift, which was the amount of notice she'd been given that Little Miss Size Eight didn't know where her dress was.

'Why don't we all just keep our own uniforms?' Jacqui, a bulldog in tight jeans, was on a roll.

'I tried that once. Half of you showed up with dirty dresses, the other half forgot you had to bring them, and one of you had popped it in the wash and made it the size of a toasted sandwich. Besides, Grey Goose uniform notwithstanding, there is no "one uniform". There are many, and only eight of you will usually need them at one time. Trust me, girls, I really have spent a lot of time and thought on all of this. I'm trying to make it as efficient and painless for everyone as possible.'

More murmuring. The girls loved to murmur. It was like gossiping or backstabbing, but quieter! What fun.

'Are there any questions, guys? Have I missed anything? Is there anything I can show you on the site?' Abby looked around the cramped room, smiling at her beautiful harem as they dissolved into chatter. People always initially resisted change, she reminded herself. Soon they'd see how easy it all was.

'Oh, that reminds me, if you introduce a good girl – and let me remind you that someone like Chantelle Lyon is *not* an example of a good girl' – the girls laughed. Chantelle was famous in Allure for sweeping into the agency dramatically, wearing her Rue Paul-esque diva attitude like a fabulous cloak, refusing to wear the uniform, then leaving mid-way through the shift because she was bored. 'If you bring in a good girl and we sign her up, you get a $250 West-field voucher.'

More murmuring, but this time of the effervescent variety.

'I'll send an email now confirming everything I told you today. It's going to be easy, I promise. Call me if there are any issues at all, there shouldn't be, of course, but, you know . . .'

The girls were already bored of the website and had started texting and standing up and slinging their bags over their arms to a chirpy chorus of 'amazing shoes' and '*love* your hair like that' and 'did you hear abouts' as they shuffled out the hallway, heels clopping, hair swishing; cleavage heaving.

Closing the door behind the last girl, Abby sighed with relief. This might just all work out okay. Jesus. She needed a beer. She wanted to have that beer with Marcus, and since she'd booked a flight to Italy in two weeks, she wanted to see him as much as possible before then. Who knew what would happen while she was away, or when she returned? Best to enjoy him as much as she could now.

27

'I reckon Chris will be massively into Charlie. *Big time.* Should we set them up? Stealthily? Like, just invite them both someplace for a drink? Watch them fall desperately in love with each other over a whisky sour?'

'I don't think she's for sale, sorry – she mentioned a boyfriend somewhere along the line. Also, doesn't Chris prefer his women to be around the age of a pre-schooler?'

Marcus shot Abby a look. He hated the 'age' jokes. Abby shrugged and showed her palms, eyebrows high. She thought he was over-sensitive about it.

Abby and Marcus were lingering over their second coffees, discussing Abby's first week with Charlie, who Marcus had met briefly on Friday night. The Java Jitters had set in for both of them, they usually stopped at one coffee, but after a shipping crate full of whisky last night, both of them were relying on caffeine just to be able to talk, walk and, in Abby's case, breathe. As usual Marcus had his legs wrapped around Abby's under the table, and his hands grabbed at hers whenever they were free. He was always so affectionate, Abby realised. That's not to say he wasn't masculine and sexy, though. He somehow managed to pick up those attributes along the way too.

'She's very cute,' he reflected, as he poured them both some more water.

'Yes, so you've mentioned. Many times.'

'Garfield,' Marcus said, a shocked expression on his face. 'You're not, you're not *jealous* are you?'

'No, of course not. You don't need to keep banging on about how awesome she is, though. I get it, that's why I hired her, remember? I have a crush on her too.'

Marcus reached over and grabbed Abby's hand, kissing it gently as he looked into her eyes.

'You're the only puss I want, Garfield. I promise.'

'For now.'

'What's that supposed to mean?' He was still smiling, but his head was cocked to one side and his tone was quizzical.

Abby knew she was being a brat, but she couldn't help it. She was in a bad mood. Very cranky and irritable. Possibly pre-menstrual.

'You're twenty-two and you boys are predisposed to procreate, to sow your seed as much as you can and with as many different women as you can. It's how we all evolved, remember? Survival of the fittest and all that jazz?'

Marcus laughed. 'Are we *really* having this discussion? Abby Vaughn. I gave you more credit than that. And we're not all here trying desperately to ensure the survival of humanity – some of us are quite happy fertilising whichever eggs come with the lady we love, and no more. And besides, you can't just tar all men with one filthy brush; we're not all despo sex-mongers, you know.'

'You were last night . . .'

'Because it's YOU, you sausage! You're a superbabe, you're amazing, you're my *dream girl,* of course I'm going to be like that with you!'

Abby crossed her arms and gazed at the man sitting across from her, being all intelligent and rational and gorgeous. It was disgusting.

'I am not your *dream girl,* Marcus. Stop it.'

'Don't I get to decide that?' Marcus asked. Abby was aghast at how relaxed he was, even in the face of her being an asshole. She almost wanted him to get fired up, just to see if he was capable of it. The only time she'd ever seen him get even a little bit annoyed was when he found out her fiancé was fictitious.

'Ohhh, hang on, I see what you're doing, you're trying to make me lose interest in you before you go off to Italy so that I'm not so heartbroken in your absence. What a thoughtful gesture. I'm flattered.'

Abby rolled her eyes. Even though she didn't really have any reason to be mad at him, she was clearly mad. She was trying to manufacture an argument for the sake of it, and there was no way of stopping her.

'Abs? Are you okay?' Marcus looked at her with concern from across the table. 'What's up? What's really up, I mean. And don't "fine" me. I hate when girls say "Fine" when actually they mean, "I'd like to rip your eyeballs out." That passive-aggressive stuff is so grubby.'

'I'm fine,' Abby said, on auto-pilot. 'No, no, I mean it, I really am. Just tired, hungover, snappy.' She smiled and nodded as further evidence of non-passive-aggressive fine-ness.

'Okay. I'm gonna go pay. Don't run off, now. You kind of seem like you might.'

It suddenly dawned on Abby that was exactly what she was doing: she *was* running off! Mentally anyway. She watched as Marcus paid the girl behind the till, a girl who had fallen in love with Marcus from the moment they arrived, and who was now flirting for Australia. In fairness, at seventeen or so, she was probably a better match for him. Abby looked at her ass-grazing denim shorts and perky bosoms and long, deliberately dishevelled hair and wondered what Marcus was doing with *her*, a stressed-out business owner who basically treated him like a well-behaved Labrador, and who had no intention of taking their 'relationship' any further than sex, sleepovers and getting sauced. Even if she was fond of him.

'Thanks, Marcus,' Abby said genuinely as he returned, shoving his wallet into the back pocket of his black jeans, which he had coordinated with beat-up black boots and a simple, tight-fitting navy t-shirt and a kind of white, red and blue cowboy scarf around his neck. He looked ready for his album cover shot, as usual. It never ceased to stupefy Abby how much thought he put into his outfits, although having seen him put them together in the mornings, she understood that creating an outfit for him was like cleanse-tone-moisturise for her. It was second nature; he was inherently stylish. She looked down at her striped shirt-dress and leather sandals and realised that she had started dressing like those dull, mumsy women who didn't feel they had to impress their boyfriend or husband anymore. She'd not bothered with makeup, instead preferring to wear her enormous Tom Ford sunglasses, which could double as satellite dishes should her cable TV ever go down. How could Marcus possibly choose *her* over little flirtrude over there? It was baffling and disconcerting and had to be a phase. He'd tire of her; she knew it. That was fine with her. If you knew something was inevitable, it couldn't surprise you when it happened, could it? Didn't matter anyway, as she had decided she was going to douse their lusty flame before Italy. She had to. Trying to prolong their dalliance was silly.

'Hey, can we maybe go past Chris's and pick up my laptop?'

'Sure,' Abby said, internally wishing the next and only destination was bed.

'I should get him a coffee, actually.' He darted back inside and Abby stood in the sunshine, trying to count how many drinks she had actually had last night.

'*Natasha?*'

Natasha was walking directly towards Abby, with another preposterously good-looking girl, both of them in underpants masquerading as shorts, and tight singlets and runners. Abby thought Natasha looked way, way, way too skinny. Her head was starting to look like it had accidentally been placed on the wrong-sized body, and that somewhere out there a large woman was going through life with a teeny little head.

'Oh, Abby! Uh, hi,' Natasha slowed to a stop reluctantly, as did her friend. Natasha looked as though she'd rather be carting coal through a mine than talking to Abby. 'This is Jade. Jade, Abby.'

'Hey Jade. So . . . Natasha, how are you?' said Abby, trying to push her rage down to below her baked eggs. Earlier in the week Holly had taken great delight in telling Abby that Natasha had switched agencies to Faces, and as yet Abby had had no luck in getting proof. It made her blood boil, especially since Natasha had just fallen off the radar and never bothered to tell Abby why.

'I've been trying to get in touch with you, actually. Someone mentioned to me that you've changed agencies; that you've moved over to Faces? I know you and I don't actually have a contract or anything, and while I'm obviously devastated, I just want to know so I can take you off the website and so on. I'm sure you understand.' Abby was doing her absolute best to be gracious and businesslike.

175

Natasha's left hand flew to her forehead, her fingers rubbing back and forth anxiously.

'Well no, it's just that, well, after, you know . . .'

'Pete's email?'

'No!' Immediately defensive the second his name was mentioned. Textbook Natasha. Her phone rang; she looked at the screen and silenced it.

'They offered me more money and more shifts.' The words tumbled from Natasha's mouth rapidly.

'If you wanted more money or work, why not just talk to me? You're far too important and valuable to me to lose over a few dollars.'

Natasha's phone rang again. It was silenced with an aggressive jab.

'I'm sorry I didn't tell you but I got really busy.' Natasha blurted this out in one go, as though leaving spaces between the words would give Abby room to spot the flaws in her story and call her on them.

But Abby, despite the rage festering in every cell of her body, didn't have the energy to draw her sword.

'Okay then. Thank you for being honest and I genuinely wish you the best over there, Natasha. You're always welcome back, of course. We'll miss you!' Natasha's phone blared again. It was silenced without even a look at the screen.

Abby smiled as widely and as genuinely as she could muster with no feeling of happiness present, while Natasha's face was etched into a fake, weak version of the same smile. Abby sensed she wasn't happy at Faces and was beginning to see the effect her dreamboat of a boyfriend was having on her life. By way of confirming this, Jade piped up.

'Uh, Tash? Pete just texted me to tell you to call him urgently.'

Abby could tell Natasha was frustrated – and now discomfited – but couldn't let Abby see it.

'Well, we better keep moving. Thanks for being understanding, Abby, and . . .' She lowered her head. 'I'm sorry about how it all worked out, y'know, not telling you myself and . . . well, you know.'

'It's fine, Natasha. These things happen.' *And I wish for your boyfriend to be taken to a South American prison and locked away for the lifespan of unrecyclable plastic.*

'Bye!' Jade said brightly as she started to walk off.

'Bye girls.'

A text from Marcus popped up on Abby's screen.

1. I'm two mins away. 2. You're the hottest woman in the world. 3. See number 2. xxx

She smiled and exhaled. *Why* was she going to give this up, exactly? Most women would kill to have that kind of adoration spewed at them day and night, and yet Abby was preparing to discard it like chewing gum that had lost its taste. Presumably it was because she thought she could do better, that's why people generally broke up with their lovers, right?

Her thoughts were interrupted by a kiss on the back of her neck.

'Sorry, darling, the takeaway queue was fertilised as we left and was boasting impressive growth by the time I returned.'

He took her hand and kissed it, and they walked on, each smiling happily. Abby because she felt beautiful, and Marcus because he loved making Abby feel beautiful.

28

Abby looked at Chelsea as she got out of her car. *Jesus!* She'd gotten even skinnier! First Natasha, now Chelsea: the moment they had boy troubles the weight fell off them like butter off hot corn. With Abby, the weight fell on, she'd never been 'blessed' with hyperactive adrenal glands, and so stress manifested in revolting diet choices and a chunky ass. It seemed somehow unfair that women in their man-hunting prime should not be given the same metabolic liberties extended to them in their twenties, when it was not uncommon for Abby and the girls to wear mini-dresses that could double as stubby holders. But why not when your body is a sizzling cocktail of firmness and tone and tan? She always encouraged her girls to flaunt their wares, and showboat those lithe young limbs with reckless abandon. They wouldn't be that sizzly forever.

'New shoes?' Chelsea could sniff out a new purchase instantly, like a polar bear finding a seal under thick snow.

'Yeah, my others were giving me shin splints.'

'From all that marathon training you've been doing?'

'YOU'RE the one who looks like she's been marathon training – you're bones in a meat suit, Chels!'

'No shit, it looks horrible, I know. I'm eating again, though. That's what happens when your boyfriend pulls off the blindfold and reveals his ready-made family, I guess.'

Abby and Chelsea had texted and spoken on the phone, but hadn't been able to coordinate a catch up since Jeremy had dropped his bomb. It was clearly still in the depths of reconstruction, if Chelsea's bitterness and doll-sized body was anything to go by.

The two women started walking at a brisk pace, the wind whipping at their legs and flicking their hair.

'How is it all going, Chels?'

'Okay I guess. I'm being very good to him. We've caught up a few times, I don't know what the fuck for, but I'm still not sure what to do. He's not chasing me half as hard as he should be.'

'You asked for space, though, right? Wouldn't that be why you haven't seen him?'

'Well YES, but that doesn't mean he's not meant to chase me and make me realise what a huge mistake I would be making to never be with him again!'

Abby couldn't help smiling. Chelsea was up to her old tricks, telling a guy one thing while hoping he'd gallantly disobey her requests the moment she turned her back, and it was strangely calming. With all of the girls' romantic dramas the past couple of months, it was nice to see Chelsea was still absolutely insane when it came to men.

'Okay, so just to be clear, you *want* him to contact you? You've decided he's worth it? Even despite little Olly and hidden wife?'

A sigh. 'I don't know, I mean, when I let him explain the whole situation it was kind of heartbreaking, you know? And I believe him that his ex is no longer in his life, and that they'll get a divorce. She's already got a live-in boyfriend, can you believe? Apparently he has a kid too, wife died of cancer or something, so they're all living together.'

'Well that's a happy-sad little situation, then, isn't it? She hardly sounds like the kind of woman you need to feel threatened by, taking in widowed men with young children like that.'

'Whose side are you on?'

'And how are you feeling about the instant family?'

'It's so weird. Like, three months ago I was planning to travel most of this year and do that yoga teacher course in Switzerland, and now I have this guy, and this kid, and this whole thing to work through.'

'Just on travel, you know I leave next week, right? Okay, back to you now.'

'I'm so jealous. Is that fake French girl you hired going to be able to handle it?'

'Chels, she is phenomenal. She's been doing all the night work and hasn't complained once. And it's complainable stuff, let me tell you. Half the girls can't understand the website, or are too lazy to try, and so insist on calling through for their jobs like before, the other half are so terrified they'll do something wrong or "break" their account, they call through for confirmation of everything, and the other half are—'

'That's three halves, Einstein.'

'The other lot are so thrilled with their newfound freedom that they forget to actually show up for their shifts. Okay, I need to finish this Jeremy conversation please.'

'There's not much else to say, it's a "we'll see".'

Abby was puffing trying to keep up with Chelsea's manic pace.

'When will you admit to him that you love him and want to be with him?

'*Do I?* It's all so hard. Why can't I ever find an easy man, with no issues or secrets? I mean; can you really see me playing step-mummy on the weekends? *Me?'* Chelsea turned to look at Abby, her face etched with an 'as if' expression.

'I'm sure he doesn't expect you to leap in with a Wiggles CD and start playing with Oliver straightaway, he'll be terrified of scaring you off again.'

'All I think about is the future, like, we'll never be just "us". Oliver will always be part of the equation, and the wife, too.'

'You have baggage too; everyone does at our age. Who knows, a life with Jeremy and Olly might be intensely fulfilling! Perhaps you can channel some of that excessive love you have for toy-sized dogs towards a toy-sized human instead.'

'I *don't want* children, remember? It's a life choice, not a flavour of the month. *Speaking* of children, how's Marcus? Dumped him yet?'

'No, no. I was actually thinking that maybe I could, you know, just kind of fade it out while I'm over there, instead of playing executioner before I go.' Abby spoke reflectively as the two of them sped along the walking track.

Chelsea laughed knowingly. 'You don't *want* to break up with him, is the issue here. You've been jammed in each other's pockets for the past few months and now you don't want to end things with him. Why are you breaking it off again?'

'Because when I'm ready to get married and relax, he'll be twenty-five and just starting to realise what an enormous, glorious world exists out there.'

'So basically you're worried he'll want to run off and screw everyone he meets. Where did this all come from, this weird, over-the-top insecurity? It's not like you, Abs, you usually don't give a shit.'

'Remember what we were like in our early twenties? When I became single I went nuts; felt like I had to make up for lost time . . . There's no way you can guess how you're going to feel at twenty-five or twenty-nine when you're twenty-two. You just can't. I even look at how I am this year compared to this time last year and I feel like a different person.'

'This time last year I was bouncing around with Dominic. *Disgust.*'

'Noooo. He was a peach! I love the way he talked to his ex-girlfriends on speakerphone when you two were driving. And how he cheated on you when you just started going out but told you that you were overreacting and it was just a "party fuck".'

'I'd actually erased that from my memory.' Chelsea looked like she may have just done a small vomit in her throat.

Abby laughed boisterously. 'And, you know, that's just Marcus; how will *I* feel in a few years? Will all his charm have worn off? Will I hunger for a *man*? Someone who'll teach me things? A well-travelled bon vivant?'

'You're being very judgemental.'

'I caught it from you. No, you know what? I stand by this, these are valid concerns.' Abby's voice had become strong and defiant the more reasons she verbalised for not being with Marcus.

Both girls heads swivelled as a young shirtless prince ran past, earphones in his ears, sweat glimmering on his toned chest.

'I can't believe you're gonna give up sex with a man who looks like that . . .'

'And you don't think I'll find a rebound or sixteen in Italy?'

'It will temporarily close the hole in your heart and crotch, but I reckon you'll be Skype-shagging Marcus within two weeks of being away.'

'And I think you'll get back with Jeremy. Maybe even move in.'

'Jesus, you're optimistic. Hey, have you spoken to Mads today?'

'No, but I had a missed call I forgot to return, actually . . . *maybe—*'

'Not preg,' Chelsea said matter-of-factly.

'*Fuck.* My heart really is breaking for those two . . .' Abby nibbled her lip, upset and sad and frustrated on behalf of her friend.

The two women were sombre as they regained their Proper Fat Burning walking speed, until Chelsea could no longer help herself and checked the screen of her BlackBerry.

29

'Mads, our silly old cougar has decided to break it off with the kid, did you know that?' Chelsea said, flicking through one of Mads's fancy architect/home décor magazines.

Abby rubbed her eyes; she'd had around three minutes of sleep last night. Not only was she utterly not ready for her trip, a new client had booked twenty girls for a lucrative gig on the same night she had fifteen girls already working for a regular, much lower paying client, which was causing a moral and logistical stroke, and her brain was fidgety with stress about the upcoming 'breakup chat' looming between her and Marcus. The thought of Marcus despising her was impossible for Abby to comprehend. She felt atrocious, both physically and emotionally. But she knew it was the right thing. As a fun exercise in torture, she'd decided to quickly workshop it with the girls before actually doing it.

'I have a friend, Katrina, who married a chap eight years younger than her, and they've been contentedly married with kids for a thousand years now,' Mads said, incredibly unhelpfully.

'And how old was she when they got married?'

'Ummm, like, thirty-five?'

Abby paused to do the numbers. 'Yeah, twenty-seven is a leeee-tle bit older than twenty-two, Mads. You have your shit together, or at least are starting to by then. At twenty-two you can barely tie your own laces.'

'See, that's the issue right there,' said Chelsea, whose tone indicated she had Arrived at a Conclusion. 'You've got it so in your head that he's a kid that even though his actions have proved otherwise, because you wouldn't have been with him for this long if they didn't, obviously, you *can't view him as anything else*. It's like he's a blue t-shirt and even though he is doing everything to show you he's a red t-shirt, you can still only see the blue.'

'Oooh, better not pop him in the wash with my whites, then.' Abby said sarcastically.

Mads sighed and looked at her friend, whose freshly-highlighted hair was messy and whose eyes were rimmed with red, and whose heart was breaking because she had elected for it to break now, in order to prevent it breaking down the track. It seemed very much like false economy.

'Can't you think about it while you're overseas? Clear your head, have your holiday and then take it up with him when you get back?' Mads's voice was soothing and gentle.

'Yeah, you're only away for, like, five weeks,' said Chels, whose head was back in the magazine she was flicking through. 'You could easily make it through that, right? . . . Oh!' Her face suddenly lit up. 'But what if you meet some gorge over there? Is *that* why you're doing this?' She peered at Abby suspiciously.

'I wish it were a reason that simple.'

'Are you feeling like it's the wrong thing, Abs?' Mads was looking at her friend, her voice soft. God she'd be a terrific mum, Abby thought, momentarily channelling her anger and grumpiness to the fertility Gods for being so stingy.

'I don't know . . . I feel rotten, to be honest. I know I'll miss him, but, I just— I can't see any point in prolonging the inevitable.'

Mads walked over and sat next to Abby at the kitchen bench, and rubbed her shoulder. As usual she had notes scribbled on the part of her hand where the palm met the wrist. She'd done it for as long as Abby could remember, and it had ruined many an outfit.

'Darling heart, maybe this is one of those situations where you have to risk a lot and stand to gain a lot.' Mads looked at Abby with a 'time-to-suck-it-up' smile.

Sensing she was safe, Mads went on. 'When you met Marcus, one of the things you said you liked about him was the fact he had no emotional luggage trailing around with him. He lived in the now, didn't have any issues with your independence, or confidence, or that you earned more than him – any of the things that have made other guys – your own age or older – so frustrating.'

'Also he gave great head,' Chels piped up, slapping the magazine closed and placing it on the coffee table.

Abby exhaled. 'You're right, Mads. You're totally right.'

'Well, I gotta go, I'm meeting Jez so he can apologise again.' Chels had stood up and was putting her beautiful tan sandals back on, delicately snaking the leather ribbons around her shapely, tanned calves.

'Is that code for a date?' Abby asked, genuinely fascinated by what might fall from Chelsea's mouth.

Chels sighed. 'Yep, it'll be a good one, too. He's all about winning me over again. I fucking love having that power.'

'You're a sicko,' Abs said, wiping her mascara from under her bleary eyes.

'I think you two are actually back on and you're not telling your two best friends in the whole world the full story. Which is both offensive and delightful.'

'You're sleeping with him, aren't you, Chels?' Abby said, excitedly, as Chelsea walked down the hall.

'Can't hear you, no reception! Good luck, Abs, bye!' Chelsea called before closing the door behind her.

'They're definitely bonking,' Mads said.

'Probably. Hey, you know, I better shove off too,' said Abby, looking at the time on her phone and taking a deep breath. 'Got to do this thing, I guess.'

'So much love to you my little button. And don't go through with it if it feels wrong! Silly idea. Terrible. Follow your heart, feel it in your toes, listen to your elbows. Now, I'll see you before you go, right?'

'Yes, of course: pizza and wine at mine as I pack tomorrow night? Is that fun?'

'Fun squared. Let me know how it goes tonight, okay? I'm extremely free for ice-cream and debriefing afterwards if you need me.'

Abby sighed as she collected her phone and keys and stood up. She pecked Mads on the cheek and set off into the afternoon.

30

Abby began to fret. They were in her car – Marcus was driving, he loved her car, said it made him feel like a gentleman, and insisted on taking the wheel whenever possible – and she was left to sit in the passenger seat and quietly ruminate on how she was going to approach The Chat as he warbled about some new iPhone app that had changed his life, taking his tally of life-changing iPhone apps to 45,280.

'Man,' Marcus said as they waited for a very old and possibly drunk man to cross the road in front of them. 'This guy is literally taking one step every five seconds. Look at him! If he went any slower he'd be busking.'

Abby smiled wanly and made a distracted, 'hmm' noise that hinted at amusement, which Marcus immediately picked up on.

'Garfield? Everything okay? You seem a bit rattled tonight.'

Damn him and his super-attuned sensitivity, Abby thought. She thought back to days gone by when she'd wished for her boyfriends to be more emotionally aware and receptive. Now she had one who was as sensitive as a helicopter lever and she couldn't deal with it.

'Yeah, yeah, just, you know, brain's full of stuff I need to get done before I leave.'

''Strue, you gotta pack all those bikinis and mini-skirts and high heels so those slimy, gorgeous Italian men lose their minds and steal you away from me.'

Abby sighed. Partly because this was his latest and favourite game, and second because his 'faux' jealousy implied that her ensuing conversation was going to be even tougher.

'I'll be in Tuscany, remember? With old couples in Winnebagos touring wineries and art galleries. You make it sound like I'll be soliciting in Roman nightclubs.'

'Sexy transcends postcodes.'

'You're a dag,' Abby said, shaking her head.

She rifled through her brain, trying to recall if they'd ever discussed what their 'situation' would be when she was overseas. She knew she'd been careful to never mention how she'd miss him, or that she wished he would come, or that Skype would save them. It was self-preserving, she told herself, for both of them. How generous of her.

Marcus pulled up alongside Abby's place and performed an expert reverse park. After triumphantly wrenching on the handbrake, he simulated smoking a cigarette and ditching it coolly out the window.

Abby gave a weak, quiet laugh.

'Okay. The ciggy ditch *always* gets a proper laugh. What's up?'

Abby felt sick, her stomach felt as though it had consumed a cask of wine and was now attempting gymnastics, and her palms were clammy with guilt sweat. She was horrible at any kind of confrontation. Much preferred the elegant Houdini. She looked over at Marcus who was smiling back at her with that dopey, loving look he seemed to have permanently etched on his face when she was around. She wanted to wipe it off with a dirty dishrag; his delight-fulness was making this a lot harder than it needed to be. It was perverse the amount of times she wished for him to be more of a prick – what did that say about her experience of men? Perhaps she nursed some deep, sick need to be treated badly. Nah, that stuff was reserved for weirdos like Chelsea.

'Come up?' she asked, the evil grandma offering candy to Han-sel and Gretel.

'Are you kidding? I'm not knocking back a chance to sleep with my girl on her second-last night before she abandons me for weeks and weeks.'

Abby winced at the words 'my girl'.

As they closed car doors and walked up the stairs, Abby realised how much she needed to open a bottle of wine. She'd had a glass of merlot at dinner, but it was revolting and bitter and had done nothing for her nerves.

'Do you feel like a glass of wine?' Abby asked, as she dumped her handbag on the breakfast bar and made her way to the fridge.

'Orrrr . . . how about I make us some Old-Fashioneds! You've still got those cherries and that sugar syrup, yes?'

Abby turned to look at Marcus, who nodded enthusiastically as he walked around the bench towards her, his arms out, ready to hold her and kiss her. Abby turned quickly towards the pantry door and opened it before he could do either of those lovely things, things that made Abby doubt she was doing the right thing by pushing away a thoughtful, romantic, loving, intelligent man who adored her.

'I'm pretty sure, yes, and you'll need bitters too, yeah?'

'Did you just brush me right there? You did! You brushed me! Abby, something's up, and you're rubbish at pretending it isn't, so come on, out with it.'

Abby slowly turned back to face Marcus, whose arms were now

crossed, his head tilted on an angle. To her surprise, she felt tears spring to her eyes. This was all so unnecessary she scolded herself, they weren't even boyfriend-and-girlfriend!

'I just, I think,' she gulped back stupid, irrational tears, 'I think we need to talk about some things.'

'Are you crying? Baby, what's wrong? Come here . . .'

He pulled her into his chest and held her closely, stroking her hair and kissing the top of her head, his breath short and concerned. It was exactly the kind of thing she didn't need. She pulled back and wiped under her eyes, taking in a monstrous breath as she did so. She was over-tired; all of her coping mechanisms were faltering.

'Can we just have a glass of wine and go sit on the lounge for a bit? And chat?'

'I'll get the wine, you go get comfy.'

Abby walked into the lounge room and sighed. There was work shit everywhere – as she'd suspected, containing it all in the office was nothing but an optimistic dream. Marcus came in, handed Abby her glass, and kicked off his shoes.

'So, what's going on?'

'It's about Italy.'

'I thought that might be it,' he said, quietly, before taking a small sip of his wine and placing it on the coffee table.

'I don't really know how to articulate it, but—'

'You want to be single and carefree over there.' A twinge of disgust had crept into his voice, which was jarring for Abby. She had assumed he would be his usual calm, understanding self, but he'd clearly already loaded his gun. Also, she still kind of considered herself as single . . . They'd never had The Talk about being boyfriend and girlfriend, even if there was an unwritten agreement that shagging anyone else would be very uncool. She hated feeling like this was a breakup, it wasn't worthy of all that energy.

'This needn't be so dramatic, Marcus.' She looked at him with an expression that was begging for rolled eyes. 'This, *us*, it was always intended to be a bit of fun and—'

'Oh come on, Abs. You know I never felt that way.'

Abby continued, ignoring his interruption.

'I admit it has become something more than just hooking up. I love being with you, and your brain, and your wit and your generosity and thoughtfulness and your . . .'

Marcus kept his gaze locked onto Abby, suddenly silent.

'But, you know, let's not make things harder than they need to be, it's not like we're—' Abby stopped. 'Look, maybe while I'm away, we just keep things relaxed and—'

'Be with other people. That's what you mean, isn't it? Keep our options open?'

Abby was taken aback by Marcus's spitting upset. The indignant side of her brain whispered that this was precisely why they should end things now: he was clearly too emotionally attached.

'Marcus . . . You're *twenty-two years old*. Aside from the fact I have a decade on you—'

'And don't you love reminding me of it every day.'

A childish interjection, but not unwarranted, thought Abby.

'Can we not get angry? Please?'

'Sorry. It's a bit hard to stay cool when you're being dumped.' He looked straight ahead with a steely glare, elbows locked, hands palm down on the lounge, and his chin down.

Well, thought Abby. This was going marvellously.

'Okay, you know what? Fine. Let's just get it all out. Us, you and me; it's a lot of fun, I love hanging out with you, but Marcus, it . . . At this time of my life, I can't invest in something that I know is . . . well, doomed.'

'What are you talking about, "doomed"?' Marcus erupted. 'How do you know we won't work, and why do *you* get to make that call? And who said anything about us settling down anyway? You're acting like I've asked to move in!'

'You know what I mean, Marcus. Making a proper go of things! Committing to this relationship!' Abby was pissed that Marcus was making out she was the only one who had contemplated a more serious future for them. *He* was the one who kept banging on about their future together, not her.

Abby gathered her cardigan around her body and spoke quietly.

'You just, you need to be a guy in his early twenties right now.'

'*Oh really.*' He was back on a roll. 'And who made you God? Who gave you the power to decide what I will do in my life, and how I will live it, and what I should be doing with it? Why do you get to choose how I'll feel in five years?'

Abby sighed. 'Marcus. All I am saying is that I know what I was like when I was twenty-two, and compared to who I am at thirty-three, I've lived a thousand lives. And I *needed to*! I needed to go through all of that, and try different jobs, and date lots of different people, and just be myself to get to where I am. Making a commitment at tha—'

'What is this commitment you keep talking about? It's a simple boyfriend/girlfriend set up! I'm not asking for your bloody hand in marriage!'

'That's the thing. I don't have time to time to be with a boyfriend – as wonderful as he might be – that I don't see a future with. I just don't.'

'I don't get it. You've told me a thousand times you don't want kids—'

'You're actually proving my point, because that's not fair to you. I know you DO want kids an—'

'No, that's MY point. If you don't have ticking clock issues, then why can't we just keep things the way they are? We're GOOD TOGETHER, Abby! And maybe if you weren't so insecure and so convinced I want to fuck every twenty year old that walked past, we could be *excellent*.'

Marcus had switched from angry-upset to sad-upset, and it was heartbreaking to watch. Also, he was right; she *had* become insecure. But Abby was too determined and too tenacious in getting all of her Important Points across to dissolve into tears yet. That would come later.

'Ouch. But I suppose you're right . . . Look, it's not you, it's me, as the hackneyed old adage goes. I can't spend three years with you, maybe move in, maybe even get married, who knows, for you to get to twenty-six and realise you're missing out on things, and to be restless, and to need to go and explore . . .'

Abby's calm and rational tone was directly proportional to Marcus's frenzied, worked-up lather.

'But you *don't know* that I will do that! How *can* you? I'm telling you I want to give us a go, and that I believe in us, and you're sitting there telling me you think I'm going to disappear so I can fuck around in a few years time. Do you even *know* how offensive that is?' He looked at her with disbelief, his brows crumpled down over his eyes.

'Marcus, this is an impossible conversation. Neither of us can know what will happen down the track.' Abby had nothing else to say. She'd said far too much as it was, and none of it had made anything better or easier or happier.

'Well, I hope you look back and you shake your head at what you *could* have had, and lost. Because while you're sitting there, planning out my life for me, and telling me how you think I might feel in a few years, I'm sitting here thinking you're the most amazing woman I've ever met, and to be able to spend a few years, maybe many years, would be far from a hindrance, it would actually be pretty fucking special.'

Marcus stood up and grabbed his shoes off the floor, putting them on aggressively.

Abby wiped at the salty streams that had began to dribble down her cheeks. She had no idea what to do or say.

He turned to her suddenly. 'Are you sure this isn't all an excuse for YOU to go fuck around? I'm not stupid, you know. I know why women in their thirties head off on these "find yourself" trips—'

'Are you for *real? Now* who's fucking offensive? Marcus, I have worked so hard for so many years, and I deserve this trip. I don't understand how you think this is some easy, heartless transaction for me . . .' Abby's words were eaten up by her sobs. She was flustered and emotional and hurt and angry. She put her head in her hands, which were balanced on her knees, and tried to calm down.

'You know what?' Marcus's voice was quiet and measured. 'I don't want to be with a woman whose overall opinion of me is that I'm so *basic* that I won't be able to honour a relationship because my dick will demand a new and exciting playhouse every Friday night. You sure know how to make a man – oh, sorry "boy" feel good, Abby Vaughn. Enjoy your trip.'

With that, he walked to the kitchen, collected his phone and stormed back through, past Abby, to the front door, slamming it as he went.

Abby snatched up her TV remote and threw it at the armchair on the other side of the room, and then she cried, and cried, and cried.

31

Abby sat down on the basic wooden bench, rearranging her flimsy cotton dress to cover her thighs as she did so. Her legs were tanned and smooth and her feet were secured into simple black sandals. Her hair was jammed under a straw hat and her skin, free of makeup and jewellery, smelled of coconut and sunscreen. A chic point-and-shoot Leica camera sat in front of her, along with a small tan leather purse containing her B&B room key and some euro. It felt delicious being so light on belongings, she thought as she applied an organic, olive-oil based lip balm she'd bought in the last town.

She picked up the menu. It was brown paper, and the dishes were handwritten: Prosciutto e melone, Insalata Caprese, Affettati e crostini toscani, Ribollita Toscana, Spaghetti al pesto, Scaloppina ai funghi . . . But Abby knew precisely what she was going to order: the caprese salad to begin, then the pesto pasta. With a glass of crisp Vernaccia di San Gimignano, and a side glass of ice, because wine was the temperature of minestrone within moments of being out in the fierce Italian sun. Satisfied her meal would help her attain that day's five Italian food groups: pasta, coffee, mozzarella, tomatoes, grapes (fermented, in liquid form) and gelato, as well as sending her off nicely into an afternoon nap, Abby placed the menu down and looked around her, inhaling her surroundings with voracious eyes and a desire to imprint the scene in her mind forever. No matter how many photos she took, they never came close to capturing the beauty of a Tuscan summer, the fields simmering with a hazy heat, the stoic, crumbling city buildings jutting into the intense blue sky and of course, the swarms of slack-jawed, sweaty tourists, all as enchanted and well-fed and camera-happy as Abby.

Abby was seated alongside the restaurant's wall, looking into one of the main avenues of San Gimignano, a precious little medieval town she hadn't even known had existed until she'd struck up a conversation with the lovely man who ran the bed and breakfast at her place in Siena, a town which she had wanted to love, but had felt was too dark and foreboding despite the lovely English-garden-style elegance of her room, and the vast, glorious views that stretched out before her as she sat in the garden eating her pastries and drinking her coffee.

Each morning in San Gimignano, Abby would sit in the room at her bed and breakfast, a dark-wood and opulently curtained villa with beautiful old dressers and intricate maroon and gold bedspreads that felt like she'd crashed a wealthy old couple's home (she essentially had) with her laptop, sipping on coffee and munching on fruit. She would stop and poke her head out the window onto the street to sniff the air, listen to the locals bellow at each other below, and feel the sun on the back of her neck, and just be aware of where she was, and what she was doing.

San Gimignano might be her favourite place in the world, she confirmed each time she ran along those country roads, the ridiculous dance music pounding through her earphones about as appropriate for the landscape as seeded mustard on jam donuts. She'd already been here five nights but was reluctant to move on.

Hungry, Abby felt her tummy and was surprised to feel not too big a mound. After all, lunch each day was a delicious mountain of pasta and crisp white wine. Gelato featured every afternoon without fail, used alongside a shot of espresso to revive her after the strain and exhaustion of a nap. Although, she *was* running most evenings; that had to be helping. Especially since she appeared to lose her body weight in sweat each time she went out there, running through fields of perfectly lined vineyards and old farmyards blazing in the evening sun, unable and unwilling to get used to the beauty of her surrounds.

Abby was expecting the weight to hit any moment: she was eating everything on the Real Life 'No' list. The fruit, chocolate-filled croissants, sticky buns and three cups of coffee she scoffed each morning as she booked jobs and updated the Allure Facebook page were a prime example.

The agency was growing at a terrifying rate, which was interesting since Abby was doing far less work on it than ever before. Charlie was magnificently reliable. She didn't skip a beat, never dropped the ball, and other sports-type metaphors that mean she never let Abby, the clients or the girls down. In fact, Abby had barely been in touch with any of the clients or girls since she'd been here – Charlie had really taken it upon herself to manage everything in Abby's absence.

Abby knew she'd be lost without Charlie. She couldn't believe her good fortune that she'd come along just at the right time. There was something incredibly thrilling about being on the other side of the globe and still able to work as normal. The Webra boys really ought to have been paid triple-fold – even Rob had agreed as he watched Allure's expenses shrivel up like a plum in the sun.

The waitress – rushed off her feet with the influx of several thousand tourists who poured off tour buses and out of hire cars each day – finally came out to bring Abby some water and take her order.

Abby took a deep breath and clumsily muttered, '*Ciao! Caprese, spaghetti al pesto par favore and uno vernaccia . . .*'

'*Si.*' She collected the menu and went to walk back in.

'Oh!' Abby said, 'and some . . . *ghiaccio!*'

The waitress smiled good-naturedly, nodded and walked inside. Abby felt like a dingus each time she ordered in Italian, but she'd come here vowing to not be a lazy, annoying tourist, and to at least try to speak the language. A young man came out with some bread in a small bowl with the obligatory balsamic and olive oil, and as he disappeared back inside, Abby nearly dropped her glass of water. He was Marcus. He was *exactly like Marcus*. Right down to his hair and his eyes and his toned shoulders. She'd always thought Marcus had an Italian flavour, not too much, just a sprinkle of oregano perhaps, but now she'd seen his doppelganger, she realised it was more like he was dipped in Napolitano sauce. Abby cleared her throat, horrified at the way she'd just made her innocent waiter morph into her ex-boyfriend, like some kind of lame apparition in a Hollywood movie. He popped back out smiling goofily as he produced her cutlery. God he looked like Marcus!

Predictably, he immediately slammed Abby back into thinking of Marcus, an activity she actively tried to avoid. The fact that she was alone all day, every day with only her thoughts for company exacerbated the cyclical, confused nature of her thoughts. Her cycle of emotions usually went from accidentally thinking of him, to trying not to think of him, to being angry with herself for thinking of him, to being angry for having fallen for someone just before her long awaited almost-sabbatical, and now wasting time on it thinking of an absent, painful lover. She replayed going over to his house to try and normalise things, the night before she flew out, and being greeted by a man who vibrated with anger and disgust, and who had about as much interest in smoothing things over before she hopped on her plane as he did in setting fire to his loft. He'd said she was selfish and that the only reason she'd bothered coming over was to make herself feel better about things, not because she genuinely cared about his feelings, or the way she had decimated their relationship with her absurd notions of how a 'relationship' should be, and how old people needed to be before she would take them seriously. She was not expecting such fury. Nor was she expecting such a blow to her self-esteem – was she really that heartless and selfish? Was he right to blame her ending the relationship on her antiquated theories and self-protective barriers? The more time she spent on her own, knocking back white wine with no one to talk to, the more she believed he was right. She was an asshole. She had broken his heart unnecessarily, callously, and now he wanted nothing more to do with her. Which of course made her want everything to do with him.

As usual, the moment Abby's reflections became morose and she realised what a bad person she was, the feisty section of her brain picked up their pom poms and made their way to centre stage, to remind her that she was awesome, thank you very much, and Marcus's behaviour only confirmed what she had suspected about him, which was that he was a child, and his inability to discuss the situation like an adult, without being so vitriolic and attacky, was all the proof she needed to know she'd made the right decision to end things.

And yet, every morning she refreshed her email on her phone, the 'checking for new mail' spinning wheel mirroring Abby's stomach spinning with hope and excitement that he might have sent her an email, and then, when he never did, her heart falling flat and becoming still, before her mouth took over and uttered a few, 'well fuck him, who needs him anyway,' type sentiments, and then her pride bounced in to remind her to definitely NOT send him one, even though she very much might like to, around 279 times a day, especially in moments like this, where she sat alone with gorgeous food steaming in front of her, knowing how much he would enjoy this, and how much she would enjoy this, if he were to be here enjoying it in front of her.

In exasperation, she skolled a huge portion of wine and slammed the glass hard – too hard – on the table. Of course, just as she did so, the godamn Marcus wannabe came back out with parmesan.

'Everything okay? Youa not happy today?'

It was the most simple sentence, and yet it bore through Abby like a hot drill. Tears flashed into her eyes, and she fumbled on the table for her sunglasses, jamming them clumsily on her face.

'Oh, no, no, I'm fine. Who wouldn't be happy in a beautiful place like this? Ha ha ha.'

She was selling, but he wasn't buying.

'Do you travel alone?'

Oh you have to be kidding me, she thought.

'Yes.'

Idiot. Why didn't she say her boyfriend was back in the room?

'Since the booka? De pray eat love booka? So many women come here by they selfa . . .' He smiled; annoyingly he was possibly even more handsome than Marcus. And looked roughly as young.

'I'm sure they do.' Abby gave a mildly condescending, busy smile and made to start eating again.

'Maybe, if you lika, you come for aperitif at my brother's restaurant tonighta? My girlfriend and sisters will be there, do not feel scary.'

Abby laughed.

'It is outside the wall, near the small churcha. I will give de address. We are there 8 p.m. My name is Andrea!' He smiled broadly and disappeared.

Abby shook her head and smiled. How quickly a lady's day could change! To be invited somewhere, to have some prospect of conversation, even if it is clunky and half-Italish, to hang out with some genuine locals – all of these things made her heart bloom. She was definitely going. Even if it was for one glass of wine. She was going. Being miserable about Marcus was a diabolical waste of a trip. He could suck it.

Wearing her new tan sandals – she'd taken great delight in choosing the style and leather she wanted and having them made – and a short, loose navy silk dress cinched in with a thin belt, Abby felt as chic as she could without dressing up or making too much of an effort. She had no idea what these people would be wearing, couldn't remember the Marcus-guy's name and suddenly panicked at the thought of what she was doing – walking down a strange, rambly path at dusk, on her way to a place in a foreign country with people she'd never met before. She'd make a horrible backpacker, she thought, she had about as much gumption as a newborn lamb.

She turned a corner and saw a small, welcoming restaurant and bar with a large al fresco area 100 metres away. It was opposite a small, pretty church, and set against a backdrop of magnificent Tuscan fields and farmhouses. There were some very fancy cars out the front for a small restaurant in a tiny town, she thought, re-applying her gloss and tousling her hair in preparation for what could only be an awkward entrance.

But Abby needn't have worried, as soon as she came into the lights, her waiter friend was leaping up to greet her. She smiled nervously.

'You came! Please, come to meet everyone . . .'

He futilely ran her through the eleven or so people seated and standing around a dark wooden bench, sipping on wine or beer, smoking, laughing. They all nodded and smiled warmly, and two of the women pulled another chair over, motioning for her to sit. A couple of kids were screaming around the tables at the other end of the restaurant, and the scent of food being delivered to other small tables of what appeared to be locals, judging by their lack of shiny holiday best, and fluent Italian, was gorgeous.

A very pretty young girl with astonishingly shiny hair came over and held Andrea's – *that* was his name – hand and smiled welcomingly at Abby. She clearly wasn't threatened by this old bat who'd stumbled in off the last tour bus, which was a relief to Abby. Abby wanted nothing to do with Andrea, as handsome as he was. It would've been an act of pure sadism.

'This is my girlfriend, Sylvana, she is de *most* beautiful.'

He kissed her lovingly on the top of her head.

'Abby, do you have husband?'

He was so *forward*. It was kind of refreshing in a way. Intrusive and awkward, but refreshing.

Abby laughed, 'No.'

'So we take you to be a single, yes?'

Abby loved the jump from no husband to single, as though boyfriends were inconsequential.

'Yes . . .' Abby wondered where this was all heading, the men in the group all seemed pretty taken, and even if they weren't, none were really her type, which was interesting since she didn't actually have a type, and they were all pretty handsome, in that slick European way. But still.

'So, some wine?'

'Thank you, that would be lovely.'

And he vanished inside to the small restaurant, with candles and very old arched doorways. It was quite a cool little bar and restaurant, unintentionally trendy in that traditional, brown-paper-menu and simple rustic candles and chill music playing, kind of way.

Sylvana, who spoke about as much English as Abby spoke Italian, gestured for Abby to come and sit with her and the women who'd pulled a chair over for her earlier. She recognised one of them as her waitress today, although with her hair out and a simple black, cotton dress with gold sandals, she looked far more beautiful. Who were these people? They didn't appear to be common town-folk, farmers and such. They looked like big-city types.

'Ciao, I am Elena,' said the waitress, smiling warmly. 'Andrea says you are travelling alone, have you been in Florence yet?'

'No . . . but I will. It will be my last stop . . . for the shopping!'

Abby had a strange way of punctuating her sentences with exclamation points since arriving in Italy. It felt appropriate some-how, her nod to the Italians' fantastic intonation.

'We live there; our family, it is a great city, you will enjoy yourself very much.'

Abby's confusion must have been visible, even in the late even-ing light.

'We come here in the summer and work, then for the winter we close the restaurant, this one and the one you visit today, and we are going to Florence.'

'Ohhh! What a terrific set up. All of you do this?' Abby gestured around the table.

'Yesa. It is what we always have done. I prefer Florence, but in summer it is unbearable, the heat. Our brother, Alessandro, he stays in Florence, because he needs the energy, but we come here.'

Sylvana said something in Italian to Elena.

'Si. Alessandro, he is arrived yesterday. Our brother, he visits sometimes, to check on the restaurants. They are his; he has in Venice too. He is a very successful man. Maybe you will fall into love with him!'

Abby laughed, imagining a bald, sleazy, wheeling-and-dealing guy driving a beat up old Alfa, chain-smoking with gold chains entwined in his hairy chest.

'Anyway. He will arrive soon, you can meet, he will tell you how is best to live in Firenze.'

Andrea placed a tumbler of wine in front of Abby, who thanked him and took a sip. It was delicious, refreshing, the perfect antidote to the warm, languid night air.

'I hope you are hungry!'

Abby *was* hungry, and as plates of parma ham and melon and cheeses and olives and breads were placed on the bench, she absorbed the moment. She was in a local restaurant, with the owners, eating fresh, local produce and drinking wine from vineyards she could see. Probably.

Everyone slowly started picking pieces from the platters and placing them on small blue, thick ceramic plates – so rustic! – and nibbling slowly. Abby was about to do the same when a man in dark jeans and a white shirt that appeared to be missing several buttons around the chest area walked in, jangling keys and smiling broadly. He had short, salt and pepper hair, tanned skin and gentle, warm eyes that were that light, piercing green that made people very beautiful, and quite often very famous. He wasn't classically handsome, but there was something instantly attractive about him. His relaxed style: brown loafers, no socks, and big, expensive watch slotted him firmly into textbook Italian hunk territory. Abby watched as he entered the group and loudly kissed and greeted people, laughing and joking in Italian, everyone moving from 40 to 100 watts in his presence.

'This is Alessandro. He has not seen some of us for since the winter,' Andrea said by way of explanation, admiration and love for his older brother beaming from his eyes.

Abby tried to politely finish her enormous piece of prosciutto before he was introduced, but it didn't matter, because he never was introduced. Instead he sat down at the opposite end of the table and, as a waiter brought him some wine from a different bottle than those already opened, he began telling a very engaging, boisterous story, which had everyone (capable of understanding Italian) in raptures. His wild gesticulation was the stuff of stereotypes, his voice full of expression, his eyes animated and engaging, and when he delivered what Abby presumed was the punchline, the entire group lost it so much their grip had to be called into question. They slapped knees and threw their heads back and guffawed and clutched at their stomachs, and all Abby could do was smile and be washed away in their sea of laughter.

She wished she knew what Alessandro was talking about, but soon enough regular conversation resumed and she had finished two tumblers of wine and was halfway through her third, and had a belly full of delicious treats, and she was so happy just sitting in her chair and the warm, silken night air, having stilted conversations with Elena and her friend, Maria about her job, and her travels and why she must go to Sicily, because that's where they holiday, and it is the best. Every now and then she caught herself looking at Alessandro, but he never looked at her. He was always deep in conversation with someone, listening intently to them talk, smiling with them. He'd kissed everyone hello when he arrived but in all the noise had failed to notice her. She tried not to be put out about it.

When she looked up at the table an hour later, it had petered down to five or so people, and Alessandro was sitting back, sipping his wine as he listened attentively to his friend/waiter tell a story.

'You like Alessandro, yes?' Andrea said with a smile in his voice from behind Abby, scaring the shit out of her. Sylvana stood with him, holding his hand and stroking it with her thumb, quietly loving on her gorgeous young boyfriend. Abby had never held Marcus's hand like that, she realised. He'd held hers in that way, devoted and adoring, but she had been to busy keeping her detached, power-holding position to be so openly adoring.

'What? No, I was just sitting here, just— *no.*' Abby guffawed and took a sip from what might have been her fifth or fifteenth glass of wine.

'*Every* woman like Alessandro.'

'That's lovely, and I'm sure he's very nice, but I haven't even spoken to him, and actually I'm—'

'Sylvana and I leave now, we will walk you home?'

Ridiculously, Abby felt irritated at having to leave not having met Alessandro. She had no idea why. Probably because he had not demanded he be introduced to the cute blonde girl from Australia. She needed to get a grip. Three weeks of being alone and missing Marcus was starting to send her sick in the head; who cares if some suave Italian hunk paid her no mind?

Abby took a final sip of her wine and reached down to the ground for her small bag. 'That would be great; thank you so much for inviting me, Andrea. I've had such a lov—'

Suddenly, a voice came from behind. 'Andrea, how can she leave when I have not even met her?'

Abby swivelled around clumsily to see Alessandro had (finally) appeared to introduce himself. She swooned a little bit inside while her ego ducked out for a pompous cigar; of *course* he'd come over eventually. Abby could instantly feel his presence . . . he was such a . . . *man*. A manly man. A grown up man, with style and confidence and the kind of accent bored housewives bestowed upon men in their sexual fantasies. He had pulled out a chair next to her as she spoke to Andrea, and she hadn't even noticed. He smelled incredible. Like leather and gunsmoke and cloves.

Abby smiled coyly and tucked some hair behind her left ear.

'Hi, I'm Abby.'

'Excuse me to be so rude tonight; I have not seen this people for some time. I am Alessandro.' He smiled good-naturedly, his eyes never leaving Abby's as he spoke.

'Hi, Alessandro,' Abby giggled, because apparently she was a twit. 'Nice to meet you.'

'Andrea,' he said, without lifting his eyes of Abby. 'Abby and I will stay for one more drink. Ciao, ciao Sylvana!'

Before Abby could protest, the two young lovers issued their buona seras, and set off into the darkness. Terrific, guys. You've left me with a man I've known for less than twenty-five seconds, when I'm drunk and will have to stumble home alone in the dark. Elena left ages ago and the woman – Maria? – Abby had been speaking to earlier was bidding her farewells.

'What makes you so sure I wish to stay?' Abby said, fuelled by indignation and the buzz of fermented grape juice.

'You look at me many times. You did not see me look at you, because I am better at the game.'

He smiled, his eyes flashing with mischief. Abby was at loss to explain how his unabashed confidence, his outrageous forwardness and his *obvious* intention somehow didn't revolt her.

'We will go back to my home for *digestiv*. Where do you stay?'

'Locanda La Mandragola . . . But *hang* on, why would I just go back to your house?'

'You know my family and I am interest to meet you, and prefer to relax in comfort instead of on this plastic chair. Anyway, we are close now.' He stood up as a full stop.

Despite her 'outrage', Abby was rather enjoying being curled up in the palm of his hand. She liked that he was so in control, taking charge. She knew she was in no danger. This was a lovely family, and they all clearly viewed Alessandro as some kind of deity.

He said something in Italian to the stragglers, punctuated it with several ciaos, and picked up his car keys.

'Whoa. You can't drive,' said Abby, immediately placing her safety-captain hat on. 'We've been drinking all night.'

'You have drunk all night. I had two wines. He smiled kindly. 'I am not a stupid man.' He looked at her, lingering for just a couple of seconds longer than a man should, so that there was no error in translation about what he thought of her. He wasn't so much undressing her with his eyes – that was for amateurs – he was placing candles around the room, sprinkling rose petals over her naked body and putting Sade on repeat. Incredibly, it wasn't creepy, or slimy or even a turn off. This was the specific and unique trick of European men, to let your 'intention' be absolutely transparent, but without uttering a single word. For Abby, it was a potent and intoxicating aphrodisiac.

Yes, she confirmed internally, to the surprise of all departments, especially 'logic' and 'self-control', I could definitely have sex with this man.

32

Alessandro drove a black Ferrari with tan leather seats and talked about his family with great affection and pride. Andrea, it transpired, was a very, very good footballer, and was on his way to playing in the Serie A for Fiorentina, which Abby sensed was a big deal.

They drove down a steep, wily driveway and pulled up at the front of a well-lit, modern villa that wouldn't have looked out of place in *Wallpaper* magazine. Abby couldn't be sure, but she thought she saw a plunge pool reflected on the roof of the upstairs balcony. It was all becoming slightly preposterous.

With the confidence and grace only a wealthy, attractive Italian man could possess, Alessandro took Abby's hand, led her straight through the living area to a room with plush day beds and vibrant rugs and beautiful coffee-table books and a long wooden bar with several stools. As he busied himself preparing drinks, Abby opened up the French doors, which overlooked the very same view she saw each evening on her run. Soft Cuban jazz played in the background and she could smell sweet white flowers. She shook her head: This wasn't Real Life. Certainly not *Abby's* Real Life. Chelsea's perhaps. She wondered if she could take a picture on her phone of this place, or even the car, and send it to Chels. Not that she'd bloody respond, she had been the *shittest* friend since Abs had been away, literally only responding to one text when Abby had announced she'd landed safely.

Alessandro walked over to Abby with two long, heavy shot-glass looking things with some ice and clear liquid in them.

'Montenegro. You will like.'

He motioned for her to sit on the sofa with him, and giggling stupidly, Abby sat down gingerly next to him, watching her small dress ride up; she was basically just a pair of legs with an Australian accent. She felt sexy, and frisky, and wanted Alessandro to look at her legs appreciatively, but he seemed not to notice, he was too busy looking at her face and being abrupt.

'Why do you cut your hair so short?' he asked.

'I like it this way.'

'But it is not feminine.'

'That may be, in your opinion anyway, but I don't really care. I've always worn it this way.' She usually didn't mind this question, but she was a little annoyed at Alessandro's attitude. Or maybe she was annoyed at the idea he didn't like her hair.

'If you like it, that is all that matters.' He smiled and took a sip.

Still didn't say *he* liked it. Abby sipped her drink to calm her irrational irritation. It was kind of delicious, in that extremely strong Italian digestive way. Thankfully it lacked the rocket-fuel-ness of grappa and the lemony sucrose of limoncello, both of which she'd become familiar with via Marcus. NO. NO. *NO*. We do not think of Marcus at this time, Abby reprimanded her brain.

'Do you enjoy?' Alessandro gestured to the drink.

'I do. And that is all that matters.'

He laughed heartily. 'So. What do you do for your work?'

'I run . . . a modelling agency. Kind of. '

'But you are not a model.' He sipped from his glass and placed his phone on the coffee table. It was a statement, a given, not a question. Was he deliberately negging on her? Abby's rational mind couldn't even make excuses for him anymore.

'No, of course not.' She tried to disguise the contempt in her voice.

'Young girls are too highly prized. Women are better; they have their head high and the confidence. It is sexy. *You* are sexy.'

He switched gears so fast; Abby was struggling to keep up. He looked at her, smiling, studying her face.

'Mmmm.' Was all she could offer. 'So, Alessandro, you live in Florence, mostly, yes?' She was doing that thing where she subconsciously mimicked whoever she was chatting with in accent and intonation.

'Si. I come back here often in summer and even winter, because the tourists go and I like peace. Sometimes I need noise and the chaos, but sometimes a soul yearns for quiet.'

'I am going to be in Florence next week, before I head home!' Abby smiled excitedly. She was looking forward to a Big City.

'Then you must stay at my home.' Alessandro said this so matter-of-fact Abby couldn't help laughing. He was a caricature, a raging stereotype. 'I won't be there, but you are welcome to stay, it is a nice home.'

AGAIN with the switching gears! The way he wavered between insouciant and intense was driving Abby mental.

'Okay, well, thanks.' She got her phone out and checked the time, it was almost 2 a.m.; she should go. What was she even doing here, with this guy who wasn't making a move, and who she now wasn't even sure she wanted to? Abby was becoming frustrated: If you decide you're up for an impulsive, steamy one-night stand with a sexy Italian, you shouldn't have to spell it out for the lucky gentleman.

'Is something the matter?'

'No, I, I just, it's late, I should be going . . .' She sat on the edge of the lounge and placed her mega shot glass on the beautiful glass coffee table. Acqua Di Parma candles. *Very* nice. He wasn't gay, was he? No, no he couldn't be. She had to remember that Italian men were stylish; they didn't need to be homosexual to wear good shoes and have taste in homewares.

Alessandro sat forward to mimic her position, his right knee touching her left. Abby felt a shot of electricity tear down her leg when they connected and she caught another whiff of his scent. She felt lightheaded and giddy being so close to him, as though she were in some kind of Mills and Boon novel.

He looked at her, his chin slightly lowered.

'May we kiss?'

She smiled and her heart stirred and her body pulsed with excitement.

'I thought you'd never ask.' She was not kidding.

He placed his drink on the coffee table and gently put his right hand at the nape of Abby's neck. He pulled her towards him gently, and kissed her lips softly. His lips parted ever so slightly and he gently licked her tongue with his: it was the smallest, most insignificant move Abby had ever experienced, but it sent shivers down the back of her knees. Abby opened her mouth to allow more of these delicious kisses and he took that as a signal to move closer towards her, and start caressing her head, his hand massaging her scalp in rhythm with their kisses. Suddenly he pulled back, his nose just centimetres from Abby's, and looked at her squarely in the eyes. His breath was sweet, far too sweet for a man who'd enjoyed multiple cigarettes, and his heady fragrance was hypnotising; Abby was mesmerised by the sensory experience of his scent and his touch and his outrageous, Enrique Iglesias film-clip stare.

'I wanted you as soon as I see you tonight.'

Who spoke like that? Abby thought. Honestly, in real life, who spoke like that? Abby conceded that it was kind of sexy in the moment, the stuff romance writers made their fortunes from, but it was also the kind of thing she wished she could record or at least write down to laugh about with the girls later.

'Liar. You didn't even notice me.'

'Just because I don't show the desire, does not mean I do not have.'

And Abby was gone again, melting into his mouth and his kisses, hoping very much that he made love with the same intensity with which he spoke and kissed.

Two sweaty, passionate hours later and Abby had her answer: Yes.

He *did* make love like that. She'd always thought you needed an emotional connection to have truly fantastic sex, but now she realised you just needed an accomplished, passionate partner and a few wines under your belt for confidence. He was a very different lover from Marcus, and even though she had forbidden herself from making comparisons, Marcus popped into her head several times during their session. Mostly because it was all she'd known for the last few months, she told herself. No other reason.

Abby looked at Alessandro's toned, tanned body as he walked from the bed – which was extremely low and trendy – to the bathroom, which appeared to be made entirely from black tiles and sans walls. It was an incredible home, minimalistic and slick, with beautiful wooden light fittings and splashes of yellow and chocolate for warmth. She must ask him about those dangling bedside lamps, Abby thought as she pulled a crisp white cotton sheet up over her naked, damp body. They were exceptional – just cords of electrical wire and large clear globes that appeared to be entwined in bendy twigs. She should probably wait until they'd stopped panting and the sweat had dried, she thought, smiling mischievously at the memory of what had just taken place in the bed she lay in. He was a Take Charge man, she concluded. The kind Chelsea always banged on about – 'I need a man who'll throw me up against a wall,' was one of her favourite shocking sex statements – but after being man-handled by Alessandro, in several rooms and double that amount of positions, she now understood exactly what Chelsea was on about.

Marcus certainly knew how to throw Abby around, but was more of an emotional, adoring lover than a strong, stuff-of-fanta-sies, Take Care of Business type that Alessandro was. She'd felt a pang of reality and a twinge of wrong when she waited, naked and pent up on the bed, as Alessandro reached for the condoms from his bedside drawer – which was under the bed and part of the frame, of course – *was she cheating on Marcus?* No, she'd decided, they were definitely separated. And weren't in a relationship to begin with, besides. He was probably doing the exact same thing, she confirmed, although probably not with an Italian man.

Alessandro returned with a towel wrapped around his waist and his hair wet. Abby noticed the hair on his chest was half grey, like that on his head, and while his body was firm, he had that little bit of skin sag on the stomach that comes with age. She really was dealing with a *man* here. A man who could be nearing fifty. Her previous record was forty, so if nothing else, she had broken that record. Oh, and climaxed on a staircase, that was also something new. He had clearly slept with his fair share of women. Abby tried not to think of herself as just another conquest, instead flipping it to be in *her* power: she had chosen to have sex with *him* tonight, because she was in Italy and she was single and it was perfect and he had a black Ferrari and a small bar fridge full of bottled San

Pellegrino. It was a terrific choice and she regretted nothing. Except for maybe that part where he asked her to do that thing with her tongue. Abby decided it was better not to think about that. Put it all down to experience.

'You will stay for breakfast?' he asked this as he applied face cream like a woman, delicately and carefully. Abby tried not to notice, because if she did it would turn her off.

Abby couldn't tell whether he was asking her to stay.

'Um, I'm not sure, I guess it might be too late to go home now . . .'

'I can drive you, if you prefer.'

Did he want her to stay, or go? It was impossible to know what he meant, and it instantly made Abby feel frustrated and vulnerable. She wasn't typically the kind of girl to sleep over, but she also wasn't the kind of girl who typical fucked a man she'd spoken less than 100 words to, either, so why stop the Eurostar of unusual now?

'Maybe I'll stay, if that is okay? And I can walk home in the morning.'

Alessandro laughed and walked over to sit next to Abby on the bed.

'You will get so lost you will wind up back in my bed anyway. I will drive you after I make breakfast. A towel?'

He kissed her on the lips gently and stood up to get her a huge, soft grey towel from a cupboard posing as a wall.

Abby didn't really feel like a shower, but he was clearly a man into hygiene, so she wrapped the towel around her body and walked to the bathroom, which had no door and offered him a full view of her body as she showered. She took a deep breath and sucked it up – he'd seen her in far more compromising positions in the past few hours than innocently standing under a stream of water; she needed to get over it. Still, she faced the bedroom as much as possible, so he didn't see her cellulite and could focus on her tits instead, which he seemed rather enamoured with, to the point were they ached a little from all the kneading and tweaking. That was new, too.

'When do you come in Florence?' he asked from bed as she tried to finger brush her hair and dry off her body elegantly, like Jennifer Aniston types did in the movies.

'I think the day after tomorrow . . . Do you think five nights is too many there?'

'Never too many nights in Firenze.'

'I thought that might be the case, I can't wait to see it . . .'

'You will stay with me.'

Abby came out and sat on the bed, wondering where she'd left her knickers in the explosion of sexual misdemeanour. She hoped/assumed he lived here alone, and that no poor soul would wake up to find them at the bottom of the stairs.

'You mean the house you won't be in?' Abby laughed. 'That's very kind of you, Alessandro. But I am so happy finding my own place. I genuinely am.'

'It would be my pleasure to host you.'

'Will you really not be there the whole time I am there?' Abby asked. She realised she quite liked the idea of seeing him again, and was a bit hurt he wasn't suggesting he would like to see *her* again. Which was interesting, considering he was a veritable stranger and seemed to not like her very much half the time. Surely holiday flings were meant to be a bit more gushing and ridiculous and teenagey and lusty?

'I can, if you would like. Show you my city.' He looked at her with those eyes, the same ones that had gotten her into this whole situation. 'But I know women like to travel alone. It is not for me to intrude.'

It was all Abby could do not to say 'awwwww'. If he was playing her, he was at concert pianist level. Her instinct – which, if she was falling into his "trap", was probably unreliable – was to say, *'No, no! You must come!'* but she decided to think about it. Let *him* feel vulnerable for a bit.

'Let's talk on this in the morning.' She smiled, dropped her towel and slipped under the sheets with him, feeling one of his soft arms wrap around her affectionately as his other arm switched off the bedside lamp from a switch she'd not noticed, probably visible only to the Italian eye. It felt very boyfriend-girlfriend, which was extremely disconcerting for Abby, and threw her immediately into a memory of Marcus and her, entwined in bed together, him trying to slip his left arm under her neck and Abby pushing it out straight away because it gave her a sore neck. 'It means I can hold you closer,' he'd argue lovingly.

Mentally shaking away thoughts of Marcus, Abby gently rolled her way out of Alessandro's embrace and faced the opposite way, with her back and naked bum against him. She felt him rise and nudge into her back, and for a thrilling moment wondered if they were about to go another round . . . how *devilish!* He softly kissed her shoulder, and a smile spread across her face . . . before feeling him roll over so that his back was to hers and fluff and settle into his pillow for sleep. Why didn't he ever chase for longer than two seconds? She lay there, eyes open and flashing wildly in the light of the breaking dawn, wondering how in the space of six hours this man had already managed to not only screw her, but get under her skin, too. He was clearly used to women fawning over him. Well, she wasn't going to give him the satisfaction. Even on a holiday fling Abby had to assert some control; it was impossible for her to completely let go.

After Marcus's transparent and generous adoration, it was a

nice change to be a little unsure, play the game a bit, enjoy the challenge and the chase.

Confirming this helped Abby fall asleep, instead of wondering why she was naked in a stranger's bed, on the other side of the world from the man she was too terrified to admit she was in love with.

33

Mads's expression was one of disbelief, even with the shitty, robotic Skype connection.

'Let me get this straight. Last week, you send me an email in which you are *unbearably, desperately* devastated about Marcus and thinking you made an enormous mistake letting him go, and today you tell me you are living in some Italian lothario's palace in Florence brimming with outlandish sports cars and vintage champagne.'

'*Si*,' Abby said, smiling smugly.

Mads had actively changed the conversation to something light-hearted after she'd reluctantly confirmed that her and Dyl's first attempt at IVF had failed. Mads's heart was a little bit broken, but her tenacity to conceive a little bit stronger. They were both exhausted. Abby felt utterly selfish blathering on about Alessandro, but Mads had demanded conversational frivolity.

'Goodness. Sounds tough, sweetlips. Hang in there for one more day, yeah?'

Abby laughed. 'I'll do my best.'

'All that hairy-chested Mediterranean sex has gone to your

head. Next thing you'll be telling me you've bought a vineyard and are staying over there to run a B&B.'

Mads was right; it was all unquestionably ludicrous. But that's what holidays were for, being ludicrous! And living dangerously! And having crazy sex! And going in helicopters to lunch!

'What, not a good idea?'

'So this . . . AleSSANdro is obviously riddled with Euro, but that's more Chelsea's bag, not yours: what do you actually like about him? Is he your future husband? Will you end up living in Florence in an enormous villa with spare rooms for your best friends from Australia?'

'Little to no chance of that. He *did* ask me to change my flight tomorrow, so he could take me to Rome, but I have to come home. I've left Charlie in charge, all by herself, for over five weeks, it seems a bit uncool.'

Not that Charlie seemed to care. She was so efficient Abby was starting to feel a bit territorial. Any time Abby started to fire emails off about things, cc'ing Charlie in on them, Charlie completely took over, leaving Abby with nothing to do or say. It should've made Abby feel at ease, and lucky, but instead she felt a bit left out. It was ridiculous, Abby told herself. Charlie was the best thing that had happened to Allure.

' . . . That was a very not-him move, though. He's no gushing romantic. He's powerful and intelligent and driven and *sexy*, but he's a playboy and he's holding *all* the cards. One minute he's telling me I could change his life forever, the next he's saying my hair is awful and why do I not grow it? He's terrific at keeping me just insecure enough to want to hang around for another compliment. Which is something I always thought I was too smart to fall for.'

'*Booooooooooring!* The SEX??'

'Oh, don't you worry about that, Mads, I bring home a veritable encyclopaedia of innovative, exciting and disgusting sexual positions. We've had one steamy little week together in Florence, yesiree.'

'OutSTANDING! So has the Italian cured you of Marcus? Has this little penetration vacation changed how you feel about him?'

Abby rested her head on her knuckle in thought, and looked at Mads's face intently on screen.

'D'you know what? I think it has. I feel like maybe Alessandro has shown me I need a man. Someone accomplished and mature, someone who can teach *me* things, y'know, inspire me.' Even as she said it, the words felt hollow to her. Detective Mads picked up on it immediately.

'I think the lady doth yank thy cranks,' Mads said, disdain on her face. 'You're doing what you *think* you should be doing, because women our age *should* be with impressive, golden raisins in their forties. We've been socially conditioned to date up in age and status since we were little girls, but you don't need anyone to look after you, or teach you things, Abby Robert Brian David Vaughn. You can do it yourself, you have for years!' Mads took a breath and exhaled slowly.

'Hormone blitz, sorry. But, Abs, do you really feel this way? Does Alessandro make you laugh? Are you having the time of your stonkin' life? I don't know, I just feel like, well, Marcus made you more *you* than any man I've ever seen you with.'

'Well, I mean we have great conversations . . . Alessandro knows so much about history and architecture and design and food, he's an amazing cook, and he—'

'And does he ever ask what *you* think? Or does he just talk at you? Older men usually want to make love to the sound of their own voice; they want an audience, not a partner.'

Abby recoiled slightly.

'Look, whatever happens down the track, this is all helpful stuff, Abs. You're starting to understand what you really want in a relationship.' She looked at Abby with big eyes, trying to jam her message into Abby's head visually as well as verbally.

'Mads, it's just a fling, just a little holiday fling, let's not analyse it too much, eh?' Abby needed this conversation to end. It was too heavy for her last day in Italy, a day that was brilliant with sunshine and begging for exploration and credit card swiping. Alessandro had shown her some incredible areas of Florence that she never would've seen by herself. She was very grateful to him. He was a generous, kind man. But Mads was right: *they didn't have much fun.*

'I've gotta go make something of my last day here, maybe buy my friends some stuff from Gucci or Celine.'

'Chelsea doesn't deserve or need gifts. Buy double for poor, childless Mads instead.'

'She has been a total turd, actually. You're right. For someone with her BlackBerry on an IV drip, she is so incredibly shit at responding to messages.'

'Well I've seen her about as much as you have in the past month so don't look to me for answers.'

'Hmmm. Must be all back on with Jezza again. You know how she gets when she's in love.'

'Yes: Invisible. Okay, I'll see you in a few days, I guess. Hey, do you need a pick up on Thursday? Text me the details. Will give me something to look forward to.'

'You're the best.'

'In all transparency, I just want my luxury leather goods.'

'Bye, Madsy.' Abby blew her a kiss.

'Ciaaaaaaooooo.' Mads waved theatrically at the camera, blowing multiple kisses and taking over the whole screen with her hands.

Abby put her laptop to sleep and grabbed her phone in preparation to go out. Of course there was no email or text from Marcus. He had not contacted her *once* since she'd left Australia. What a thoughtless brute, she thought, before remembering she was in another man's home and had been for six nights now, and couldn't really be angry with a boy she had totally blindsided with her 'issues' and then dumped a few days before jetting out to have a sexy Italian fling.

Still, she thought as she applied some sunscreen and makeup. *He* didn't know that. Abby looked at herself in the mirror. It was easy, considering it took up the entire wall of Alessandro's bedroom. She looked good: she was tanned and her hair had gone lighter in the sun. Her skin was glowing, her eyes shone bright – she looked healthy, happy, relaxed. Or very well sexed. Either way, she was in fine form to 'run into Marcus' should she see him around this weekend back home.

Alessandro had told her to dress up tonight; he was taking her to his favourite restaurant for sunset cocktails and dinner. In her Home Head, this meant a 6 p.m. pick up, but her Italy Head knew that Alessandro meant 9 p.m.

As Abby fastened her bra and pulled up her floral romper, she battled a mixture of emotions. She was excited to be going home, but gloomy to be leaving Italy, and Alessandro. She still got a thrill when he came in the door, or called her, or insisted she get in the shower with him because he liked making love to her when her hair was wet. He was her Italian fairytale, and Abby didn't generally find herself the protagonist in fairytales.

As Abby popped on her sunglasses and grabbed the house keys her phone chimed with a new text, no doubt from Alessandro. But in fact it was from Chelsea.

I'm 7 wks pregnant. And totally fucked. DONT tell Mads.

34

Alessandro was taking Abby to Hotel Villa San Michele, which pleased Abby very much. She'd wanted to go there after reading about it in *Travel + Leisure* magazine, well before Mr Fancy Shoes had come along. It was going to be her blow out meal; she was going to go there all by herself, an independent, successful, sassy solo traveller showing the world she didn't need a man to enjoy an expensive meal and a bottle of wine (and possibly even an overnight stay) in a chic, luxurious haven.

Abby was trying to act normal, but she was profoundly rattled by Chelsea's news. They'd fired a few texts back and forth, and Abby discovered that Jeremy – who Chelsea was definitely back on with, and even considering moving in with – had seen the pregnancy test and was adamant she keep it, and that they give it a go. But Chelsea did not want children. Plus, she wasn't sure she was ready for that big a commitment to Jeremy; for all she knew he collected babies from different women as sport. That she'd accidentally fallen pregnant while poor Mads couldn't no matter what lengths she went to felt horribly unfair, and to Abby's astonishment and pride, this was the thing Chels was most upset about. Abby calmed her friend down as much as she could from the other side of the world and via SMS, and promised Mads would understand, and that they would all discuss it once Abby was home.

Abby took a long sip of her champagne in an attempt to get back to the moment, and filed away her friend's conundrum until the morning. She noted that Alessandro looked especially handsome this evening – perhaps it was that he'd done up all of his shirt buttons? – and seemed to be in a particularly convivial mood.

'I like this dress on your skin,' he said admiringly, or in some cultures, inappropriately.

'Thanks, Alessandro,' Abby smiled at him genuinely, partly because she was thrilled to finally be the recipient of a pure compliment, and partly because receiving Alessandro's full attention was still dizzying to her.

Abby was wearing a new soft, short, silk peach dress that kindly offered Alessandro – and each of the waiters – an exciting reminder of the delights of cleavage, yet, with its flowing, floaty shape wasn't at all tacky. She'd teamed it with tan-coloured heels and a delicate gold bracelet she'd bought at Zara that looked far more expensive than it was. Abby finally felt herself relaxing, the sultry night air and alcohol working in tandem to soothe her anxious mind. Really, Italy had gone more than perfectly: Allure was being babysat by an efficiency demon, and she'd bought Chels and Mads sexy knickers and camis from Loretta Caponi, the most magical shop she'd ever been in, complete with artisans sewing angelically on the actual shop floor, breathtaking frescoed ceilings and beautiful handcrafted linens. And, most importantly, she had made it the entire time without one email, call or text to Marcus. In addition, she'd also somehow landed the kind of summer romance gold-diggers and teenage girls could only dream of. She looked across at the man responsible for her high-class dip into Italian loving and smiled. She was feeling unusually sentimental tonight, possibly as a result of the rapid-fire succession of champagne refills.

'So, how much, on a scale of one to ten, will you miss me, do you think?' She knew it was an inane question, but felt like being playful.

He looked at her, smiled and took a sip of his champagne, before reaching across the table to take her hand.

'I am with you now, and that is where my mind is. But, since you must know, I will miss you, yes.'

Abby felt a flash of affection run through her. He'd come a long way since the first night. Watching him watching her smile and blush, Abby saw Alessandro's Aloof Hero façade drift over the balcony to the masterfully manicured grounds below. Despite warming up over the week, Alessandro's compliment-output switch was still essentially set to 'economical'. Marcus, on the other hand, was magnificent with compliments; he sprinkled them over Abby as though they were icing sugar on strawberries, giving them as little gifts all throughout the day, making Abby beam.

As it did 780 times a day, Alessandro's BlackBerry rang. To her amazement, Abby watched him press 'ignore'. Well. *That* was a first.

'It is our last night together, the work can wait.'

A waiter appeared to take their order, his eyes squinting in the piercing sunset, and Alessandro ordered in Italian without asking or consulting Abby as to what she would like or want. She almost spoke up, but bit her tongue in an effort to be a good dinner guest, and not distract from his benevolence in bringing her to this glorious restaurant. As she let that strange and subservient thought wander through her mind, she realised how foreign her silence was.

'Actually, Alessandro, I would really love to try the gnocchi.'

She really did. It was the restaurant's signature dish, and she'd been looking forward to it. Alessandro stopped speaking and looked at Abby across the table, bemused.

'Trust me, Abby. You will like this food I order.' He smiled as a full stop and handed back the menu to the waiter. The waiter gingerly reached for Abby's menu, which still lay open in front of her. She thought about demanding her gnocchi, but decided against it. It wasn't worth the drama. They were, after all, holiday romancers, not one of those awful long-term couples who sat in beautiful restaurants in the most picturesque locations in the world, bitching and hissing at each other and then sitting in silence, thinking murderous thoughts and ordering that enormous and specific amount of wine that is the signature of those having a wonderful time, or a hideous time. She snapped the menu shut and smiled at the waiter.

'*Grazie.*' Abby thought about what Mads said about older men, how they called all the shots.

'What time is your flight tomorrow?'

'9 a.m. I'll book a taxi for 6 a.m.' She was packed already; she wouldn't be late, no matter how little sleep they got tonight.

'I will drive you,' he said.

'No, no, it's fine, you've done enough, really.' She meant it.

'It is my pleasure to drive you.'

She smiled and accepted he was not going to take no for an answer. Abby took a deep breath, and focused on the view over Florence. It was breathtaking, even despite the hazy layer of heat and pollution resting above the city.

'I'm going to miss Italy,' Abby said, smiling woozily as she took in the warmth of the evening air, the sound of the people at the table next to her laughing, the joy of not having her phone on the table, the scent of Alessandro's fragrance.

'So stay!'

Abby smiled and shook her head.

'Then come back next year. I will take you to Sardinia, we have the boat there.'

'That *does* sound nice . . .' Abby said, because it really, really did.

'Maybe I come to Australia. I have a cousin there, Federico. He always tells me come to see him. You can show me your city.'

'Oh, it's nothing like this, I assure you! You will find it quite dull.' Abby smiled and shook her head.

'But you will be there. That is not dull.'

He looked at her with interest; Abby felt he sensed her deflection. She *was* discouraging him, if she was honest. How awkward if he came to Australia and she was back with Marcus; what would she tell him? Both hims? Why did she assume she would be back with Marcus?

'Let me get a photo of you,' Abby said brightly, desperate to change the topic.

She took out her camera and aimed it at Alessandro; he confidently eyeballed the lens, his lips unsmiling.

'Okaaay, now do something fun! Make a face or something.'

'What does this mean, make the face?'

'Something funny!' She pulled a dapper face, using a grissini as pretend cigar.

He stopped for a second, thinking, then raised his eyebrows and shoulders, as if to say, 'who, me?' It was terrible.

Abby took the photo anyway, and laughed to herself. A befuddled expression crossed his face, and he pulled out his cigarettes, lighting one up with the matches on the table.

'You are funny girl, Abby.'

And you are *not* a funny girl, thought Abby, but he was a grown up, she reprimanded herself, and this is what they were like. Perhaps Abby should be taking leaves out of his book, instead of making them into paper planes.

The food (and an outstanding Barolo) arrived, and right on cue, Abby became ecstatically hungry. Despite her annoyance that she hadn't been allowed to have the gnocchi, Abby relished the meal – scampi and thyme risotto, baked sea bass with ginger and basil polenta, beef carpaccio, artichoke and asparagus nestled in feather-light puff pastry . . . Bloody Alessandro; managing to produce the perfect Italian meal without a whisper of pasta. Show off.

'It is delicious, yes?'

He *phrased* it as a question, but it was simply a statement wearing a fake moustache.

'It's delicious.' It really, really was. 'It's the perfect last meal with you.'

'The last meal for now.' He smiled at her, lingeringly, and touched her thigh under the table softly.

'That's right. For now.'

Lie. Well, maybe.

'You have been so, so kind and generous to me, Alessandro. I've loved this week. *Thank you.*'

Abby smiled and leaned over the table to kiss her lover.

35

It was a short and comfortable trip home, consisting of two trains, one bus, three flights – one delayed by three hours – two four-hour stopovers, and a sick, grizzly infant interrupting any decent sleep that might have had the audacity to sneak in on the final twelve-hour leg. Abby used the opportunity to reflect on handsome, enigmatic Alessandro, who had presented her with a beautiful bracelet when he'd dropped her to the airport, and had smelled and looked as good as any man could at 6 a.m.

Mads insisted on an afternoon tea party to welcome her friend home.

'*Look* at you, you sexy little strand of spaghetti!' Mads said admiringly as she placed a plate of pastel-coloured macaroons on her coffee table. 'Look how tanned you are! And have you lost weight? That's not right; you were in the United States of Wheat! It's scandalous.'

'What'd you get us?' Chels asked as she repositioned herself on a light wood armchair. 'Okay, I actually cannot sit on this fucking chair one second longer – I don't care if it's Eames or fucking God himself made it, Mads, it's the most horrible thing I've ever sat on.'

'Are you kidding me? It's heavensent! I ADORE it. We found it at a garage sale – do you even know how much a genuine Danish solid wood rocker costs these days? And this is proper art deco, ladies, not a replica from the fifti—'

Chelsea gave up and flopped onto the sofa perfectly, her newly dark hair swept up into a top-knot, showing off her perfect skin and impressive cleavage, which was falling out of an olive green singlet. Abby tried not to look at Chelsea's stomach as she plucked a lilac macaroon from the platter and bit into its chewy, soft deliciousness. She assumed from the cordial mood that Chels had definitely not yet made mention of the small human growing in her stomach.

'So what's the story with your Italian Stallion?' Chelsea said, ignoring the macaroons that would obliterate her calorie count for the whole week, choosing instead to sip on her green tea.

'Will you stay in touch? Will he come out here and swoop you up into his Ferragamo-clad arms and whisk you away from us?'

'Nahhh. Well, actually, he did threaten to. But we were in summer fling mode, people say a lot of shit they don't mean when there is no fear of actually making good on it.'

'Would he, though?' Mads asked.

'Maybe. But probably not. We had a really good week, we really did, and the goodbye sucked, it felt a bit . . . real, I guess. But so did my fling with diamond necklace guy.'

All three girls dissolved into giggles.

'You had sex with him in a storeroom at a nightclub, Abby Vaughn. I can't even believe you did that . . .' Chelsea shook her head, bemused.

'I was young and wild,' Abby said, smiling at the memory of her Contiki-tour mischief.

'Speaking of young . . . any goss on Marcus?' Chelsea asked.

'Nothing. Nada.'

Now she was home, she couldn't even try to suppress thoughts of Marcus. Memories of him were *everywhere*. Had she really done irreversible damage by breaking up with him? Was he seeing someone new? The very idea made her heart descend in an instant and yet he was entirely within his rights to do what and whomever he pleased. After all, Abby had TOLD him he wanted to sleep around, and TOLD him he was young and should be exploring the vast sexual landscape available to a gorgeous, funny, clever young man with beautiful shoulders, and TOLD him he was too young to be settling down with an old crone like her. What a *dickhead* she was. Why the fuck had she said those things? Was she trying to convince him or her that he should be doing these things?

'But, I dunno, I was thinking I might try and catch up with him sometime.'

'*What a surprise!*' Chelsea cried.

'This is magnificent news,' Mads said, beaming. 'Be bold, my travel-weary comrade. Nothing to lose. Look at Chels and Jeremy – patched things up beautifully.'

Chelsea squirmed almost imperceptibly, but Abs caught it. Abby looked up at Chelsea from her position on the rug, who caught her gaze and dropped it just as fast. Abby, already dealing with monstrous fatigue and now the sugar shakes, felt ill to her stomach. Chels had to say something. This was the moment. *It was now.* Mads would be supportive, of course she would. Abby tried to telepathically signal this to Chels, staring at her as she did so.

'What's going on?' Mads's eyes darted between her two friends.

'Nothing,' they said simultaneously, which meant 'everything'.

'*Guys!* What?'

Abby exhaled deeply and busied herself with a thread on the rug.

'Oh, for fuck's sake, Abs, dog me out much? You're hopeless!' Chelsea sounded justifiably angry.

'Wha—' Abby pathetically made to protest.

'It's okay, whatever. I'll just come out with it. Mads? I'm in a situation. And I've been too scared to tell you . . . because I'm terrified you'll get upset. I had planned to write you an email this week, but I guess I should just come out with it now.'

She shot a micro-glare at Abby.

Mads's eyes were now the size of limes. 'Well you've terrified me with that introduction – what the hell is going on? Are you sick? Do you need a vital organ? I'll give you whatever you need—'

Chelsea rearranged herself on the sofa so that her legs were straight in front and her hands clasped in her lap. It was unsettling seeing ferocious, bold Chelsea become small and anxious, like watching a WWE wrestler picking daisies.

'It's, well, I've fucked up basically,' she said, solemnly.

A deep breath and then: 'I'm pregnant, Mads. I'm two months' pregnant.' Chelsea ran her fingers over her hair, smoothing it nervously, repetitiously. 'It was an accident . . . Jeremy wants to keep it, but I don't know if I do.'

Mads's face went white; her eyes cool and lifeless, both hands covered her mouth in shock. Abby's instinct was to get up and comfort her, but she wasn't sure if that was the right thing to do, considering Chels was also having a horrible time. She watched the scene unfold like the ghastly tragedy it was.

Mads's voice was small and muffled under her hands. 'You're, you're pregnant?'

Chelsea nodded slowly, despondently.

Abby sat up, fingernails jammed in her mouth, eyes zipping between the two women. She had no idea where this was heading, but it was safe to say it was several postcodes from where she thought it would.

'And, it was an accident,' Mads stated, her hands now cupped on her cheeks, her voice becoming stronger.

'Yes, bu—'

'And, let me get this straight, you're,' Mads raised her fingers up to make sarcastic quote marks, '*not sure if you want to keep it.*' There was poison in Mads's tone; her eyes had narrowed to become angry slits. Two green antennae bursting out of her scalp would've been less unusual than this seething, simmering rage.

Chelsea knew better than to utter a word. She'd known Mads would be upset, but she had no idea she'd reach this level, and at such warp speed. So she just sat there, blinking, waiting for the verbal violence.

Mads suddenly stood up and walked to the table, then back to the rug, then back to the dining table, where she rested her hands on the back of a chair and tried to gather her thoughts. Finally, she looked up, and at Chelsea.

'Do you even KNOW how much a throwaway sentence like that hurts me?'

Her eyes were glazed with tears, but her voice remained strong.

'I mean, would it have KILLED you to at least fucking pretend to want the baby, knowing the horrific time I've been through try-ing to conceive? I could be happy for you, I could be genuinely happy for your pregnancy, if you didn't have to pretend like it was a FUCKING HASSLE, Chels. "You're not sure if you want to keep it?!" I mean, give me a godamn fucking break . . .' Mads shook her head, breathing heavily, gathering strength for her next tirade.

Chelsea became smaller and smaller on the lounge, pulling into herself, trying to, Abby presumed, slip through the crack in the cushions and disappear. She wasn't going to say a thing, and she couldn't. Mads's pain and anger vibrated from every cell in her body; there was nothing that could be said to calm or appease her.

'It's so fucking typical, isn't it. You don't want a baby, have never wanted a baby, and you're handed one on a fucking platter without a whisper of effort or thought. I, on the other hand, want for nothing more in this world than a baby, and I cannot, no matter how ravaged my body or marriage become, fall pregnant.' As she spat her words at Chelsea, she crossed her arms and her eyes became small and glazed.

'It's just textbook fucking Chelsea Patton, isn't it.'

'I realise you're very upset, Mads, and with all of my heart I am sorry. I am genuinely and deeply sorry for how I delivered this news. And it breaks my heart that you can't conceive, of course it does, you're like a sister to me, I hate seeing you so sad and feel so helpless—'

Mads mumbled something inaudible and shook her head. Chelsea ignored her, battling on with her monologue.

'But, and none of this takes away from what you're feeling, of course it doesn't, but can you appreciate this is a bit fucked for me too? I've—'

'Don't you DARE try to make this about woe is you, oh, your poor life,' Mads said, warningly.

'Mads? I heard you out, now you hear *me* out,' Chelsea was gathering momentum; Abby was becoming more and more terrified for her wellbeing with every word she spoke. It didn't happen more than a few times a decade, but when Mads lost her shit, she wrapped it in camouflage and tossed it into the Amazon Jungle.

'I am in a new relationship, and I am pregnant. The man who wants to have this baby with me already has a wife and a kid, and he seems to have left them without too much thought. All of that of course is on top of the guilt I feel even being pregnant knowing what you've been through, and, you know, your situation . . .' She rubbed her forehead awkwardly, clearly wanting to skip that part. 'But who's to say he won't get bored of *this* family in a couple of years?' Chelsea's eyes were glassy and full of anxiety. 'It's hardly a silver fucking platter, Mads.'

She wiped a tear from her eye, which Abby gratefully took as her cue to stand up and get a box of tissues from the bathroom. She prayed there would be no punches thrown in her absence.

When she came back into the room, offering the box to Mads, who had taken a seat at the table, and then to Chelsea, who hugged her knees in close on the sofa, both were quietly sniffing and wiping under their eyes, but neither of them took one. Abby set the box on the coffee table; placed her hands on her hips and looked at her two friends with sadness.

'Guys. I think that maybe—'

'Do you know what, Mads? I would have this baby and hand it over to you in the delivery room if I could.' Chelsea looked at Mads, who refused to look back at her, shaking her head sadly instead.

'Oh don't be godamn histrionic. And fucking moronic.'

'I mean it.'

Mads snapped her head up to face Chelsea. 'Oh, yeah okay, Chels, great idea. Hey, why don't I call Dylan *right now* and tell him everything's sorted, I found a baby in my friend's belly that we can have!'

She was about to go nuclear. Abby needed to step up.

'*Okay!* Enough. Come on, we're all adults,' Abby said, not entirely sure that they were.

'It's impossible to get through to Mads when she's so upse—' Chelsea started, frustration beginning to seep in.

'I just need to be alone, actually,' Mads said decidedly, standing up to encourage their exit, her eyes locked on the floor.

Chels stood up, collecting her bag off the coffee table, looking wounded and shocked, like a little girl who'd just been told all the girls at school no longer liked her.

'Mads, can we please talk about this? I can't leave you being so upset . . .'

Mads was silent, head down, playing with a loose thread on the tablecloth.

'Chels, let's leave it for now. We love you, Madsy. We'll call you later.' Abby steered Chelsea, who was crying again, by the arm and together the two women walked out the front door.

Wide awake at 4.02 a.m., Abby walked from the bedroom to the kitchen for a glass of water, peeking into the office as she did, which Charlie had been working from so diligently in her absence. It was, like the rest of the house, absolutely pristine.

Desperate for a mental distraction following the scene at Mads's and the consequent vent session with Chelsea directly afterwards, Abby lay in bed and composed a long email to Sean on her laptop. Then she wrote an epic one to her mother, describing her trip, and the numerous trinkets she wanted to present her with this weekend. Still sleep evaded her. Desperate for slumber and incredibly bored, Abby began mentally composing the perfect, nonchalant text to Marcus, who she had decided was not only completely over her, but probably already seeing some 21-year-old honey. It seared Abby's heart to think of him out partying, having gorgeous, no-strings sex with cool, hot girls who looked like they'd just stepped out of *Nylon* magazine. Her whole Alessandro thing somehow didn't count by comparison, and anyway, Marcus would *never* know about him. Abby knew it was in bad taste to want to make him jealous, but being in good taste seemed so ineffective by contrast.

Abby took her phone off the bedside table and started tapping out drafts.

> Marcus, how are you? I was wondering if you were around
> this wee

No. Too dull.

> If a lady were to ask a gentleman for a coffee this weekend,
> would a gentleman be available and/or interested?

Too friendly. And jokey.

> If my number hasn't been changed to 'ignore and delete'
> in your phone, and you decide to read this and respond,
> would you maybe meet me for a co

Awful. Too convoluted and quasi-self deprecating.

> My fingers are sore from drafting clever versions of this
> text, so: I'd love to catch up with you, is a coffee possible in
> the next few days?
> Honest, Australia.

Fuck it. Abby hit send, momentarily forgetting it was 5.30 a.m. and he might very well think she was out and boozed and thus reasonable to ignore, then switched her phone to silent, so she didn't listen for its bzzz all night like a psychotic girl waiting for a text from the guy she's into, despite being precisely that. Abby was disappointed she still needed to do such things at her age, wasn't all of that gamey stuff and torture meant to have ended in your twenties? Abby lay in bed, eyes blinking in the darkness, waiting in vain for sleep to flow over her.

36

'And that's how I accidentally got CashCard as a client.'

Charlie looked genuinely bemused as she relayed the story of landing an enormous gig for Allure, purely by chatting to a nice old man at the bar, while she waited for her boyfriend at a Caribbean luncheonette. Once Abby had finished teasing Charlie for being such a hipster that she ate at a 'Caribbean luncheonette' she swamped her business partner with praise.

'Charlie, do you even know how many pies those guys have their paws in? Sport and concerts and the te—'

'I know,' Charlie interrupted. 'Lawrence said he's keeping on some other agency as well, for some things, thinks they're more an actual modelling agency or something, but he definitely wants our girls for like, VIP golf days, or the celebrity box at the football, or – you'll love this – playing hostess at one of the million concerts they sponsor. He was using Elite models, but said that the girls were always too precious to actually *do* anything, like serve drinks, or chat, or smile.'

'Well, what great news to come back to. Charlie, you're just terrific.'

Abby's phone buzzed.

I think I can manage that, yes. How's tomorrow at 11 at Alfies?

Marcus! The lack of kisses and friendliness was a kick in the shins, but Abby had to remember the actual situation, and not the one she coveted. She asked Charlie to hold that thought for one moment, and frantically replied.

Perfect. And thank you.

She almost added 'I'll wear my lobster suit so you recognise me', but thought it might be pushing it. He was still upset with her. Probably didn't want any of her terrific jokes at this stage. Excitement squelched through her arteries.

'Sorry, go on,' Abby said, grinning at Charlie.

'Less awesome news is that I lost a few girls . . . Does that happen a lot? I was kind of scared to tell you.'

'Any of the good ones?'

'Uhhh, there was Jacqui . . . and Amy, who had only done about two shifts, decided it "wasn't for her". Oh, and Tara.'

'*Really?* Jacqui? And Tara? Shit. That bites. Do we know why?'

'Didn't say.' Charlie's eyebrows and shoulders were up.

'That's weird that they wouldn't say why . . . Oh well. It happens, I guess. Three is a lot, though.'

'Did I do something wrong?' Charlie sounded defensive rather then apologetic.

'Oh, no, no . . . Did we get any gains?'

'A few nearlies, but not quite Allure standards, I'm afraid.'

That was a bit odd, Abby thought. They were getting almost twenty applications a week when she left. And good ones, too.

'Oh. Okay then, well I'll go through any new submissions today.'

'Also, uh, we kind of lost the Tag Heuer account to Faces.'

'You're shitting me,' Abby said in disbelief. Tag Heuer had been a constant and pleasant client for over twelve months. Why would they have switched all of a sudden? Maybe leaving Charlie here alone wasn't the world's greatest idea after all; things were falling apart.

'Di didn't say . . . was really weird actually. Must be a money thing. We *are* kind of expensive, I guess. Anyway, I've got a meeting now, but maybe we can get lunch after?'

Abby prickled at Charlie's comment about Allure being expensive. Also it was very strange that Di didn't send her an email and just left like that. Abby had a fantastic relationship with her.

'Did Di email about it, or—'

'Oh, it was all on the phone, unfortunately. You know how she loves a chat, all darl this, darl that . . .' Charlie was speaking rapidly, and busying herself looking for something in her bag.

'So strange . . . I should call her—'

'Oh, so no point; trust me. I tried.' Charlie's intonation signalled the end of the conversation. 'So, lunch? Moko's?'

'Yeah, cool, sounds good,' Abby was in a daze.

'Sorry again about Tag. Hopefully CashCard will triple what she gave us.'

Charlie smiled at Abby and swivelled back round to her laptop, which she packed into its sleeve, popping her Chloé messenger bag over her shoulder and standing up.

'Oh, hey, before you go, you haven't seen my two little Hermès bangles at all have you? I can't find them ANYWHERE and it's doing my head in.'

'No . . . Sorry, you sure you didn't take them to Italy?'

'Yeah, no . . . I remember almost taking them but then thinking

I'd lose them so I left them here, in the bathroom I thought . . . Oh well, I'll find them.'

'I'll help you look later,' Charlie flashed a smile and powered out of Abby's house, and Abby was left alone, to wonder why she felt like her own company had run away from her, and scold her brain every three minutes or so for sneaking over to the area marked 'Marcus', when it was told in no uncertain terms to sit on the grassed area marked 'Allure'. She called both Chelsea and Mads, but neither answered. She'd give them one more day, she decided, then she was going in.

At 11.03 the next morning, Abby walked into Alfies wearing a sleeveless olive green silk dress she'd picked up at D&G and her tan trench coat. She was a little bit cold, and her new suede heels were a little bit ruined, and her hair was a little bit demented from the pouring rain, but she was unflappable, because she was seeing Marcus today. She was sure she looked decent, but it was actually her giggly smile and the glint in her eyes that raised her above the commoners today. Abby was vibrating with excitement and nerves, unsure of what new information she would possess in an hour's time.

Marcus was seated already, one ankle resting on a knee, tapping away on his phone. It was a scene Abby wished she could freeze in time, not just because Marcus was looking dishy with his scruffy hair and an almost-beard and a sexy, high-necked black coat, but because if things went badly today, this was the last moment she didn't know that, and she still had some hope.

'Good morning,' Abby stood awkwardly at the table, wondering whether this was a kiss hello or sit straight down moment. She started to remove her jacket for something to do, when Marcus stood up, his eyes taking her in appreciatively, and kissed her on the cheek. His smile was weak, nowhere near as dazzling as the one Abby was used to, but she pretended not to notice.

'Hey there . . . Italy sits well with you, huh? Most people come back looking like gnocchi . . . you look more like a little grissini.'

Abby laughed, luxuriating in his compliment as she placed her jacket on the back of her chair and sat down. She prayed he couldn't see her fingers shaking. Men don't compliment women unless they are attracted to them, right? No, of course not.

'Thank you . . . Have you ordered a coffee yet?' Abby's mind was hyperventilating with anxiety and fantasy and it was making it hard for her mouth to do its job.

'Yes, and yours – soy capp, yes?'

Abby's insides melted a little. He was so considerate. How could she have forgotten how thoughtful he was?

'Perfect . . . Thank you.' she cleared her throat, trying to clear some of the nerves with it. 'So how are you, what's happening?'

'Yeah, really good, thanks . . . work is still work, but that's to be expected. Nothing else super-exciting going on, really . . . But who cares about me; how was Italy? What are the headlines?'

Oh, you know, thought Abby, ate some fettuccine, drank some wine, saw some statues, hooked up with some guy for a week of it, an older guy, who's successful, experienced and self-assured, just like you always said I would probably end up with, but that's not the point, he wasn't for me. *You are,* Marcus, you are. Now TELL ME YOU WANT ME BACK THIS SECOND.

'It was pretty special,' Abby said, finally. 'It was a bit strange being alone for so long, but there were so many places to see, and things to do, galleries and teeny gelato shops with queues ten deep, and field trips to beautiful vineyards and, you know, I was working the whole time as well, so I definitely wasn't bored, and th—'

'Any epiphanies? Life-changing moments?' Marcus didn't realise his offhand question was the entrée to a very heavy main course.

Abby paused, biting her lip. Well yes, Marcus, if you must know, there was one, and it concerns you. Abby took a quick breath and decided to leap. These platitudes were killing her. And coffee would only send her even further into a jittery spiral. The time to come clean was now. *Now.* Abby exhaled theatrically.

'Funnily enough, yes in a way. I did.' Embarrassingly, her voice broke like a wimpy, pimply teen. Marcus's expression turned to one of concern.

'Are you okay, Abs?'

His kindness almost set off the ludicrous tears of anxiety and nervous energy and jet lag that were perched in her already glassy eyes. She took another deep breath. This was getting preposterous. This was not telling someone they had cancer, it was telling her ex-boyfriend she'd made a mistake and wanted to try again.

'Marcus, I missed you. I *miss* you. I thought of you, without exception, every single day I was away from you. I wrote a thousand emails and texts to you that I never sent, and I imagined you being there with me non-stop. It killed me that you never contacted me, even though I know I didn't deserve it, and I know it's not "cool" to admit that, but I don't want to play games, Marcus. You deserve honesty and you deserve respect and I hope that by telling you all of this, you feel you're getting that.'

'Long black; soy capp.' The heavily eye-lined waitress placed two coffees on the table.

Abby ran clammy fingers through her hair. 'I know this is full-on, and I could've perhaps done it a better way, but I wanted to do it in person, and man up, because I need to tell you that I apologise. I severed something beautiful that I sincerely wish I could resurrect.'

'Jesus, Abs. Not here to talk about the weather, are you?' Marcus blew air through his mouth in a silent whistle, his eyes showing apprehension and mild incredulity. He stirred sugar into his coffee slowly, his head shaking almost imperceptibly.

'Marcus, I'm sorry for just dumping it on you like this. And look, you don't need to say anything now. I just, selfishly I suppose, wanted to let you know how I'm feeling, and you can do with that information as you please.'

A lengthy silence, and then Marcus, still looking down, said, 'I'm not sure I can do anything with it, Abby.'

The soundtrack Abby's brain had supplied to the conversation suddenly changed from one that hinted of optimistic, romantic conclusions, to one that pre-empted disaster. Abby sensed that all of the guts she had spilled on that little café table were about to be swiftly swept onto the floor, and into the bin.

'I thought about you while you were away, of course I did, and I considered contacting you, but I didn't Abby, and that's because you hurt me, you know? I was really fucking hurt.'

Abby sat stunned, unable to move, and very, *very* disenchanted with where this was all heading.

'Abby, I'm sorry, but right now I can't— this won't— it'd be wrong to start anything up with you again.'

An invisible heavy-weight boxer punched Abby in the stomach, rendering her unable to breathe, see, comprehend. Then suddenly, clarity: 'You're seeing someone,' Abby said, dead-faced.

'*No!* No,' Marcus said, quickly. 'You told me, Abby, that I needed to be young and free and travel and live a bit, remember? That was massively offensive, as I told you then, and I will tell you again now. But on some level, well,' he looked around, as though hoping to find his script on the specials blackboard, 'I guess there was an element of truth to it . . . I *am* twenty-two . . . I *am* young. I am in a good position and stage of my life to be a bit loose and a bit free.'

Abby crossed her legs and arms in sync, not realising she

instantly gave away her anger in doing so. She loved being right, but if she decided her original perspective was incorrect, she preferred to be wrong.

'So let me get this straight,' Abby said. 'You now *agree* with what I said, but you're still angry with me?'

'It's not as black and white as that, Abs. When you get dumped because the woman you've fallen in love with believes you should be out there having fun, and then never contacts you again, well after a while, I guess you start to start to think she was right.'

'Unfuckingbelieveable,' Abby muttered and shook her head, a grimace of astonishment on her face.

'You realise you can't be pissed at me over this, right? It was YOU who planted the seed in the first place and—'

'I'm *not* pissed.'

Marcus leaned forward to rest his elbows on the table, trying in vain to lock Abby's eyes onto his, but she refused to look at him for longer than a few seconds at a time. He, on other hand, was calm and cool-headed. The irony of Abby's childishness was not lost on her.

'Abby, I was crushed. You know I took us a lot more seriously than you did. So I thought a lot about where we're both at, and what you'd said, and I spoke to Chris and he really helped me get some perspective an——'

'Oh, of *couuuurse* Chris was there for you. I'm sure he had a harem of twenty year olds just chomping at the bit to meet you.' Abby was being vitriolic and horrible, but she couldn't stop the words firing from her mouth. She'd always thought Chris had too much influence over Marcus. Of course, if she were honest with herself, it was nothing more than insecurity on her behalf that Chris would eventually tell Marcus he could do better than Abby.

Marcus was doing that thing he did when Abby was flying off

handles. Which was to sit quietly, looking at her, waiting for her to calm down.

Abby sighed. 'I'm sorry. That was an awful thing to say. I'm sorry. I know how big a role Chris plays in your life.'

'No, I don't think you do. He's pretty much a father to me, Abby. And for the record, Chris actually said I should chase you. He saw how miserable I was.'

Abby was immeasurably glad she hadn't said anything more about Chris. Especially since, amazingly, it sounded like he was in her corner. For once in her life, Abby Vaughn had no idea what to say.

'Anyway, that's all beside the point. Abs, I'm just— I think I need to stay on this path for now. I'm going to travel a bit before the end of the year and maybe take on a project with Caleb which will take up all my time anyway and . . .' His sentence petered out to silence.

Tears trickled into Abby's eyes, and hollowness spread through her body. Marcus meant it. He really meant it.

'Abby, are you okay?'

She looked around the café, buzzing with happy, slurping people having high-spirited, creative meetings, and she wanted to throw her shoe at them. She took a quick breath in and cleared her throat.

'I'm fine, well, I will be. You've made up your mind, there's nothing else I can say. I can see that. I fucked it all up. And I— it was— I never— Forget it, I should go.' She pushed her chair back and stood up.

'Abby, you can't do that, please tell me what you were going to say, come on. There's no need to be so dramatic.'

'I don't see the point, Marcus. You know how I feel, I know how you feel, and it's all just a bit gutting, to be honest. Let's keep with the no contact, okay? It's not useful for either of us to stay in touch.'

Marcus was looking at Abby with broken eyes, knowing how much pain he was putting her though, momentarily forgetting she'd pushed him down the exact same slippery slide five weeks earlier. And as she put her coat over the body he'd fantasised about constantly for months and walked away, his mind was furiously trying to confirm he'd done the right thing.

37

Feel like I'm leaping off the fucking cliff w no parachute:
I'm having a baby, I've moved and I have a stepson –HOW
DID THIS HAPPEN??? W the fuck happened to my life???
Seriously!!

Mads still won't speak to me. I've called emailed text . . . I
even left a letter in her mailbox --- nothing.

Its been 3 weeks now and not one word from her

Abby had never witnessed Chels admit things were out of her control, it was like hearing a librarian asking everyone to please talk louder. But her single, sassy, flashy life had indeed been flipped on its pretty, blow-dried head.

Honey, I know you're scared and freaking out. But you know everything will work out, right? *Of course it will.* You are Chelsea fucking Patton. Everything always comes up rosy for you. It's your thing. You've made these decisions because they felt right, in your gut or heart or big toe, so have faith in them. Jeremy is a <u>GOOD EGG.</u> He will support you. He loves you. It will be a "journey", but you'll get through it together . . . And don't forget, you are bringing a new human being into the world! This is a very happy and exciting time of your life! Please remember that, honey, it's important that your little belly human can feel your love. And sorry to be a downer but you gotta remember how much some people would give for this privilege . . .

I'm here for you, as always, whenever. Can come over tonight it you want for Thai and a walk?

Mads will thaw out. She's just in pain. And it's not you she's angry with, it's the situation.

I'll call her now. My two broken friends need to be fixed. xxxx

Ps As a bit of cold comfort: Marcus still hasn't made any contact. Since when did we become so unpopular?? It's so over. Schooled by a kid! Touché.

To: Abs work email
From: Chelsea Patton

Make her talk to me again pls. asap.

You know the kid is playing you, right? Giving you a taste of ur own. You held all the cards and don't forget you dumped HIM. Let him feel like he's in power for a bit n he'll come back. Trust me --- I know men. xc

It was surprisingly good advice from Chelsea. Maybe Marcus was just letting Abby sweat for a bit. She was suddenly overwhelmed by a wave of missing him: that she might never lie in bed with him at night, or never feel him kiss the back of her neck as she slept, or see him perform intoxicated, hilarious acrobatics with salt shakers at a restaurant table. She took a deep breath and steadied her head by placing it between her hands on the table. She was not as strong as she thought she was. She *had* treated Marcus badly. She deserved to feel pain and melancholy. She was emotionally dyslexic, and it had taken a man ten years younger than her to expose her. In the only show of strength she could muster, she went onto Facebook and, trying not to notice the new profile picture of him looking ridiculous climbing up a palm tree somewhere hot and delicious, deleted him as a friend. Should've done it ages ago, she chided herself, but still felt secretly smug that she'd beaten him to it. It was amazing what time and the deafening sound of no contact from him could do. She had, in the days following their coffee at Alfie's, expected him to come back to her. Clearly she was prone to both reckless opti-mism and megalomaniac tendencies, because aside from a polite text on the day they'd met, saying he was sorry to upset her, and it was great to see her and bullshit, bullshit, bullshit; nothing. It still made Abby a bit angry, but it didn't make her sad. And she was proud of her strength: She hadn't called him drunk, she hadn't stalked his Facebook, and she hadn't even sent him any transpar-ent, I'm-totally-fine-with-this-have-a-great-life texts. In a funny way, the anger helped, propelling her through, reminding her to have an Excellent Life because he sure as hell was, and that to waste any more time thinking about him was preposterous. After all, he was just a *kid*. Even he'd admitted it in the end.

Abby called Mads, but she did not answer her phone. Abby would go around there tonight, like Dylan had suggested. They'd had a long email back and forth and he was not coping too well, no one was – they'd never seen Mads in such a funk. Well, thought Abby, in every friendship there came a time when a good friend pulled a sad friend out of her slump. And tonight was it.

Two hours later, Abby looked around the flower market, searching for Charlie. They had to choose a floral theme for the girls to wear in their hair and around their wrists and necks for a new designer swimsuit boutique launch tomorrow night.

Abby saw Charlie, looking cool and effortless in flat ankle boots and a short cream lace dress, poring over some freesias, and walked over.

'Hey, Charlie!'

Charlie turned around, hand on her heart, eyes closed.

'You scared the godamn pancreas out of me . . .' She caught her breath and smiled. 'How's tricks?'

'Yeah, good thanks. Hey, I was thinking orchids. Do they have any?'

'Mm-hmm. Not that I've seen so far.'

The two girls walked around the stands slowly, smelling different blooms, bunching small flowers together to get an idea of the final look.

'Oh, hey, someone on Skype was calling yesterday afternoon while you were out; I forgot to tell you. Rang a few times actually.'

Abby smiled. 'I think I know who that might have been.' She realised with interest that Alessandro's contact was now exciting to her. For the first week or two after returning Abby was polite and friendly in her responses, but not what you'd call 'encouraging', or 'at all interested'. She hoped it wasn't purely an exercise in ego boosting.

'Will Smith?'

'Sadly no. I had a bit of a thing with this Italian guy while I was over there. We've been Skyping a bit.' Abby smiled as they stood

behind a heavily pregnant woman choosing lilies. Apparently someone had forgotten to tell her baby it needed to eventually leave the
uterus, because it appeared to already be the size of a two year old.

'*Reeeeally!*' Charlie said, a grin on her face, her eyes wide. 'Has
it got any legs?' she asked, as she held some white lilies alongside
deep magenta orchids.

'I don't know,' said Abby, as she trailed behind Charlie. 'We just
chat about life, work . . . the time difference is killer. I'm at least a
glass of wine down because it's evening for me, but it's his *morning*.'

'Boners are always biggest in the morning. So what's the point
of it all? Will he come out for a summer romance? Will you ride red
Vespas and eat gelato every day?'

'Maybe . . . He has some cousin out here and keeps hinting he
might come visit him. Not me, of course. Him.'

'Ciao Abby, it's Luigi, I'ma ata the airport! Are you free for some
pizza and maybe soma garlic breada too?'

Abby laughed at Charlie's atrocious accent. 'I don't think he'll
visit. Honestly.'

'Do you like him?'

'I have *fondness* for him, I guess, yeah.'

Charlie, gripping several bunches of bright flowers, was nearing
both the end of the foliage hunt, and patience.

'Well with things finished with Marcus, you're free to be fond of
whoever you wish,' she said, distractedly.

'Mmm.' Abby held a small posy of dusty pink David Austin roses
to her face and inhaled their deliciousness before placing them
back carefully. She remembered how Alessandro had brought her
flowers when they were in Florence, three bunches: one each for
the bathroom, bedroom and lounge room, so that she 'saw beauty
wherever she was'. He really was incredibly charming, Abby realised. Maybe she *should* encourage him to visit, what harm could it

do? No. No, no, no, she confirmed: You can't revive a summer fling. It's a big fat triangle that never fits into the Real Life circle.

'These are definitely the winners, aren't they?' Abby nodded and Charlie placed the blooms on the counter, and the florist began stripping and snipping the deep pink, orange, white and red blooms they'd be adorning the girls with tomorrow.

'*Charlie!* Hi!' An attractive woman in dark jeans and navy striped top called to Charlie, waving. It was Diane Grove, from Tag.

Charlie looked startled. 'Diane, hi,' she said weakly.

'Di! *Hi!*' Abby moved into Diane's vision and went in for a hello kiss.

'Oh, Abby, hi . . .' Di was stiff and awkward, seemingly forgetting that you need to lean in and offer a cheek for a hello kiss. How bizarre, Abby thought. Probably just felt bad about leaving the agency, she thought. Fair enough.

'How's things?' Abby beamed at Di, gearing up to mischievously woo her back to Allure in a few well-constructed sentences.

'Oh, good, thanks . . .'

'You're already missing us, aren't you?' Abby said, cheekily, grinning like a drunk.

A look of puzzlement spread over Diane's face. 'But I haven't—'

'Sweet tropical breezes, would you *look* at this guy!' Charlie squealed loudly, bending down to pat Diane's ludicrous French bulldog.

The hair on Abby's arms stood on end. Something strange was going on. Abby looked at Di, who looked equally confused. Abby decided to dive in. If she was being fucked over, she wanted to figure it out now.

'So, how's it all going over at Faces?'

If Diane was tipsy with confusion before, she was now bordering on shitfaced.

'Abby, I'm sorry . . . but I don't quite know what you're talking about—'

Charlie bounced back up, a psychotic smile on her face.

'Di, it was lovely seeing you, we have to go unfortunately, but it was really great running into you.' She threw eighty dollars down onto the florist's bench, picked up the bundles of flowers and grabbed Abby by the arm to lead her away. Di was left standing, mouth agape, eyebrows furrowed in bafflement.

Abby allowed herself to be dragged ten metres before planting her feet down and shaking Charlie's grip off.

'Okay, what was that? What just happened?'

'Nothing! I mean, *you* know Di . . .' Charlie said, rolling her eyes and shaking her head as though Di had just caused a scene, which was perfectly normal, and everything was cool.

'Yeah, I do, and that was not regular Di just there.'

'I guess it's weird seeing you because she left Allu—'

'Do you think I suffer from arrested development, Charlie? What's going on?' Abby's voice had become slightly shrill and blood was rushing to her head as though it were an exit in a fire. She looked at Charlie like she was faced with a stranger.

Charlie switched the flowers from one arm to the other and sighed. 'Abby, you're over-reacting. It's just the usual ex-client stuff.'

'So why was she so thrilled to see *you*?'

'Uh, she was the same with you, Abs.' A hint of insolence crept into Charlie's voice.

'Were you wearing a blindfold and headphones? She was terrified of me! Charlie, just please, whatever you've done, we can work it out.'

Abby stared at Charlie, who gazed back at her with a look of perfect calm.

'It's honestly nothing. I just, well – to be honest? – I think she was annoyed you were overseas for so long, and so I tried to calm her down, which is why she's still cool with me. Abby, I'm sorry. But I had so much going on and it was just easier to kiss her arse and send her off nicely, you know? Rather than bother you with it while you were on holiday—'

'I *wasn't* on holiday,' Abby said through clenched teeth. 'I was working the entire time, you know that. She could've— *should've* emailed or called me. I have no idea why she didn't, and I gotta say it shits me that you didn't involve me.' Abby sighed and frowned at her business partner. Something was still amiss, but Charlie wasn't going to give anything away. Abby would simply contact Di herself tomorrow.

'I wouldn't contact Di, probably. She's still a bit pissed.'

Nice try, doll, Abby thought. 'Hey, I've gotta go, are you right with those flowers? Or shall I take them?'

'Um, no, it's fine, I'll take them . . . Hey Abs, are we cool?' Charlie's elfin face was the picture of concern, but Abby wasn't interested.

'Yeah, course. Okay, I've gotta go, see you at mine in the morning.'

As Abby walked away, her intuition buzzing wildly that all was not well, she started to wonder if she knew who Charlie Fennessy was at all. And just how awesome a decision it had been to let her into her business and home.

38

'I'm *exceptionally* impressed with how Allure is tracking, Abby.' Rob sat across from Abby in his jeans, Converse and crisp white t-shirt and sipped on his coffee as he looked over her figures on his laptop. He was looking even fitter than usual, Abby thought, but then, she thought every man was looking fitter than usual, because she was in a dry spell.

'And if you ever let Charlie go, I will personally fine you five thousand dollars.'

'Yeah, she's been great . . .' Abby said as enthusiastically as she could muster. She held her tongue regarding Charlie's 'brilliance' while Rob went on about how she had attracted 30 per cent new business since coming on board, which not only made Abby feel jealous and territorial, but desperate to know what Charlie had been doing that wasn't accounted for on spreadsheets.

'See, that's what I'm talking about,' he said, scrolling down spreadsheets, shaking his head, 'That's the golden rule: 20 per cent of your clients will bring in 80 per cent of your income, and right now, that client is CashCard.'

He was right about CashCard: The girls had been extremely

busy with their new client who, like most clients with a lot of money and little interest in reality, wanted the prettiest girls every single gig, of which there were three a weekend, and because they paid more than any other client the girls always wanted to work for them. That Sabrina had met her now-boyfriend – handsome, clean-cut, wealthy Formula One race car driver, Alex Lanbery – while working for CashCard, had poured through the ranks of Allure like spilled tea onto a keyboard, and now every Allure girl wanted to work the CashCard gigs. Some had even requested their photos be changed on the Allure site to better reflect their looks, and some had told the CashCard regulars to call them if they ever couldn't make it, even at the last minute. It was sickening, but as Rob pointed out, it was lucrative.

'Well, I've gotta get going, Abby: I'm off to an accounting convention.'

'That's bound to keep you on the edge of your sleep.'

Rob laughed. 'Was there anything else you needed for now?'

Abby smiled tightly, wondering if this would be the moment she'd look back on as the chance she had to tell Rob about her suspicions of Charlie, and potentially save her business from being completely ruined or extorted.

'Nah, I'm good. Have fun with your number nerds.'

'I will, trust me,' he smiled, and then walked quickly out of the café.

Abby remained at the café, enjoying the warmth of the sun on her back and the flavours of her coffee, and composed an email to Chelsea, imploring her to physically go to Mads's home and sort things out. Abby had met Mads for Japanese last night, and as was now customary when the topic of Chelsea was brought up, Mads had gone mute, and refused to engage. Abby had never seen her friend so bitter, so angry; so interested in drinking vodka on the rocks. Both girls needed each other's support; this stand off was starting to become farcical. And Abby didn't have the energy to play desperate mediator any longer.

At 11.30 a.m. Abby walked into her home to hear Charlie talking animatedly on the phone. Abby walked past the office and into the lounge room to dump her bag, and saw a bouquet of David Austin roses perched in the centre of the coffee table. Obviously a make-good present from Charlie. How funny she'd chosen the exact flowers Abby loved; Abby couldn't recall ever having told her they were her favourite. Back in the office, Charlie was wearing a bright red jumper over a white Peter Pan collar, a black leather skirt and black patent brogues.

'Hey,' Abby greeted Charlie absently once Charlie had hung up the call. She hadn't been able to get through to Diane yet, and unearth whatever it was that Charlie had done, so until then things would remain civil.

'Morning!' A triple-sized smile from Charlie.

'And check this.' Charlie produced twenty-five stunning little headpieces made of flowers for the girls to wear at that evening's event.

'Wow . . . They're pretty spectacular,' Abby said, standing up to look at them.

'Thanks; stayed up watching *Girls Just Wanna Have Fun* making them. Craft and eighties movies: Stereotypes 101. Oh, hey I just got off the phone from this girl called Jean I met out last week, she's this cute jewellery designer with some football hero boyfriend whose team plays at Southfield stadium. She reckons we can easily get the contract for the VIP box, because the girls they use now are atomic skanks.'

'Must be the one club CashCard don't sponsor. Do we need to do anything?'

'I'm sending her links of some appropriate girls now. Holly will do it. So will Kate, if we up the hourly a little. And if they ever work out how to use the website.'

Was that a dig at the website or the girls? Abby wondered.

Suddenly, Charlie shook her head and covered her eyes with her hands. 'Oh fuck it, I'm rubbish at keeping things from you!'

Finally, Abby thought! She was going to reveal everything about Diane and Tag.

'I didn't even know whether to tell you this, and it's probably not even useful information, but I thou—'

Jesus. So dramatic, Abby thought.

'Come on, spit it out.' Abby smiled in what she hoped was a warm fashion.

Charlie exhaled. 'I saw Marcus last week.'

'Oh.' Abby's voice was as calm as a poker player's, but her heart was performing the kind of flips Russian gymnasts could only dream of. Just his name made her skittish. If Charlie had seen him last week, why was she only telling her now? They'd even talked about him yesterday. Charlie was fast losing her glimmer.

'Do you want to hear stuff about him? Be honest. Think before you answer. You're doing SO GREAT. And sometimes when you hear stuff it can set you—'

'Pssshhh. It was ages ago. We've both moved on. *Ohhhh*, he's moved *on*, moved on . . .'

'Well, I don't know. I mean, okay, well he was with a woman, and they were having breakfast . . . thing was, she was, um, a bit *older* than him.'

'Typical,' Abby snorted. 'So, were they together-together? Were they touching hands? Was she feeding him his hard-boiled egg soldiers?'

'I didn't pay enough attention. I just saw him sitting at a table with a woman. I'm sorry, Abs.' She gave Abby a wincing, apologetic look. It served to only further irritate Abby.

Abby crossed her arms. Fuck him.

'. . . Should I have spoken to him?'

'No, no, of course not.'

'For what it's worth, they weren't making out or anything.'

'It's fine, he's moved on. If he'd wanted to get in touch with me, he's had ages to do it. Every day, there are twenty-four hours, and in any one of those he could've taken three minutes to send a text or email, but he chose not to. So she was definitely older? Like, my age older? Or, you know, in her forties?'

'I would say . . . maybe mid-forties? She was quite fit-looking so it's hard to say.'

Abby sighed and slumped back onto her stool. She was irritated that Charlie had not revealed anything about Tag Heuer. And now she was annoyed at how much this Marcus information had affected her. She secretly thanked the Gods for Alessandro, who was the perfect diversion and pep up when she hit the occasional Single-Girl lows.

'The Italian will keep you distracted,' Charlie said, as if reading Abby's mind.

Abby gave a weak smile.

As Charlie walked out into the hallway, Abby took a moment to think about what she'd just learned. Marcus could jam it. Real men made contact. He was a kid. And this was over. Gone. He could enjoy his life chasing mid-life-crisis tail. Abby picked up her mobile and deleted his number once and for all. It felt tremendous. Then she searched for 'DIANE GROVE' and grabbed her handbag and keys.

'Just going to get coffee, you want?' Abby bellowed up the hallway.

'I'm sweet, but thanks!' Charlie hollered back from the bathroom.

And Abby set off to find out what exactly cute-as-a-kitten Charlie had been up to.

39

'Charlie's a *saboteur*? What, did she thieve the nuclear bomb you keep hidden in your underground lair?'

Mads was simultaneously alarmed and delighted. The Charlie stuff was exactly the kind of salacious distraction she needed. Mads and Abby were the only customers at Ricky's, a cosy café with shitty local art on the walls, deep second-hand sofas and incredible coffee and baklava. Abby had decided to mastermind a surprise Mads and Chels catch up. The war had gone on long enough. It was time to make things right.

Abby sadly noted that Mads still wasn't wearing any of her crystals around her neck. She had stopped wearing them after the blow-up with Chelsea, Dylan had said, because they were bullshit; the universe was as flawed and arbitrary as everyone had always told her it was. Hearing that had broken Abby's heart, but seeing the lack of colourful stone had been worse: Mads was giving up hope. Or already had.

'I think she is, yes. She's somehow taking Allure down while making it look like she's helping the business. I need a PI. I'm pretty sure she is stealing my clients. Sh—'

'But she's so charming and has such snappy dress sense! Although I suppose in accordance with popular spy cinema, most super-villains *are* extremely well-dressed . . .'

Abby was thrilled to hear Mads's effervescence and sense of mischief returning. Since Chelseagate Mads had hit an all-time low.

'I spoke to two of the clients she'd told me had moved on and neither said they knew anything about it, but that they had been told to deal directly with Charlie from now on, and Charlie only. Why would she do that? It makes no sense, unless she is secretly one day going to reveal to them all she has her OWN AGENCY and they should all stay with her, and not Allure.'

Mads's eyes were wide in disbelief.

'I also think she's stealing my girls,' Abby said as she sipped her tea. 'She said we had no admissions the whole time I was in Italy, which is total nonsense, we'd been getting almost two dozen a week when I left. But because she has access to the back end of the site, I think she was going in and erasing their applications – after taking down all their details, of course – before I even had a chance to see them. Now not only do I have no idea how to tell her I know what she's been up to, but I've just lost my only employee. A really fuckin' good one, too. Well, sabotage aside.'

Mads leaned over her ankles and adjusted the buckle on her Mary Jane heels as she spoke.

'Get what you just told me in writing from one of those clients and forward it to her. Make the subject line: *You're fired.* Easy. As for staff, hire a temp. Find someone from an agency and let her look after all the admin rubbish while you do the Big Girl stuff.' She flicked back up, her face flushed red, a problem-solved expression on her face.

Mads had a point, two of them in fact. Abby wondered what Charlie would do once she'd been busted. Decapitated possums on the doorstep, perhaps. Abby looked at her phone nervously: 4.13. Chelsea was already thirteen minutes late, and Abby knew Mads had to leave soon. Abby peered towards the front of the café, and was amazed and terrified to see Chelsea pushing the door open at that exact second; scanning for Abby.

With deep strides and her signature hip-wiggling strut, she saw Abby and smiled as she got closer.

Then she saw Mads.

And Mads saw Chelsea.

Abby quickly stood up, hands palm down to both sides as a sign of peace and everyone relax and please, no scratching or biting.

Chelsea stopped dead, clutching her enormous snakeskin handbag in tight to her stomach, her eyes flitting between Abby and Mads wildly, trying to figure out if she should be flighty or fighty.

But it was Mads who decided for her; she stood up and slung her bag over her shoulder, glaring at Abby as she did so.

'*This* was a shitty plan, and *you* are a shitty friend,' Mads said to Abby, a look of disappointment on her face.

Chelsea immediately responded: 'Don't worry, I'll go.' As she turned on her heel to go, Abby's voice rang out shrilly through the café.

'*Guys!* Please, don't leave. You can't leave . . . Just, Chels, come on, sit down. COME ON. *Sit*. There.' Abby pointed to the seat next to her, which was directly opposite Mads.

Abby could see Mads's chest rise and fall as she quickly tried to calculate her next move.

'Mads, you too. Please. *Please?*'

'She won't stay,' Chels said, nodding her head told-you-so-ishly towards Mads. 'Hates me.'

Mads said nothing, her mouth was scrunched tightly, her head shaking rapidly, multiple exhales filing from her mouth.

'PLEASE, you two,' Abby pleaded, surprised to feel tears prickle in her eyes. 'Come on. Just five minutes is all I ask.'

Sensing Abby's desperation, Chels finally moved, walking haughtily towards Abby's couch.

'Well, I'll stay,' Chelsea said to Abby, nodding slowly. She looked directly at Mads. 'Because *I want to fix this*.'

She collapsed onto the sofa, sighing. A small bump was visible under her tight dress, which Abby hoped Mads wouldn't see straightaway. After sixty seconds of the kind of will-she-won't-she tension reality TV shows were built on, Mads gave in.

'Abby Vaughn, you are a treacherous witch,' Mads hissed, as she sat back on her sofa and crossed her arms and legs defensively.

'Thank you. I'm doing this because I love you both. And you can huff and puff all you want, but *you two need to talk*. You need to get through this. I'm sorry to deceive you into talki— Well, actually, no I'm not. Extreme measures for extreme circumstances.'

Abby looked at the two women, and was delighted to see Chelsea looking authentically engaged in what was going on – there was no BlackBerry in sight, just a serious, solemn woman sitting on a sofa looking as though she was preparing for a particularly intense chess game. Mads looked less involved, and much more fidgety. But at least she was still seated and present.

'I'm going to order you two some tea and then I'm leaving,' Abby said, as she picked up her bag. 'You *will* give all our years of friendship the respect it deserves by getting everything you need to out, okay? We all love and support each other, remember? We have to. You need each other right now. We all need each other, always. *Especially* when times get shitty.'

Chelsea was still staring at Mads, but now Mads was looking down, picking her deep plum nail polish off.

'Alright, alright, Pol Pot,' Mads uttered. 'We get it.'

Chelsea looked at Abby and rolled her eyes. 'Abs, we *get it.*'

'Okay, well, good luck. Bitch about me in my absence if it gets things moving.'

'Can't you stay, Abs? Despite your grotesque subterfuge, I want you here.' Mads looked up at her friend wistfully.

'I can't. I have to find out if Charlie's stabbing me in the business back.'

'Wha—?' Chelsea asked, frowning up at Abby.

'Long story, Mads can fill you in once you've kissed and made up. Okay, I will call you later. Please be nice to each other.'

Impressed with pulling off her dramatic coup, Abby turned and rushed out, mentally crossing her fingers that Mads and Chelsea would be at least civil to each other. Once she had walked the three thousand blocks to her car, her phone chimed with a text. If it were Mads or Chelsea saying they'd left, she'd be stomping straight back there to slap faces.

> Abby I know you wont believe this, but I am just landed in your city. Can I see you? A.

Oh, this HAD to be a joke.

It wasn't happening.

Couldn't be.

Not today.

Once, just once, Abby wanted to know what it felt like to have all of her balls up in the air at the same time without something fucking up or causing disruption and making the balls thud to the floor.

Abby re-read the text and the name attached to it. Just as Mads, Chelsea and even Charlie had predicted he might, Alessandro had done it, he had flown out to surprise her. Abby sat with the engine off in the driver's seat, one hand still held her phone, the other generously offering up a selection of fingernails to anxiously nibble. A woman pulled up aggressively beside her, using sign language and eyebrows to ask if Abby planned on leaving any time soon. Abby shook her head no, then quickly typed out a text.

Alessandro! Are you joking? Are you really in Sydney!?

Abby stared at her phone as though it were about to reveal the winning lotto numbers. It chimed. Abby inhaled and read her screen.

I arrive last nite to the 4 seasons. Can I take you to dinner tonite? 8 p.m.?

Abby's free hand flew up and slapped on top of her eyes. She was speechless, her head shaking like a small dog on the rear dash of a car. She *did* want to see him, but her almost heart-attack knowing he was in the same city seemed to suggest otherwise. It was a holiday fling! And holiday brain operates at around one-fifth of regular brain; holiday flings are senseless hook-ups, in the true meaning of the word.

To be fair, she had *probably* given him more of a signal of interest than she should've over Skype lately. But she liked the attention! And she was a bit lonely. Abby certainly didn't expect he would get on a bloody plane and fly out here to see her. No, Alessandro was obviously just here for work, or to visit his cousin, Abby confirmed to herself as she started the engine and pulled out.

At the next set of traffic lights Abby quickly punched out a text.

Of course Alessandro. I would love that. x

She looked at the time on her dash: 5.03. She wondered how the girls were going back at the café . . . She desperately wanted to tell them about Alessandro being here. She would have to wait till the three of them were all normal again: this freeze-out was so frustrating.

Abby didn't have time to further investigate Charlie now, either. And had dirty hair, hairy legs and a distressing bikini line.

'*Fuck,*' she said, summing it all up perfectly.

Despite usually requiring a month-ahead booking, Alessandro's concierge had secured them a late sitting at Bonsai. It might have been because it was a Tuesday; it might have been because Alessandro tipped like a homeless man with an imaginary hat, either way, the two of them now sat facing each other in the city's most exclusive restaurant.

Abby had met Alessandro at his hotel bar earlier, wearing a short, tight black dress that suggested she might take payment for sex, and a pair of heels that she'd always felt were too high until this very moment. She wasn't sure why she felt the dress code was 'Hot Twenty-one Year Old,' but evidently she was out to impress. Abby was loathe to admit it as she waited, but she couldn't stop thinking about Marcus seeing her with Alessandro. It was ridiculous and embarrassing to confess, even to her internal monologue. But Marcus would immediately assume that it was her boyfriend, and they were together. Like when Charlie told her about seeing Marcus with his cougar at breakfast, presumably after a night of over-the-top sex, fat-free whipped cream and episodes of *Mad About You*. Gross.

Alessandro had stood waiting for Abby in the lobby, looking astonishingly handsome. He'd cut his hair very short and had a short, sexy smattering of facial hair. He looked very, very good, in a Handsome Man In A Luxury Leather Goods Advertisement kind of way: dark charcoal pants and a black shirt. Abby's nerves skittered through her body when she saw him. She felt lucky that he was waiting for her. Smug even.

'I am the luckiest man in this city tonight,' he said as took her hands and pulled her in to kiss her on the mouth.

'*Welcome*, Alessandro!' Abby said, smiling widely as she pulled back.

'More.' He uttered the word so softly, so sexily, and came in gently to begin kissing Abby again, this time for longer, inciting memories of their first kiss in San Gimignano all those months ago.

Abby, aware that they were in a public place, took a deep breath in and pulled back again. He smelled so masculine, so captivating, and as she took in his smiling face she could sense new warmth in him. His mouth was stretched wide, his eyes twinkled – he seemed very, very happy to see her. She felt like a bitch for presuming he would show up in white shoes and silky, open shirts: He was a successful, intelligent, chic European man; he knew how to adapt to his environment! And what was the worst that could happen, anyway? He was only here for a week. She could, and would, enjoy his company for that period.

'You are more attractive than I remember,' Alessandro said, after gracefully inhaling a dozen oysters as his entrée. 'Attractive' was as good as it got from him, Abby remembered. This was a hyperbole-free zone.

'And you are more *surprisey* than I remember! So what is this trip here about, mister?'

'I come to see Federico.' Alessandro said, as he sipped on his whisky. 'He is making his business to grow, and he needs help, he almost lost a big deal last week and so I flew here to help. It is family; you must help. It is my first time here, but already I like. It is relaxed. People are your friend.'

Abby smiled, feeling relief that he hadn't come all this way to see her – knowing him he would never admit such a thing anyway – but it was also affection: what a generous and kind man he was. He really was. He might be missing the wit and playfulness of A Certain Other Person, but he was sexy and thoughtful. She would simply have to ensure their time over the next few days was *fun*; perhaps with him out of his comfort zone he'd be more gregarious. She certainly was, she thought, recalling going back to his place after knowing him for thirty-seven seconds. And then having sex with him on his stairs.

'What a lovely thing to do, Alessandro.' She smiled her sparkliest smile and sipped on her champagne; he had ordered for them, as usual. It was Dom Perignon, as usual. Things could be worse.

'Having you here made it easy. Because I have missed you, Abby.' He looked at her in a way he never had before, with feeling and intention. Abby cleared her throat and looked away. Her nervous tic did not go unnoticed.

'It is just me?' he asked.

Abby tapped her index finger nervously on her champagne flute as she wondered what she was supposed to say here.

'Alessandro, I wouldn't be Skyping and emailing with you if I didn't have feelings for you . . .'

'You have boyfriend.' He had made a pyramid out of his fingers, and his elbows rested on the table – his detective position.

'*Noo!* No. Do you think I would be here with you now if I had a boyfriend?'

Abby was flustered though, and Alessandro picked up on it. She took a long sip of her champagne and shook her head.

Alessandro laughed. 'A husband maybe?'

Her mind flew to Marcus and their first night together, when she had lied about her fake fiancé. Thoughts and feelings for Marcus had repeatedly bobbed up all day, and quite frankly, Abby had had enough. He was certainly not sitting there with his forty-something girlfriend thinking about her, so why should she sit here with her forty-something lover and think of *him*?

'No husband, no boyfriend, just a busy, busy job I'm afraid.'

'Must you work tomorrow?'

'I must. I really must. I have an early meeting, in fact.' She screwed up her face. She did not, but she *did* have an employee to fire and needed to write the accompanying email.

'Stay with me tonight.' There it was, that sexy, commanding lack of question marks that had driven Abby wild, in both a negative and positive way, in Italy.

'We'll see,' she said, smiling in what she hoped was mysterious allure; although it was absolutely, 100 per cent guaranteed she would be in his hotel room within hours. It had occurred to her as she had been swearing about the fact she couldn't get in with her waxer this evening, and so had to resort to trimming her own bikini line with the office scissors, that she was really, really looking forward to sex. Alessandro had been the last man she'd been with. She would bet her left breast that she was not the last woman he'd had. Not by a Roman soccer field.

'When do you have to be back in Italy, Alessandro?' Abby asked, wanting confirmation that it was set in stone, and he wasn't going to try and stay for a month. The speed with which she fluctuated between wanting to be naked with him, and wanting him safely back in Italy was brainbending. But she wasn't foolish enough to miss what was going on: her heart was still with Marcus, even though he didn't want it.

Maybe THAT was it, Abby thought, triumphantly. It wasn't

that she wanted Marcus, she was just put out that he didn't want *her*. Yes. Yesyesyes, she thought, finishing off her drink and placing the flute down, already seeing the waiter swoop in to refill it in her periphery vision. That's what it is. *It's all ego.* Idiot! The ego was only happy in the past and in the future – it couldn't survive in the present. And that's exactly where her thoughts about Marcus always ended up: in the past missing him, or getting despondent that her life ahead would not include him. But when she was present and in the moment, *Marcus wasn't there.*

But an Italian prince and a glass of vintage champagne were. It felt magnificent taking back control of the situation, and being the boss of her feelings about Marcus.

'Tuesday.'

Abby did the math; that was only a few days! Now she was quite happy for him to stay a little longer, what difference did it make?

'And are you working over the weekend?'

'I am not sure. Do you have some plans we can do?' He smiled, knowing his minxy, carefree Abby was hatching a plan.

'I do. Can you keep from Saturday lunch till Sunday night free?'

His smile was now at a very environmentally unfriendly 200 watts.

'Of course. For Abby, I can do anything.'

Abby was going to stop over-thinking every little thing; how often did you have a handsome, powerful, Italian gentleman – confirmed by every woman and quite a few men doing terribly obvious double takes of Alessandro as they walked into the restaurant – fly across the globe to land in your city, and want to spend time with you? She and Alessandro were going to have a beautiful couple of days.

40

'You poor, poor lamb, are you okay? I can't believe you had to be lavished and romanced by a sexy Italian for a *whole weekend.*' Mads was not quite able to comprehend the phenomenal, indulgent weekend her friend had just had.

Abby laughed as she speed-scrolled through all of the brunettes on the Allure site, pausing occasionally to scribble something down. Clients were supposed to do this themselves, she thought. That's why we set up the website in the first fucking place. The second Alessandro was gone she would hire a temp. And then, finally, she would tell Charlie she knew exactly what she was up to, and fire her.

'I'm managing, I guess. Oh, Mads, it was so insanely decadent. And he wouldn't let me do a thing. Well, I mean, I booked the hotel and the chopper and everything because he wouldn't know where to start—'

'He just handed over his ruby-encrusted AmEx at the end?'

'I *think* they're actually pink diamonds, but yes. Pretty much.' Abby smiled woozily at the thought of the weekend she and Alessandro had shared, complete with twelve-star mountain ranch, endless

French champagne, ninety-minute massages and 1200-thread-count-sheet sex.

'But did you have *fun*? Gold-plated golf carts and jacuzzi-loads of caviar aside . . .'

'Well,' Abby said. 'I mean, he's never going to suggest we get blazed and watch *The Simpsons,* but we had fun, yes . . .'

'This would make a terrific premise for a movie, you know. The young, sassy bird from 'Straya, who pines for her teenage lover—'

'Whoawhoawhoa, I no longer pine for him, thank yo—'

'And her sixty-year-old Mediterranean lover who secretly longs for a sedate life of golf, 6 p.m. dinners and comfortable recliners, and the journey they take each trying to convince the other that they're something they're not, but in the end, all that really matters is that they have access to helicopters and plunge pools.'

The two women laughed, and Abby loudly sighed the specific sigh that comes from a happy lack of sleep.

'Oh keep it down, sex glow. He leaves tomorrow, right?'

'Yep. I'm cooking for him tonight, would you believe . . .'

'*You!* Cooking! Sweet baby Jesus, you DO like him.'

'Mads, I actually think I'm going to really miss him.' Abby meant it. Alessandro had come out of his shell, the backhanded compliments had dried up . . . he appeared to genuinely feel something for Abby. Maybe without the pressure of work he was able to relax more, or *maybe* it was the benefit of a home-ground advantage on her behalf that had allowed her to enjoy her time with him so much. She felt less like a 'kept woman' when she was choosing the restaurants and had her own home to return to.

'Maybe you'll move to Florence to be his shiny exotic wife and drive your Lambo to Prada every day. Imagine that. Chelsea would faint with jealousy.'

Abby had wondered when Mads would bring up Chelsea; she

knew the girls had left the café Friday on okay terms, but with Alessandro in town she hadn't had a chance to find out the exact details.

'Speaking of Chelsea . . .'

Mads exhaled. 'We're cool. We all know I over-reacted when she told me she was pregnant, but I was in such a dark place, Abs, it's hard to explain. I'd never felt that low.' Abby picked the phone off the desk and held it to her ear. This was no speaker-phone conversation anymore.

'Poor darling. And you closed yourself off to us, we couldn't even help you . . .'

'But that's just it – you *couldn't* help me. I had to sit in that space for a bit, and toil through everything I was feeling, and be furious and bitter and despondent and wearied and . . . It was really, really horrible. Dylan didn't know who he was sharing the house with. There was talk of anti-depressants.' She blew air quickly threw her lips in disgust.

'I knew I'd come out the other end eventually. Last week was the first time I started to feel a bit okay actually, and fortuitously that was when you chose to launch your kamikaze Chelsea attack. A week earlier and I would've slapped your little cheeks.'

'She loves you, you know. She spoke of you every day you didn't speak to her.' Abby's voice went quiet.

'I'm happy for her, Abs. I'm concerned she doesn't know what the high hell she's gotten herself into, but we'll help the little rascal. And I'll just have to live vicariously through her pregnancy, I expect.'

'Who would've thought Chelsea would be living, unwed and pregnant with a man and his kid?' Abby mused.

'Mmm,' Mads said, a touch of sadness still in her voice. 'More evidence that you can harbour intense hope and desire for something but the universe is indiscriminate with who receives its gifts.'

'Well, you're handling it beautifully Madsy. I'm proud of you. Hey, what crystal are you wearing today?'

Abby held her breath and closed her eyes, hoping the answer wasn't sad and hopeless.

'Um, it's rose, actually. For self-love. A little heart. Dylan bought it for me on the weekend.'

Abby welled up a little. She was back into her magic crystals. Things were finally returning to normal.

Abby's call waiting beeped, it was Rob. That was never a good sign; he was an emailer. This was serious.

'Oh, shit, sorry Mads . . . It's Rob; I should take this. I'll call you later? Love you.'

'Bye toots.'

'Abby, it's Rob, how are you?'

'Hi Rob . . . To what do I owe the joy or terror of this phone call?'

Rob sighed. 'Are you in the office? Is Charlie there?'

The hairs on the back of Abby's neck pricked up; she already knew where this was heading.

'No . . . told her not to come in today. Why, what's up?' Abby said, guessing she knew exactly what was up.

'Well, she's not the dreamboat we thought she was, I'm afraid . . .'

Half a day and an outfit change later, Abby was busy faking a delicious home-cooked meal, all bought from the local deli to look authentically homemade. She'd carefully selected absolutely nothing that could lead to curious or investigative, ingredient-based questions. Abby had 'prepared' oysters, a simple potato, chive and onion side dish, a green bean salad, some Parmesan and parsley-crusted flathead that required a couple of minutes being pan-fried – outstanding for authenticity – and some aioli. Smashed brownies with berries and vanilla-bean ice-cream would follow for dessert, and all of it would be supplemented with bottles and bottles of Australian wine, firstly so Alessandro could try them, and second so that they could both get quite tanked and any awkwardness about never seeing each other again would be diluted, if not eradicated entirely.

At 5.54 p.m., a sleek black BMW 7-series pulled up out the front of Abby's, and a handsome gentleman nursing a bottle of wine and a densely packed posy of elegant flowers stepped out. He uttered something to the driver, who nodded and cruised off into the fragranced, spring night.

Abby flung open the door and smiled from ear to ear, seeing Alessandro on her doorstep. She kissed him passionately on the lips and pulled back as he handed her the flowers.

'You're *early!* Come in, come in . . . Oh, look at this posy . . . Thank you, Alessandro, that's very sweet of you, they're so beautiful.'

'They are not nearly as beautiful as you.'

Smiling bashfully, Abby stepped aside to let him walk through, her swishy, berry-red dress springing around her thighs as she did so.

While 'cooking', Abby had already put away two glasses of wine. This only served to amplify her affection towards Alessandro. She hated thinking about him leaving tomorrow morning, because she was fairly sure she didn't want him to. Just like when she was about to get her hair cut, and then it suddenly started looking terrific, and she didn't want to cut it off after all.

'Your house is just how I imagine,' he said, walking through to the lounge room, past the closed door of the messy office and into a kitchen that, to the naked eye, looked as though it had been used approximately 80 per cent more than it actually had.

'Please, take a seat on one of my genuine Australian bar stools. Can I pour you some wine? I want you to try some of my favourites tonight. Send you off in local style.'

'And with the hangover,' he said, grabbing a plump green olive from the nibbles Abby had laid out and popping it in his mouth, smiling.

'Well, yes, but who cares; you're flying first class, you can sleep it off.'

'It's true. Something light to begin?'

'*Buonissimo!* I have the perfect riesling.' She excitedly opened her fridge, which, like the rest of the apartment, was sparkling clean thanks to a gratuitous overpayment to her cleaner to have him come in this morning, and grabbed a slim, dark green bottle, pouring two moderate glasses and plopping them down on the bench.

'Come to me . . .' Alessandro said, taking her hand and pulling her around the bench so that she was standing directly in front of him, her legs between his, which were splayed open on his stool, his ankles resting on the foot bars. He gently took her in his arms, wrapping them around her so that she had to place her wine glass down and rest her hands on his shoulders.

'What have you done to me?' Alessandro asked, his skin smelling like cedar and gunsmoke and leather, his eyes looking into Abby's, searching for an answer as to how she had fallen into his lap that night in July, in the town he grew up in and in the restaurant he owned of all places.

He kissed her, mouth closed, gently, softly, tenderly. It was unexpected; Abby was not used to him being, well, *loving*. She figured it was just part of the never-see-each-other-again business; he'd done a similar thing that final night in Florence. Was he falling for her? Was she falling for him? No, surely not. Just holiday flinging again. She was over-thinking things, as usual. Abby forced herself to be present, feeling his kisses, and his hands gently slide up and down her back, slipping under the flimsy silk of her dress. She pulled back from his kisses and looked at him. She didn't want this to go any further: They were going to have a civil, romantic meal before they got down to biz.

'Oysters?'

He smiled and shook his head as she wriggled out of his soft grip.

'I will get you.'

Abby presented him with six oysters and a small dish of red wine vinaigrette, as she stood over the stove, gently pan-frying the fish. Alessandro happily slurped his oysters, chatting away. She was a little embarrassed about her bumbling around in the kitchen, but kind of didn't care at the same time. He loved simple food and bare wooden benches back home, why wouldn't he appreciate some simplicity here? Especially served by a blonde in a sexy red dress.

'Uh, I hope you're hungry, because I think I cooked way too much fish.' Abby finished arranging the kind-of crumbly fillets onto the two plates already abundant with salad and fresh-from-the-oven potatoes, and presented them to her audience.

'Abby! I am the lucky one tonight, no? It is the best to have someone cook for you.'

Abby kissed him on the lips. 'It is the very least I could do for such a generous man.'

After dinner, dessert and more wine than was necessary or healthy for two adults, Abby wanted to have a cigarette on the front steps. Alessandro thought it was vulgar to sit on steps, but as there was nowhere else to do it, and Abby forbade smoking inside, they picked up their wine glasses and headed outside.

As daylight savings was in full and glorious swing, the sun was still languorously lighting the sky, and an almost-full, very bright moon was creeping up to thieve the position of prominent sky feature. Abby flopped down onto the top step, as she had done many times in the past, usually alone, but sometimes with Marcus. Alessandro delicately hitched up his jeans, confirming his no-sock-loafer policy, and sat down next to Abby.

'*Jeeeeez*, what an amazing night . . . look at that moon! Oh, we've really turned it on for you, haven't we? And look, if you peer through those buildings over there? You can see the bridge.'

'The one I see from my hotel room all day?'

Abby punched him playfully in the arm, and as she turned to him, he grabbed the back of her head gently and pulled her in for a kiss. They kissed, dreamily, lovingly, pathetically, pent-up, for several minutes, Alessandro's hands sliding down to her thighs, hinting at all kinds of mischief. When he slipped his hand underneath to her panties, Abby pulled back, smiling like the boozed fool she was.

'*Alessandro!* Cut that out. I have neighbours, you know.'

'Then we can bow at the end.' He kissed her amorously on the side of the neck, gently pulling her closer to him at the small of her back.

'Come on, let's have that cigarette,' Abby said, resuming her most enjoyed and best-suited position of flirty sexual warden.

'I love to kiss you,' Alessandro said, looking at her with the eye equivalent of a boner.

'Why, thank you. Tell me, Alessandro, did you really come all this way to see Federico?' Abby couldn't resist.

He paused, taking a drag of his cigarette.

'I missed you, Abby. I like that you have your work and you don't need me. It suits me. If I were to see you every few months, that would make me very happy.'

Abby was sure there were some authentic feelings in his bizarre and mildly offensive comment, but it seemed to be overshadowed by his love of efficiency and the desire for a casual relationship. Surprisingly, she understood where he was coming from. Perhaps that was the way to go: get on with your life and career and then have an intensely romantic fling four times a year. It didn't exactly smack of romance, but there were worse options for two busy people who were fond of each other.

'Spend summer with me, I can take you to the islands, we will get the boat.' Another Italian summer; that could be a beautiful idea . . . It could become an annual thing, she thought. And if he came over here again in a few months for a week, is that so bad? On the other hand, while Abby felt very tender towards him right here and now, with her insides bubbling with wine and the knowledge he was leaving tomorrow, did it have legs? Was it worth enduring the deprived gratification and annoyance that accompanied a long-distance relationship, even if it were a loose one? She looked at his face, his light eyes, and the lips she had become rather attached to. She could do a lot worse.

Maybe it was the lifestyle that appealed to her, the fantasy, the luxury, the terrific sex and the lack of Real Life hassles. She didn't know. Abby had a gnawing feeling their relationship report card would read: *Good on paper, terrific potential, exciting and engaging, but lacking authenticity and feeling. Needs work. B–*.

'Let's just be in the present for now,' Abby said, kissing him quiet.

The present was beautiful. To wish to be anywhere else would be criminal. Abby kissed him lightly on the nose, then on the lips and then leaned her head against his shoulder and took a deep breath in. He put his arm around her and pulled her in close. Whatever this is, it's nice, she thought. I am a lucky woman.

41

U miss him already, don't u. Did he offer to fly u over??

Do miss him a bit, yes. And yes, he did offer. Might even
go! Imagine that.

Abby was feeling gloomy that Alessandro was back in Italy. He'd
already followed up about flying her over in a few months, but Abby
had been too busy to confirm or deny or even decorously hold him
off. On the flip side, she couldn't stop thinking about how weird
and defensive she'd felt when Alessandro had noticed Marcus's
razor in the shower the other night. Still she couldn't bring herself
to chuck it out.

Have u fired your bunny boiler business partner yet?

No. Told her I was sick and not to come in last few days
while I sorted everything out. But am about to unleash all
fury.

Good. fucking nutjob. Kid practice with Olly here all wknd – come over pls xc

Abby took a deep breath to calm down and mentally filed through everything bubbling away in her brain. She'd barely slept last night; she was that horrible blend of wired but tired, which meant there was little slumber, and when it finally came, it was filtered through many stresses. It was legit, though: she was about to confront Charlie about what she'd been up to: her very own Events and Promotions company, called – *how original* – Charlie's.

She opened up a folder in her inbox marked 'Charlie' and began printing off the emails and attachments within. She had to hurry; Charlie was due in twenty minutes to 'collect some uniforms' for an event that night, at which she would probably try to convince both the client and the girls to ditch Allure for her own seedy side-project.

With great thanks to Rob and the new, very efficient IT guy at Webra, her grand You're Busted moment (tolerated but not advised by Rob) consisted of a neat manila folder Abby had poisoned with the words 'Join Charlie's! The newest agency in town!' that held the twenty-seven applications potential girls had made to Allure while Abby was overseas, which she'd asked Webra to find, because nothing was ever really deleted in cyberspace. Then there were the emails she'd received from some of those girls when she'd emailed them asking to come in for a meeting, saying that 'Charlie had already been in touch,' or that, 'Am signed to Charlie's now, thanx anyway! Xx.'

There were also emails from Charlie to Rob, advising him that 'unfortunately' CashCard were looking for another agency, but she was 'too anxious' to tell Abby, and would he? Also she'd requested the current Allure financials, and history of Abby's longest-standing clients. There was also the email Charlie had sent to Diane at Tag, telling her that she would be their sole point of contact now and that, because some clients deserved extra special attention ('Like yourself, obviously, Di!'), she was now heading up a boutique sector of Allure that they were casually referring to as 'Charlie's'.

Finally, and most damaging, was the correspondence from Abby's contact at Grey Goose, who had forwarded her the emails between himself and Charlie. The emails had enticed him away from Abby and Allure with the promise of even better girls, at a better price, if he just dealt with Charlie privately. Charlie had even done a few jobs for him, making sure to use girls who'd never worked for Abby. It made Abby shiver with fury.

She put everything into the folder and left it on Charlie's desk, furnished it with a post-it note asking that Charlie leave her keys and all Allure tools of the trade in the office and to leave immediately. She was going to add something about 'or legal action would be taken', but didn't even really know what that meant, it just sounded scary. She gathered up her laptop and handbag and left the house, trying not to think about all the work she had ahead of her with Charlie out of the picture and no other staff. Not to mention having to explain to all her clients and girls what had happened, and trying to get them back. Of course, if they did leave her for Charlie, well she didn't want them anyway. No, she definitely did, actually. But it sounded tougher the other way, and she'd be prepared to fake it until she fell in a heap.

It was a phenomenal turn of events, Abby thought as she drove down her street aimlessly, with nowhere to go and nothing to do except wait for Charlie to discover she'd been discovered. She was angry with herself for being too caught up in her personal life and travel to see what was going on, and for allowing such a virus to infect the business she'd worked so hard to create. Abby had thought she was a pretty good judge of character. But then Charlie slithered in and ruined all of that with her shady backstabbing and revolting business thieving.

Abby desperately needed to drink something strong and sedative. As she drove through the streets, trying not to feel too glum, she also began to crave a cigarette. Filthy habits for a filthy day.

The sun was shimmering in the sky, a spectacular sunset was about to take place, and Abby couldn't help thinking, in her exhausted, mildly melancholy state that she should be enjoying it somewhere with Marcus. His appreciation and dedication for the landscape, the sky, the sea had always inspired Abby. She wondered if he was still with his cougar, if he was travelling, if he'd moved on from the rockabilly look to ski-chic or butcher style or whatever the people in Brooklyn whose music and fashion and blogs he so admired were doing now.

In an instant, Abby knew where she should head for the hour or so she had to fill. And if she happened to take a cider and some cigarettes with her, what of it?

Half an hour later, Abby had nervously parked her car on what looked like a very illegal shoulder of a major freeway, determined to remember the exact way Marcus had showed her to get to his lush little oasis. There was another car, an old Toyota 4WD parked there: was it a ranger? Or a car full of deros drinking rum from brown paper bags? She looked down at her own brown paper bag and smiled to herself sheepishly. There was bound to be someone else up here on a night like tonight, she figured, walking gingerly towards the old gate. It was breathtaking.

As she hopped over the old fence and came into the clearing her suspicions were confirmed, there was a couple sitting on the grass fifty metres away, hugging their knees, their backs to Abby as the faced the impressive view. They'd definitely thieved the primo position, in fact it was almost the same spot she and Marcus had laid, but there was enough space for everyone.

As Abby walked towards them along the teeny dirt path, she watched as they stood up and shook off their picnic blanket. Terrific! They were leaving; she could enjoy a contemplative hour up here alone. As they came closer, Abby noticed the boy was wearing a hat just like Marcus's. And was roughly the same height. And had cuffed jeans, which was Marcus's staple. And had Marcus's face. And was Marcus.

Abby's body was rooted to the earth, unable to do a thing. *Why wasn't his car parked up there on the shoulder like a warning beacon?* Jesus! He hadn't seen her yet, but if Abby turned around and ran off to her car now, he'd definitely know it was her. Oh fuckfuckfuck, Abby screamed internally, why do I have to run into him now, of all days, of all places, and he's with a WOMAN. A bit of a daggy one, to be honest . . . Abby ran her fingers through her hair and furiously swallowed the small amount of saliva that had kindly decided to stick around. She'd have to face him. There was no other option. *Fine*.

Marcus was mid-conversation, about ten metres away when he finally looked up and saw who was standing in front of him. His face went blank and his girlfriend followed his gaze to Abby, trying to piece together what the big deal was with this strange blonde up ahead.

Marcus's left hand shot up to his face in embarrassment. That was weird, Abby thought; after all, it was his secret little spot and Abby was intruding, if anything, he should be pissed off.

The couple got closer and closer, and Abby saw that a faint smile had fallen over Marcus's face.

'Well, what have we here? Abby Vaughn, sneaking into my little secret headquarters with her dirty little longneck of VB . . .'

Abby smiled nervously, clutching her brown paper bag in close to her chest.

'I'm sorry, I just, I swear I haven't been up here since, well, since you showed it to me,' she dropped her head respectfully to Marcus's date, who she was sure was *loving* watching this little scene unfold. Abby shot her a warm smile and stuck out her right hand. Goodness, Abby thought, she *was* a bit old, even by Marcus's standards. Very fit, tanned, and with a face that was undeniably beautiful, but still . . . She must be the one Charlie saw him with. Abby's brain computed it all in nanoseconds. Wow. So they were really on, it seemed. Breakfasts . . . romantic secret city lookouts . . . If nothing else, at least Abby now knew she was about twenty years too young for him. *Such* a dog move for Charlie to tell her that, she reflected. *Bitch*.

'Hi, I'm Abby.'

A look of understanding washed over the woman's face.

'Abby!' She cupped Abby's hand with both of hers and shook it warmly, smiling deeply into Abby's eyes as she did so.

'I've heard so much about you.' The woman looked at Marcus, her eyebrows jammed up as far as possible, still holding and shaking Abby's hand as she did so.

'Uh, you can probably let her hand go now,' Marcus said.

The woman dropped her hands quickly and giggled. Abby noticed she had a few beautiful silver pendants around her neck, and a stack of woven bands around her wrists. So she was an 'Earth mother,' was she? Probably all into tantric sex and incense and buckwheat.

'Tell you what, I'm going to head back to the car to make this call I've been meaning to make all day. I'll see you back there, Cussy, and don't rush.'

Cussy? Jesus. What the hell kind of nickname was that, Abby thought as she smiled broadly to the woman and watched her dart

289

past towards the freeway, her shapely calves strapped into leather sandals, and her small silhouette faintly visible under a simple, green cotton dress.

'She seems nice.'

Marcus laughed obviously. 'She *is* nice. She's the best. I can't believe you two finally got to meet, and up here of all places.'

'Marcus, look I'm glad you're happy, Charlie told me you were seeing someone, but why would we want to meet each other? That makes no sense.'

Marcus folded his arms defensively, his face utterly confused.

'What are you talking about?'

Abby sighed. Why was he being so piggish? This didn't need to be a fight.

'Your girlfriend? I assume she was the same one Charlie saw you with in a café a while back.'

Marcus's hands flew to his cheeks, slapping them loudly as they made contact. 'Oh, this is *magnificent*. You think that woman is my girlfriend?'

'Well, we both know you like older women.' Abby crossed her arms and looked out to the view, her upset building. She'd been looking forward to that cider for hours, but never more than this exact second.

'Abs, that woman gave birth to me. That's *Gayle!*' He laughed uproariously, his head flipping back at the sheer hilarity of the situation.

Abby pursed her lips, flushing violently red from her chest to her scalp. On one hand, she was ecstatic that Marcus wasn't in love with a woman who had a tattoo of a dolphin on her arm, and on the other, she was furious that she'd messed up her first meeting with Marcus's mum.

'Damn,' she uttered quietly.

'I can't wait to tell her, she'll be *ever* so flattered—'

'Please, don't – it's creepy. Jesus, Marcus: why didn't you introduce her as Gayle! I would've figured it out then!'

'I kind of like that you were jealous, now that I think of it.'

'Jealous, *pfft*. More like nauseated. No offence to your mum.'

'Charlie tells me you're dating a silverback yourself, so you're not exactly in the best position to judge . . .' He was looking at her not with teasing eyes, but questioning, is-this-true eyes.

'What do you mean "Charlie tells me" – how often do you two catch up, exactly?'

'Nice segue. I don't know, I guess we email a bit, run into each other at Capelli's sometimes?'

'Email: why?' Abby's face was crumpled in confusion.

'Uh, because I'm helping her with the site for your new agency, obviously? It's cool, she told me you didn't want to deal with me and I get that.'

Abby let out a frustrated groan and covered her eyes with her free hand.

'Whoa-whoa-whoa, what's going on?'

'I cannot fucking *believe* that girl! I don't have a "new agency", she's been stealing my clients and my girls! AND she's been fucking emailing *you* to create a site for all of it!'

Marcus frowned, 'Really? That doesn't seem like Charli—'

'Don't even finish that. You won't *believe* the shit she's been up to. She's a fucking lunatic. I'm sorry, I have to open this, I'm at risk of cardiac arrest.'

Abby opened the brown paper bag and pulled out the cider, twisting the lid furiously in order to open it, before cutting open her finger and realising it was not, in fact, a twist-top after all.

'*Fuck!* Fuck, fuck, fuck.' She sucked her finger, and Marcus stepped in and took the bottle.

'Still as patient as ever, I see. Give me that, you gorgeous little dunce.' He took out a bottle opener that was attached to his keys, and flipped it open.

'Sit for a moment. Come on. You're all worked up.' Marcus sat down with his legs out in front of him in the grass and motioned for her to do the same. Abby sighed and sat down next to him, a million murderous thoughts careening through her brain. Why had she been so elegant about her dismissal of Charlie? She should've set her fucking car alight.

'Sorry, I just, it's full on, you know? I've never been done over before. And I hate that she was emailing you, and that you thought I'd told her to, and oh, just, it all sucks a bit, basically.'

Abby swigged hard on the cider, gulping down the sweet fizz.

'She did seem a bit rattled when I showed at your place, now I think of it.'

'My place? What, *when?*'

'Ages ago. Few days after we had that friendly chat at Alfie's. Ohhhhh . . .' A look of understanding washed over Marcus's face.

'She didn't tell you, did she?'

'No. She did not.' Abby's teeth began involuntarily grinding against each other.

'I also dropped over some of those David Austin roses you love the other week – she never told you they were from me, I'm assuming? I guess it doesn't matter, as long as they made you happy.'

Abby sat there stunned at what she was hearing.

'Marcus, why did you do that? Why *would* you do that, you never called or emailed or . . . I had no idea you were even feelin—'

'I just realised Mum didn't bring her phone today,' Marcus said chuckling, flinging his keys around his finger, changing the topic.

'Wonder what's she doing up there right now. She's always been very pro-Abby, you know.'

'That's nice to know.' Abby said, taking the cue that his feelings weren't on the table for now. 'Especially since I thought she was sleeping with her son.'

'Husshhh. We don't speak of that probably. Bit gross.'

'You know, I only just fired Charlie today, right now, literally this hour. It's so . . . fortuitous? Well, kind of, that I ran into you here and you told me that. Really cements my decision. I'm so angry that my intuition didn't pick up on her tricks? I thought I was good with my gut instinct.'

'That the same gut instinct that told you you'd messed up by dumping me?'

Marcus looked at Abby, his hat causing the sun to fall only on his beautiful lips, and Abby felt her stomach start to swirl.

'I guess so . . .' Abby looked back at Marcus, wishing him telepathically to say that *he'd* messed up by telling her he didn't want her back. Why else did he bring flowers and come to her house? Her brain couldn't even compute the possibilities.

'Doesn't matter anyway, you have some Italian Prince Charming now I hear, old and wise and not averse to helicopters and Ferraris.'

'I can't tell if Charlie did me a favour or a disservice by telling you that.' Abby smiled reticently, the sun making her blue eyes light up with ambers and yellows.

'Well, I'm heartbroken, if that helps you figure it out.' He grabbed the cider from Abby's hand and took a swig before handing it back.

'I can't tell if you're kidding. Can you not kid for a moment? I'm confused enough as it is.'

Marcus went on. 'So, is he everything you wanted and needed? Older, rich, experienced, worldly, three marriages and five kids under his belt?'

'Marcus, please. What's going on? Why the flowers? Why the—

How come you didn't try harder to contact me?'

'I could've texted I suppose, but I quite fancied the rawness and honesty and hero status that came with knocking on a doorstep and asking for another chance. But Charlie made it clear you were taken. I *now* realise that anything she said is to be investigated under microscopic scrutiny, but I didn't know she was all *Clockwork Orange* back then. So I took it to be true. And, well, I backed off.'

'Marcus . . . I had no idea . . .' Abby looked at him as he looked down, playing with some grass. How had this nearly not been discovered? If she hadn't come to the clearing today, they would've never known how each other felt. It made her queasy thinking of a future not knowing Marcus sent her roses, or maybe still had feelings for her.

'You hurt me, Abs, I needed some time to work through it. And I was angry; you saw that. I needed to hear you admit you wanted me, and then show you I didn't want you, I suppose in a fucked-up way.'

'And be single. Come on. Admit it.'

'The girls out there are revolting, Abby. They're stupid and juvenile and self-centred and desperately low on self-confidence. All of the things that made my Abby shine, they lacked. I hate them.'

He was being dramatic, but Abby let what he was saying sink in anyway. They'd both hurt each other, now . . . maybe it was time to see if they could mutually fix things? It felt like it was an even playing field again.

'So, has the Italian stolen your heart?' He twisted his head to look at her, just as a single strand of blonde hair fell over her eye, in the exact way he'd always adored.

Abby looked at Marcus, her eyes searching for a sign that she was doing the right thing.

'No. I wanted him to take it, if I'm being honest. Wanted to not think about you anymore. But you can't force that stuff. The heart wants what the heart wants. Or, you know, who.'

'Hmm.' Marcus said, and they both sat there silently in the set-ting sun, feeling the energy of what was unfolding envelop them.

'Do we still have a shot at the title, Abs? You and me?' He looked straight ahead as he said this, too frightened to look at her lest her expression reveal the sad truth that no; they did not. 'Have we found ourselves in a scene from a movie for a reason tonight?'

'It might not work, you realise,' Abby said, matter-of-factly, tak-ing a sip of the cider.

'Might end in a week,' Marcus said, practically.

'And, well, as much as you hate to hear it, the age difference might eventually be a legitimate issue, even if we don't want it to be . . . I have to be up-front about that,' Abby said, honestly.

'I understand that, Abs,' Marcus said earnestly.

'I won't make an issue of it anymore, though. I promise you. I've learned my lesson.'

'Good. I'd like that.'

'We have no reassurance whatsoever things will work out,' Abby said in a warning tone.

'I know.'

More silence.

'And then there's the fact I've been dating my mum.' Marcus smiled and looked at Abby, who was smiling back at him. He gen-tly slipped his hand into hers and entwined his soft, brown skin around her fingers.

'Can we try this, Garfield? Slowly-slowly? Day at a time? Hour by hour? What do you say?'

Abby looked into Marcus's eyes and felt her breathing quicken, her heart trying to keep its cool as a million fireworks exploded within it. She nodded, a rogue tear slipping down one cheek. He leaned in to kiss her softly on the lips.

Acknowledgements

Thank you, Kirsten, tireless publisher and editor of mine! Your enthusiasm and guidance has been exceptionally helpful, as it always is. Thank you Tara and Pippa (for your assistance in mischievous deadline nudging especially). Thank you to my many excellent and smoking hot girlfriends who've dated and fallen (carefully) in love with gorgeous younger men. Your insight and anecdotes were not only intensely entertaining, but extremely useful and instrumental. Finally, thank you to *my* younger man. You took me from New Zealand to New York to write this, and saturated me with love, support, fun, delight and snacks every single day of the way. *I love you hard.* Deal with it.